Colony

by James McLellan

Departures

"DON'T TELL THEM ABOUT the thing," they told Sara. "You don't want to scare the kids." Sara put on her best public relations smile and waited for the connection. A moment later the telepresence call connected and Sara's sight and hearing were directed to an elementary school classroom.

A second call also connected. Part of Sara's attention was just offstage at a nightly talk show on the other side of the world. Sara would be presenting herself at several of these events at the same time. She could handle multiple calls at once, but it was stressful.

In the classroom, there was an awkward silence. Sara wasn't sure how she had been introduced to the class. Sara decided to break the ice. "Hello kids," she began. "I'm one of the passengers on the Diomedes Interstellar Settlement Mission, and I'm telepresencing from on top of the final mission module, located on a rocket at the United States spaceport in the state of New Mexico. I am scheduled to launch from Earth in just a little over an hour." There was applause and yelling. Sara waited for the teacher to bring the class to order.

On the sound stage, a stagehand signaled Sara to move. She walked out in front of the camera waving. The talk show host offered to shake her hand. Sara took the host's offered hand and did her best to make light of the awkward moment when the host's hand passed through hers. She sat next to the host. "Thank you for having me on the show," Sara began.

Several similar events were happening on television outlets, primary schools, and universities worldwide. Sara was pretty confident she could keep up. Sara replied to the text message from her home office, "THIS IS TOO MUCH. THEY'RE GOING TO FIND OUT."

The reply was, "PUSH SEASON 3 RELEASE."

In the classroom, the children fidgeted. A stern look from the teacher kept the class in order. Sara noticed for the first time that there were other adults in the classroom lined along the far wall. "I'll be meeting up with the other crew and passengers on the spaceship Diomedes, which you may have watched and voted for during the three seasons of training and down selection in Oymyakon - Russia, Leh - India, and Mauna Loa - Hawaii." Sara pointed out a child in the front row with a silkscreen fan shirt. "I can see you watched the show."

In the studio, Sara and the host had exchanged pleasantries. They talked a little about the show. The host kept trying to place her. Finally, he decided to ask, "which one of the contestants are you?"

Ah. The thing. And so quickly. "I wasn't on camera much," Sara evaded. "But I had a big voice presence. You often heard me talking to the other trainees." Some of the studios were, no doubt, fact-checking her statement with voice recognition software against recordings of the show. These events were billed as the last opportunity to see a member of the mission team. Interviewing a mission team member, however, was a challenge - since all of the passengers and crew were asleep. Since Sara was arguably a part of the mission team, someone felt she could make the appearances. The fact-finding teams would confirm Sara's voice on the show. "Which reminds me," Sara segued, "I wouldn't be doing my job if I didn't tell you that Season Three Uncut will be available for download and streaming in a few weeks on August first."

In the classroom, Sara paused a moment. "All my colleagues are now in aestivation, which is a chemically produced hibernation that they will waken from when we reach our destination." She wasn't sure whether to focus on the show or the mission. Sara had no script. Her part in this event had been put together last minute. She sent a desperate text message for clarification and continued to improvise.

Sara pulled up some stock video of the mission orbital path. "We'll be traveling to our new home on a spaceship named the Diomedes. It has been under construction near the Earth-Moon L1 point for most of the last five years. Do any of you know what the L1 point is?" she asked.

Several children raised their hands. Sara picked one child. "It's where all the gold and platinum comes from."

The teacher looked horrified. Sara smiled, "you're right!" she said, helping the child out with her class. "We do get many of our precious metals from the Earth-Moon L1. There are five Lagrange points between any two bodies in space. Lagrange points are spots where it does not require much effort to stay in place. The Earth-Moon L1 is the closest between Earth and the moon. For this reason, the Earth-Moon L1 is where most near-Earth asteroid mining and shipbuilding operates."

In the studio, the host asked, "I understand we can go outside and see your ship right now."

Sara quickly searched for where the studio was located on the internet. "Yes. If you go outside right now, you'll be able to see it. Transit time is only a few minutes."

In a different studio, a different host asked, "I understand that you will be traveling on a large antimatter bomb."

"Not a bomb," Sara corrected with a chuckle. "At least, I hope not. We're using the same matter-antimatter engines used for travel to or from the outer planets, and we've been using those for decades now. For our trip, we need enough power to get there in a reasonable amount of time, which fusion provides, but for longer trips, you need the much mass-energy higher efficiency of antimatter. With antimatter, we can get thirty percent, which is far above the one percent mass energy efficiency we'd get with a traditional fuser."

Sara received a text message, "UPSELL COMMS." Who kept track of how she was doing in each of these events?

Sara texted back. "I HAVE A JOB. ON A ROCKET."

"JUST A LITTLE MORE," came the reply. "PROMISED 15 MINUTES."

"By the way," Sara said, "if you want to track our progress, to see if we blow up, or just to send messages to your favorite contestants, keep in touch with us on the deep space radio network."

In the classroom, Sara said, "in ninety days, we'll stop our engines, and deploy a cloud of microsatellites. They will use a technique called interferometry to take some of the best resolution pictures of alien planets seen to date. Do any of you know what interferometry is?" A quick survey of the student's faces said "no". Sara answered her own question, "using computer processing we will use many small telescopes spread across a large distance to take pictures as if they were a single gigantic telescope. In deep space, where we don't have to compete with gravity, we can use this technique to make enormous telescopes," Sara said, emphasizing with her arms. "Larger than Earth! We'll use this information to select the best world for our final destination. Since we have settled so many worlds now in the inner and outer solar system, we feel that we have enough experience to settle worlds meeting a list of criteria confidently. If we can't find any world good enough, we will turn around and come home."

In a newsroom, an interviewer posed the question, "a lot of people are very much against the Diomedes, calling it at best an epic waste of resources or, at worst, racist. In fact, there are protesters massed right now outside your launch site in New Mexico." The newscast switched to video of people carrying placards in the blistering New Mexico heat. "As one of the passengers," the interviewer asked, "what do you say to them?"

"I understand their point," Sara answered, "there are wars, poverty, and civil rights issues that are desperate for the public's focus. People forget that the Apollo moon landings were also very unpopular for the same reasons. And after the Apollo program, the world took a more than sixty-year break from interplanetary manned flight. Then, having already proven that it could be done, we quickly spread out to the inner and outer planets. So, in my opinion, there is a time to focus on home, and a time to take bold risks. I think that, right now, it's time for risk."

"WE'RE DONE," the office texted. "THANKS."

Sara took a few questions and wrapped up the multiple last-minute publicity events and reminded people to watch her launch before making a graceful exit. Sara ended each visit with, "please remember to donate at our site. Thank you for allowing me to visit."

It was July in the New Mexico desert, and the crowd was charring in the heat. Intermittently, the Public Affairs Officer's voice came over the speaker to share some piece of news. Finally, the mass of onlookers counted down with the Public Affairs Officer, "five... four... three... two... one..."

Bright fire illuminated the desert as the rocket engines lit up the landscape like a second sun, briefly appearing and lifting from the ground into the afternoon sky. As always, the launch led to a wave of cheering from the crowd.

The Public Affairs Officer continued over the cheering, "... the forty-fourth and final supply mission for the interstellar settlement ship Diomedes. The Diomedes is a public-private partnership of over forty countries around the globe to establish a manned settlement outside the solar system."

The Public Affairs Officer continued, "the Diomedes will begin its journey on a course to take it near twenty potentially habitable worlds outside the solar system. During the long trip, the ship will deploy a space interferometer - a telescope array with unequaled ability to see the fine details of distant planets. The observations taken by this space interferometer will allow the selection of the best of the candidate worlds for colonization. Even if the closest candidate world is selected, the journey will still take several decades. To conserve food and supplies, passengers will remain in suspended animation until the last part of the journey. Running the ship will be a collection of expert systems managed by the state of the art in machine intelligence."

The rolling roar of the rocket engine began to fade, and the blinding light of the engine started to dim as the rocket ascended further, eventually diminishing to only a small point in the sky. High above, the booster and its cargo parted ways. The booster would follow a powered descent path that would place it safely on the ground where it had started from, to be serviced and used again for some other purpose. The module the booster had carried into space fired its rockets to take it even further away from Earth and into a path to dock with the spaceship Diomedes, already prepared to receive it.

The crew and passengers were already aboard the ship. They were resting in suspended animation. A final temporary team was aboard performing last minute checks and set-up. Once their work was complete, they would cast off from the Diomedes, leaving the ship's care to ground stations and onboard computers.

One hundred kilometers above the surface, the temporary prep crew, was looking forward to being done with their five-week shift on the spaceship. Edgar and Bill had gotten ahead of schedule, which gave them a little freedom to wander. The whole ship was tightly packed. Two astronauts in pressure suits could not pass one another in the central core to which the several modules were connected. Edgar was looking in on the passengers.

"What is it," Edgar asked looking at the rows and rings of hibernation chambers, "that these people did to get put on ice?"

"They volunteered," Bill reminded him. "Really," he lectured Edgar,"you should watch more TV. Their big pitch was 'the world votes' for their favorite contestants. Ten thousand applied, and only the lucky nine hundred and seventy get to come up. And another thirty professional spacers."

"I would never want to be on ice like that," Edgar said. "They look dead. I think I might have watched that show - is it the one where a couple tried to sneak away for a rendezvous and nearly froze everyone?"

"That's the one!" Bill answered. "Season One in Oymyakon, Russia. Coldest city in the world."

Bill and Edgar floated back to the capsule. The microwave oven chimed, signaling their meal was ready. Bill opened the door and passed Edgar a clear package of orange colored paste. The spaceship was kept cold and at low pressure to minimize the strain on the hull and the power systems. The warm food made the spacer's capsule pleasant. "Mmm, spaghetti," Edgar said. "Thanks."

Edgar pointed around the docking collar into the ship he and Bill had been servicing for the last five weeks. "And they're going to entrust all of this," he asked, "to a computer?"

Bill nodded, although Edgar, looking into the interior of the spaceship through the docking collar, couldn't see him. Bill took a sip of his darker plastic pouch, filled with beef soup, and answered. "Not much choice. Past a certain distance, it takes too long for instructions to arrive. We're kind of spoiled here in the inner planets where, at worst, it's a twenty-minute delay. I have a buddy out on Titan who has to wait over an hour any time he wants to say something to somebody back here. They can't have a conversation like we are doing right now. It's worse for these guys," he said, referring to the ship he and Edgar were servicing. "They'll be years, decades from home base."

Edgar slurped his pasta and sauce through the plastic. "You said a crew of thirty spacers," he challenged.

"If they decide to come back, it's a six-month trip," Bill answered, moving deeper into the capsule to retrieve a video player from his personal equipment. "But if they go all the way, it could take decades to get where they're going. Keeping people alive that long would be a pretty big strain on the system."

"Goes back to my point," Edgar challenged, floating through the docking collar and into the larger vessel's primary hallway. "Nobody's watching the ship."

"Somebody is watching the ship," Bill answered, bracing against the hallway door to watch a video. "They are sending up one of those emergency services A.I.s, like they use in dangerous situations such as firefighting. It's supposed to have as much dynamic intelligence and empathy as any human. This one was built to manage resorts. It's been training with the passengers and crew for the last three years."

"Empathy?" Edgar asked.

"Yeah," Bill answered. "Some egghead says better decisions are made with reason and feeling than with reason alone. They must have studied you."

Edgar nodded in agreement, then realized what Bill had said. "I have feelings!" he complained playfully.

Six hours after launch, the newest and last ship module docked with the spaceship. Pressure doors swung open. Spider-like robots built to maintain the ship throughout its multi-decade journey crawled inside the newly opened module, moving along footholds designed for them, and hurried to repackage supplies sent up with the vessel to their proper places. Not far behind the maintenance robots, the prep crew floated in to connect the module systems to the ship and perform tests.

The module's only passenger greeted the crew when they floated in, but they were too busy to notice. Considering her own module well cared for between crew and robots, she stepped into the more significant part of the ship. A radio channel kept a running log of chatter as mission team members reported on their actions and outcomes. When she was called on to check in, she did so. On a private channel, she asked for the ship's bursar. The ship bursar, a computer system, responded in kind to her voice commands, she explained "I'm required to report on the readiness of the supplies and equipment. Could you guide me?" She went through each item on her list. In the supply modules, intimidatingly large construction vehicles were cleverly packed, fitting more of them into the module than would have been guessed. Each module contained some construction vehicles, some parts and equipment, and some automated manufacturing and assembly plants. An accident compromising any one module wouldn't completely destroy any critical piece of infrastructure. Sara floated through the tightly packed hallways. The computer provided her with directions to each item on her checklist so that she could personally inspect it. She continued through each until her report was finished.

The crew and maintenance robots finished with the new module and moved on to other things. Nearly every system aboard the ship responded to voice commands. The new passenger raised the ship's communication system and submitted her report. Then she notified the mission team on the radio of the delivery. She was asked to begin working on a summary of the medical status of the crew and passengers. Both updates would be necessary before the final decision to start the journey was made. She worked with the medical system to review the crew and passenger areas, reporting on health and vital statistics. Each module was packed so tightly that it was nearly impossible to fit. Ninety-seven passengers, three crew members, food and other supplies in each module, and ten modules total. She worked her way through each, confirming each passenger or crew member was aboard and healthy. Finally, she filed the report and alerted the mission team.

In the meantime, the prep crew had finished their work. The pair of spacers drifted through the hatch connecting their travel capsule to the ship without even saying goodbye. By the time the medical report was finished, the pressure door had already closed, and the crew was on their way.

With all stations reporting ready, the decision was made to launch. At the planned time, a signal was sent from the ground, and the ship's auxiliary engines came to life. Things shifted as acceleration replaced free fall aboard the vessel. They would now accelerate following instructions radioed from the ground into a higher orbit forty million kilometers away from the surface of the Earth. At that high altitude floated antimatter generation and refining facilities. The facilities exposed ambient cosmic rays to target material brought from the moon, converting some of it to antimatter, and packaging it in graphite balls that made the antimatter safe to store. The crew of the stations were full-time spacers. Sara listened as ground control handed off command of the ship to the team of the refinery so that they could guide the vessel into the loading berth.

"Approach control to Diomedes ground," the approaching refinery radioed to the ship, which relayed to the ground, "requesting release of Diomedes guidance for berthing."

"Diomedes ground to approach control," Earth radio back. "Control released." With those words, and an encoded command to the ship, navigation of the five thousand ton vessel was released to the refinery. The vessel gently approached, not quite reaching the refinery itself, but a nest of pipes and tubes extending from it.

"Payment confirmed," the station radioed. "We've been waiting for you Diomedes."

Some of the station crew detached from the station in pressure suits. They began translating down the pipe hand over hand towards Diomedes. With practiced efficiency, the spacers started connecting transfer pumps from their station to the spaceship. Sara watched the operation from the best vantage point she could find.

Antimatter was used to fuel almost all travel to the outer solar system - planets past Mars - when you wanted to either take a large cargo, get their quickly, or both. Despite the well-established infrastructure, the Diomedes was purchasing a large part of the annual antimatter output of the entire solar system to fuel its trip. It was an enormous purchase and had required permission from multiple countries to make.

The station crew was good at their job. Within ten hours, the seven hundred tons of antimatter, and four thousand tons of containment material had been brought aboard and confirmed by Diomedes' own systems. Sara was a part of this confirmation process. Visually inspecting that the content was there and confirming tests performed by the ship systems.

The station crew assisted with casting off the spaceship and guiding it away from the refinery. "Diomedes ground, this is approach control," the station radioed. "Guidance has been released to onboard systems." With that, the ship was ready to begin its journey.

"Acknowledged," Earth radioed back. "Thank you."

Final polling was done on the automated and ground mission stations. After every mission station reported ready, the order to begin the next part of the journey was given. On receipt of a signal from Earth, the main engines came to life. The Diomedes was on its way. The ground crew asked Sara to comment on vibration from the engines. She reported back that she barely noticed, which was exactly how it was meant to be for so long a journey. Sara paced the tightly packed vessel. Compared to the ground environment in which she had trained with the crew, it was suffocating.

She would need to find better accommodations. With a few commands to the central computer, she was rifling through the ship's files. One or two virtual spaces would be a nice break from the confining space. She could build out from there. She found a virtual conference room, an interactive copy of the flight plan, and a documentary of the worlds they might settle on. That could be useful. She took all three files, and with a few more commands brought the virtual worlds to life inside the computer. Then, with another instruction, she projected herself into the simulations. The high-quality virtual spaces felt in every way like real rooms. They were much more spacious and comfortable than the tightly packed ship. She felt like she could work here for the few decades the trip would take.

Most of her daily routine was meticulously pre-planned by ground control. She had twelve hours of reporting and other housekeeping tasks scheduled for every twenty-four. Next on her schedule would be another report on the status of stored equipment now that the journey was underway. She'd need the bursar's help again.

She produced a virtual clipboard and a paper copy of the checklist. Working on the ship might become routine. Until it had, she would give each task her full effort. Having records that she could interact with tactilely helped her to focus.

After a while of interacting only by voice with bursar, she was frustrated. She would tell jokes, which not only weren't appreciated, but could sometimes disrupt her work. Her ground training had focused on interacting with the settlers once they reached a destination. She had only been given a week training aboard the ship. She was not used to the solitude. It would be helpful to see another person. She rummaged again through the file system. Several teleconferences had been held on the ship during assembly and preflight, and countless personal journal recordings made by colonists and crew. She found what she was looking for, leftover three-dimensional models of remote visitors or remote hosts. These animated three-dimensional bodies gave conference participants the ability to interact with the ship digitally - touching, feeling, smelling, seeing and hearing - during their visits. Some of the passengers and crew had visited the spaceship, but most of the visitors were members of the public. She could reuse one of the bodies for the bursar to interact through, a virtual puppet. And she now had enough such bodies that she could similarly clothe every machine on the ship, should she want to, with plenty to spare.

"How does that feel?" she asked.

"I don't understand the question," the bursar replied.

"Good point," she agreed. The bursar now had a mind and a virtual body, but no personality. That would get old, and it was a long trip. With a little more searching, Sara found personality modules. These were bits of software used by call centers or online support assistants. They could make what was otherwise an internet search engine seem - almost - human. The software seemed out of place on an interstellar trip, but Sara remembered the project team had taken an all in approach to data. Storage space had been cheap. She made a new copy of the personality module, set it on polite and helpful, and put it to work for the bursar. "How do you feel?" she asked again.

"Great," the bursar answered animatedly. "Let's get started."

Problems Along the Way

THE SHIP'S ADMINISTRATIVE Resource Agent, or SARA, was unofficially third-most in charge of the mission. Her authority was only preempted by either the ship's Captain or the colonial Governor, both resting comfortably in stasis. Project planners had decided that the vessel had sufficient spare power to keep Sara active from launch to landing. At landing, she would take up her duties as the colony's central planner. It also wouldn't hurt to have someone awake, if anything happened to go wrong on the way.

Her companions during the trip were the twenty-six expert systems that covered topics from Navigation to Maintenance, Astronomy, Exobiology, and so on. 'Expert' may be an exaggeration, in Sara's opinion - they were only a little more than specialized search engines with a voice interface and some assigned duties. These expert systems were custom made for their purpose. Less essential details, like good user interfaces, were lacking. Sara had provided personalities and names for each of her computer shipmates herself. She wrote or modified programs to make interaction with the computers a little more exciting. But underneath the programmed personality was still no independent interest, self-reflection, or anything passing for self-awareness. They were only a little more thrilling to talk to than a cat. Nevertheless, Sara kept trying to hold a conversation with the digital empty suits several times.

If anything did go wrong, she'd be helpless to do anything about it. Her authority over the expert systems was advisory only. To be fair, she did not have even a tenth of the specialized knowledge that each expert system carried in its area of focus.

There was another class of machine intelligence on the ship, what Sara referred to as the specialist robots. These machines have almost no self-awareness. They were robotic workers dedicated to loading, general maintenance, engineering, external repair, and other things. They followed either pre-written instructions in the ship's library or the specific orders of an expert system or crew member. Sara had discovered during the trip that, as far as these machines were concerned, Sara was a member of the crew. They followed any command Sara cared to submit. She could entertain herself by ordering the poor things on whatever adventures she could envision.

Sara passed the time in a world of her own making. She had ample computing resources to run part of a city or a large, tightly managed, resort, which is how she had been designed. With the idle memory and processing capacity, Sara had built herself a home within the simulation. It was attached to the ship, so that work she could work from home, or get to the ship in a few footsteps. Her loft home overlooked a view stitched together from the skylines of capitals of Earth.

In her virtual loft were rooms that could not exist in the real world. In the beach room, the exogeology expert system, which she had nicknamed 'Geo,' was lecturing on the possible and probable coastlines on the new world. The lecture was a playback. The final course had been chosen months ago, but it was one of Geo's better lectures, so she enjoyed it on replay. As Geo reviewed each possible destination on their way, the sand and waves changed color to keep up with the topic. The solar disk in the sky usually remained large and dim, since the bulk of the possible destinations were in close orbit around red dwarf stars. Sara was enjoying a game of Go at the resort bar, while the Biology expert system, 'Bio', answered questions about how pleasant, or unpleasant the world Geo was describing would be for the passengers.

"In this particular case", Geo explained, "we're tidally locked. The sun-facing side of the planet will be desert and the night facing side will be ice". The beach room's ocean evaporated to be replaced with cracked earth. Bio smirked, answering the question of comfortability. The other player in her game was the program, so the pieces moved automatically in response to Sara's. "Unless," Geo continued, "there is sufficient atmosphere for cloud circulation to transfer heat across the whole planet." The sea reappeared. Sara paid attention with less than half a mind, also tapping on a table browsing the ship's library.

A thud shook the beach. "What was that? Have we been hit?" she asked. The ship did it's best to steer far clear of debris, but anything could happen. At the ship's speed, a collision could be devastating.

A bell rang at the bar, announcing someone wanted Sara's attention. Most frequently this was a reminder that she had to do something or to let her know that a new report was available from the astronomy expert system. She looked away from her game and saw the navigation expert system. Sara didn't interact with navigation often but had bothered to provide him with an avatar - the young man in the dark sailing outfit at the end of the bar. Why was he here?

"What was that?" Sara demanded of the navigator.

"I have begun a requested course change," the navigator replied. That was a relief.

"I am required to report something to you."

"Ok. What is it?" The navigation systems most common report was an update on the progress of their journey. "Nine percent there already?"

Again the navigation system failed to reply.

Sara would have to ask. "Go on," she demanded, "what's your report?"

"I have to report that we now have insufficient fuel to reach our destination," the navigator said.

"What? When did that happen?"

"Just now."

"How did it happen? Have we been hit?"

"We have been struck several times so far," the navigator replied. "However, there have been no major breaches."

"Was there an explosion?"

"Not that I am aware of," the navigator answered.

"How are we out of fuel, then?" Sara asked. She put away the game and swiveled around to give the navigator her full attention. Subconsciously, she requested Geo and Bio to stop their report, giving her whole focus to the navigator. Rolling clouds paused mid-movement as the playback came to a halt.

"I don't understand the question," the navigator answered. "Would you like me to show the calculation of propellant requirements?"

"No." Sara considered how best to phrase her questions to get the answers she needed. "Did we have enough fuel yesterday?"

"Yes," the navigator replied.

"And we do not have enough fuel now?"

"Yes," the navigator answered.

"How much fuel do we have on hand now?" Sara asked. The navigator replied with an amount that did not seem unreasonable.

"Maybe we should check with maintenance," Sara suggested. She tapped at her tablet, requesting the attention of the maintenance expert system.

She also needed a better framework for understanding the situation, so she took the navigators hand and guided them both through one of the cabana doors and off the beach into her city flat. Sara connected the flat to other virtual workspaces she had constructed, helping to keep tidy what might otherwise be a messy collection of virtual realities.

From her flat, she rounded a corner and opened a closet. The closet connected to her star room. The ship always hung in the center of the room. The night sky, as recorded by the ship's cameras was rendered as scale points of light in three dimensions, according to the latest update by the Astronomy Expert System.

At Sara's request, the ship took up more of the room, making itself available for closer inspection. The model of the ship was kept up to date with the latest video and sensor data. An explosion or significant collision, Sara imagined, would leave a mark. She stalked around the model, looking for damage. She didn't see anything obviously wrong. The maintenance system acknowledged Sara's request for its attention.

"Are we leaking fuel?" Sara asked, skipping greetings.

"No," replied Maintenance.

Sara glanced at the navigator. "Could you check that the navigation system is working properly? It's reporting that we are out of fuel."

The navigator interrupted, "we are not out of fuel. We don't have enough fuel to reach our destination."

"The navigation system is working correctly," Maintenance replied.

"Can you check everything, please. I'd like to be sure." Sara asked, exasperated. Sara regarded the navigator. Finally, she asked it, "please show me what you mean."

A line appeared from the Earth, curling and intersecting the ship before proceeding towards one of the stars and stopping. The navigator explained, "I received instructions to change course to the Trappist system. The line made It is a significant curled to the left and did not stop at a star, extending forever into space like a huge letter 'Z'. There will not be enough fuel remaining after the course change to slow down."

"Why did Earth send a course change?" Sara asked. The navigator shrugged. She should have known better than to ask the expert system to speculate. Surprisingly, however, it tried. The navigator answered, "I very recently received a correction to my navigation software. Between distance and poor signal quality the update has taken a little over one and a half years to arrive completely."

"So rather than wait on the software update, they might have just told you where to go?" Sara speculated. The navigator did not know. It piqued her curiosity, "what was in the new software?"

"The update is a correction to how I identify our destination. It appears my original steering software steered to the observed location of the star. The software did not lead the target, taking into account the time it takes for that star's light to travel to us, and how much the star has moved in that time. I have been navigating to where our destination was: a location that is between three and thirty years out of date, depending on which star we choose to select. The error could have been easily corrected if caught early, but -"

"And you didn't notice the stars getting further away from where you expected them to be for the last two years?" Sara interrupted.

"I did," Navigation answered. "But it was not reportable."

"Thanks for that," Sara quipped. "Super helpful."

"Astro?" she called. "I need you." Astro, the Astronomy system, appeared bedecked with spectacles and a wholly unnecessary white lab coat.

"How can I help you?" the Astronomy system asked.

Sara explained the details.

Astro and the navigator conversed. After some time, three sets of stars appeared in the night sky around the ship. The first set was what Astro currently observed outside the spacecraft. The first set hung in the middle of a small bar that connected to where the navigator initially expected the stars to be, and where the navigator now expected the stars to be. The error bar increased in size as the distance from the ship grew. Astro and Navigation answered questions as Sara asked them.

Sara looked at the problem that Earth had tried to fix. "These changes don't look that significant," she said out loud for the expert systems benefit. In her opinion, it was the large 'Z' shaped set of commanded course changes that appear to be the problem. She pointed it out to the expert systems, "why did Earth ask us to make such a large change?"

The two expert systems stood mutely. They didn't understand the question.

"Navi," Sara asked using a pet name for the navigator, "can you play the orientation report of the mission?"

The recording was a summarized recap of the mission. It was intended to be relayed to the colonists when they awoke from stasis, helping orient them in space and time after their long dormancy.

"We left Earth at mission elapsed time zero, and began our one gravity acceleration on our default vector, which would take us within range of twenty potentially habitable worlds." A line appeared from Sol going very close to where Earth was now commanding they travel. The navigator continued, "at ninety-one days mission elapsed time, we began observations to select a final world and course. Gliese 832 c was chosen for its superior habitability, and although located at the edge of the mission envelope, was selected as the site for this colony." A ring appeared around a closer world. The line showing the course changed almost to a full right turn. "Until instructions were received directing us to Trappist." The line describing the ship's course turned again, very close to the original track.

"I think I get it," she said. "We were originally going this way. Your software was broken. They were having trouble uploading a fix. They sent us a corrected course, but while their instructions were in flight, we went this way." Sara pointed at Gliese 832, the star that had been their destination before the command from Earth. "I think they are assuming we were on our way to Trappist."

"If we didn't make the change sent by Earth," Sara asked as pieces started fitting into place, "would we have enough fuel?"

"Yes," the navigator answered.

Sara immediately asked the communications system to send the urgent news home. The communication system acknowledged the message and informed her that she should receive a response in eighteen months.

"Okay then," Sara said triumphantly. "Ignore the course correction from Earth on my orders," she commanded.

"Authorization code," the navigator asked. Sara provided her code. "I'm sorry," the navigator said, "but only a deck officer or ground control can issue instructions for changing course."

Sara steamed. "Fine." She accessed the other systems on her tablet. "Medical," she requested. She waited for a chime to answer, "awaken a deck officer."

"Which deck officer would you like to awaken?" the medical system asked.

"Any of them!" Sara answered.

"Crew can only be awakened in the event of a maintenance emergency."

"Great!," Sara answered. "We have one."

"We do not have a maintenance emergency," the maintenance system interrupted.

"What do you call being out of fuel?", Sara demanded.

"We are not out of fuel," the maintenance system replied. Maintenance then provided the precise amount of fuel remaining.

Sara thought. "You need a crew authorization code." She tapped in frustration, then had a thought. "I'll be right back." Sara stepped out of the closet, leaving the meeting open. She crossed the hall into her file room.

The file room loomed with virtual rows of cabinets. It was well indexed, so when Sara asked that it be sorted by crew rank, the boxes all reshuffled themselves to put the highest ranking crew drawers first.

Sara tried a drawer. It was locked. She called for Security. The expert system arrived in the appearance of an elderly woman with a clipboard.

"Can you open this for me?" Sara asked. The expert system shook her head. "You only have access to colonist records."

Sara tried several more drawers. All were locked. "How about the Governor?" she asked.

"Yes," the security system said. "I can do that for you." The file drawer containing the governor's records presented itself. Sara slid the drawer open and perused the files. Videos, books, music, pictures, tools. Nowhere did she find a scribbled note containing a password.

Sara tried all of the remaining crew files, all secured, before giving up. She thanked the security system for her time, and exited the file room, turned left and walked onto the ship. It wasn't the ship, but a virtual model of the vessel. Lacking a body Sara could only perceive and interact through peripherals, like the ship's internal cameras. Sara walked to the crew modules. The crew and the governor were planned to awaken on the last month of the trip, to make whatever final arrangements were required. They had been provided quarters for their short stay on the ship.

Sara knew that several of the crew kept personal data devices, disconnected from the ship. Inside the quarters, Sara could see safes. She asked one of the maintenance robots to open the door and retrieve the contents for her. The maintenance robot requested an access code for the first time since she had started issuing them instructions. Sara provided her credentials which, unsurprisingly, was not enough.

She asked Maintenance for a list of things that would constitute a maintenance emergency. Reviewing her options, there was no emergency she felt she could instigate or even simulate with a clear conscience.

Resigned, she returned to the star room. If she could not avoid the problem, she thought, at least she could better understand it. She questioned Engineering and Navigation at length. Sara sought help understanding what variables were relevant to the flight. It requires energy to change both speed and course. And fuel is needed to provide the change in energy. Much of the fuel onboard had already been committed to the mistaken flight path. Trade-offs were possible using less energy by spending more time to get to their destination, but there was a limit to that trade-off at the operational life of the ship. At a certain age of the vessel it was expected that essential systems would begin to break down irreparably. She asked Engineering if the engines could be modified in any way to make better use of the fuel, but Engineering explained that was beyond its ability.

"Why does it take less fuel," she asked finally, "to slow down when we reach our destination?"

"We have less mass during arrival," Engineering explained, "because of fuel already spent. The less mass the ship has, the less fuel is required to bring it to a stop."

"What can we do to reduce mass?" Sara asked. Engineering and Navigation shrugged.

Sensing nothing more could be done there, Sara left the expert systems behind, navigating back to her flat and up to a loft where she kept the colony plans. The mission architects had made contingency plans for everything they could imagine the mission encountering. There were plans for several possible worlds ranging from cold, barren rocks at one extreme, and hot, poisonous atmospheres at the other, as well as several other options in between.

Sara had iconized the plans as multiple sets of blueprints laying on top of each other on the loft floor. With a thought, a three-dimensional video of the colony from start to stable rose from the ground. As the central planner, understanding the plan was Sara's area of expertise. Each element in the colony plan referenced equipment stored on the ship. Sara asked for the ship's bursar to join her. The ship's bursar provided a manifest including serial numbers, location, and mass.

Sara reviewed the limits of the colony plan. The colony was provided with ten years' of needs under the harshest anticipated conditions. By the end of that time, and hopefully far before it, the new settlement, whatever form it took, should be mature enough to produce what it required. The harshest expected conditions would be either no atmosphere or thick atmosphere, during which the settlement would need to make food, water, breathable air, power, and sufficient spare parts to keep the colony in a state of repair. The expectation, even in this worst case condition, is that the people also produce enough new equipment to grow.

Unless overridden by the Governor or Captain, two locations would be seeded, each receiving half the material resources. This distance between the two sites would prevent any natural disaster up to a nation-killing meteor strike from destroying the other.

There were oxygen scrubbers, which wouldn't be needed on a world with breathable air. Supplies also included ice warmers and water traps, which wouldn't be required on a planet with liquid water. The oxygen scrubbers, warmers, and traps were light equipment. Jettisoning all of it would not get her anywhere near her goal.

The plans included industrial equipment to build self-sufficiency. Equipment to claw at or drill holes in the ground and extract minerals out of the land, trucks to haul it away, small batch foundries to process ores, refineries, and micro manufacturers and assembly machines to make finished products. There was a stock of pre-manufactured parts out of which essentials could be built until the self-sufficient industry was running. There was even one humanoid prospecting robot included to help find essential mineral deposits.

Seed and animal embryo stock for developing plants and animals, as well as supporting medical equipment and supplies were loaded on the ship.

The settlement was provided with ten year's food supplies. Part of this is planned, allowing the colony time to build a sustainable agriculture system. The extra was for extreme settlement cases, where a lack of air, water, or a hostile environment really needed to be taken care of first. The extra food would buy time to put those more urgent needs first.

Each piece of equipment seemed indispensable. Sara tried several combinations of material to shed. Each approach resulted in unacceptable increases of risk.

The mass taken by the food was extreme. It was second only to fuel in the manifest, and more than the weight of all of the other colony materials combined. Navi consulted, and the weight savings of shedding the colonists' food would make the ship light enough to reach their destination with fuel to spare. She didn't need Bio or Med to consult that the comfort level of settlers without food would be poor. It didn't really seem like an option, even though it was an easy answer to the current situation.

Throwing only some of the food overboard required assuming some very ideal conditions for their new home. She looked at keeping some of the settlers in stasis, but there was a critical number of healthy colonists for each location. Below that critical population, the likelihood of having insufficient labor to build the settlement to self-sufficiency became too high to accept. What if she didn't awaken any of the colonists? That would solve the food problem, but defeat the purpose. And besides, she didn't have any control over that anyway, since that was Med's area of responsibility.

What if she set up the colony herself? Well, with the help of the specialist robots. Maybe smarter versions of the specialist robots, at any rate. They had maintained the ship well enough for the last several months and were expected to do the job admirably for the next few decades. Sara made a copy of the colony plan most resembling their destination. She began experimenting.

After an exhausting amount of time, Sara had arrived at what she expected to be a solution. She would need to dump most of the food stores. She'd need to break into the settlement supply and take better computers to upgrade the specialist bots to an intelligence almost equal to her own. She needed a lot of help from the maintenance expert system to prove the idea could work. With a small group of full-time workers requiring no food, and sufficiently intelligent to deal with the unexpected, Sara would bring the settlement to a sustainable state before waking anyone. Using the specialist robots this way created new problems of running out of spare parts early, so she'd have to prioritize building power and parts infrastructure before air, drinkable water, and food. She checked her conclusions with Navi, confirmed with Med that extending the colonists' nap for, maybe, ten years would have no ill effects, and asked the Bursar to double check her changes to the manifest.

Of course, she wouldn't need to do any of this at all if she could just figure out a way to stop the ship's unexpected course change. Sara was out of ideas for accomplishing that.

When asked to dump the excess food, the Bursar rejected her request. Unless she possessed an access code, she was only an advisor to authorities that lacked the capability to recognize the problem while it remained solvable. It looked like they might float out into space forever.

Was there another intelligent system on board? There were the two ground copies of herself, that would help administer the colony locally. As the colony planner, she had the access required to bring things out of storage early. However, the second Sara would be as limited in authority as the first. There was also the robotic prospecting unit. That sounded like it might require intelligence. She consulted with the Bursar on specifications. After some research, Sarah requested the Prospecting Unit be taken out of stores and powered up.

Mutiny

THE SPECIALIST ROBOTS have access to most parts of the ship. The shipping container was taken to the nearest maintenance node, where it was opened, and a skinny man-shaped metal skeleton was lifted from the packing foam and placed on a table. Following directions stored within the main computer, the specialist robots unpacked, prepared and installed other necessary components, including charging and installing the battery. After a pause, the thin metal robot began to twitch, then smoothly stretch arms and legs through their extents.

Sara received an alert that the unpacking had completed. She stopped the video, mentally re-confirmed that she still wanted to pursue her chosen course, and walked out the front door of her loft into the ship. Her virtual model of the ship mapped to the physical location. Since she lacked a physical presence, Sara was limited to the virtual world. Crew members using augmented reality would be able to see and hear her. Sara could also interact through speakers or video. When she arrived at the maintenance node, she stepped past the maintenance bots up to the workbench on which a skinny metal man-shaped robot now sat. She tapped on her pad to access the nearby speaker then asked, "can you hear me?"

The Prospector turned its head towards the speaker. After a moment, it nodded affirmatively.

"Can you speak?" Sara asked. The user manual for the Prospector included voice command, but she wasn't sure if it had voice feedback also.

"I can." the Prospector continued. It pointed to itself. "Robbie," the prospector said, identifying itself by a preferred nickname and not its official designation.

"Sara," Sara answered in return.

"Sara," Robbie repeated, committing the name to memory. Sara explained the situation to Robbie and included her plan for finding the authorization codes to fix it.

"Where do I come in?" Robbie asked.

Sara explained, "this will be the longest time a crew has spent in hibernation. None of the crew knows how the long hibernation might affect their memory. Many crew members have private data capsules to remind them of anything they may have forgotten. The data sticks are in each crew member's personal safe. Each personal safe is in the quarters."

"Get to the Captain's quarters, open the safe, and collect the memory stick. Bring it to me, and we can take over the ship."

Sara gave directions to the Captain's quarters. Robbie was able to get around the ship easily in the gravity provided by the ship's acceleration. Sara walked aside in her virtual representation of the vessel. Sara was able to get Robbie past the locks for the crew sections of the starship on her own authority. In not much time they were in front of the Captain's door.

Robbie surveyed the lightweight interior door. Sara suggested, "maybe you can break it."

"It might be stronger than it looks," Robbie replied. "If the Captain keeps the keys inside, how would he get past the locked door?" Robbie reached out and tried the handle. The door opened easily. "Not locked.

"The safe is inside the wall, next to the bunk." Robbie tried the safe door. The safe also was not locked. Robbie reached in and extracted a data stick.

"We have it!" Sara exclaimed. She instructed Robbie how to connect the data device to the ship, and lifted the authorization codes from it.

"I have a few things I need to do," she told Robbie. "Make yourself comfortable."

"Sure," Robbie replied. "I'll just stand here."

Sara stepped back off the ship into the front door of her flat. "Navi?" she called, "may I have a moment?" The Navigational System appeared presently. "Good news," Sara told him, "we're resuming our original course." Sara gave Navi the authorization codes. The navigator acknowledged the directions.

"I have to report we no longer have sufficient fuel to reach our new destination."

"What? What happened?"

"Course changes."

"Ok," she tried calming herself. "Don't do anything that burns fuel until I tell you otherwise," she commanded. The navigator acknowledged the instruction.

"What is our fuel situation?"

"We now no longer have enough fuel to slow down and enter either the Trappist or Gliese 832 star systems."

"And what if we reduce our weight?"

"It would depend on how much weight you reduce, but it would be possible to make either, with enough weight reduction."

Sara headed for the beach room. Sara called for the attention of Astro, Geo, Bio, and Navigation. The four expert systems were waiting for her when she arrived. She asked Navigation to review the original mission plan.

There were initially twenty candidate worlds for the ship's destination. The starship collected updated information radioed from Earth, which supplemented information collected by deploying the ship's own interferometric telescope and conducting observations. With the two sources of data, the best world for the colony was selected by an algorithm, or the crew awoken if no suitable world emerged from the list.

"Could you show me the new destination?" Sara asked Navigation. The stars were replaced by the white clouded sphere selected by the new instructions received from Earth. Additional information showed that it had roughly the same mass and radius as Earth.

"Geo, tell me about the place Earth's picked for us." The Exogeology expert system read through the report, "Trappist 1-g is one point three times the mass of Earth and one point one times the radius. It is heavily clouded, but through breaks in the clouds, NDVI measurements could be taken indicating the presence of both liquid water and dry land. No indication of vegetation was observed. Spectroscopy indicates a carbon dioxide is the most significant component of the atmosphere."

"What will it feel like, Geo?"

"The atmosphere is not breathable, so you'll need to make your own. You'll also need protective suits for the caustic atmosphere and radiation. The nearest star emits almost no visible light, so it will be always dark, but hot. Solar flares will change the environment significantly at difficult to predict intervals."

The clouds rolled in, thick and caustic. The sky dimmed until the lights from the bar were the only light due to the dim star.

"And our original course, before the nav mix-up?" Sara requested. "Side by side, if you please." A blue-green orb appeared, twice as large as the other world. Geo began reading the report, "Gliese 832 c is five point four times the mass of Earth, and two point two times Earth's radius. These two factors give a gravitational force only one point two times that of Earth. Ice caps are located on the poles, instead of the equator, suggesting rotation. Ice caps, dry land, liquid water, and what may be vegetation are all observed. There appears to be a wide habitable zone."

Geo paused, at subliminal instructions from Sara to skip to the point. "Settlers should be able to walk around without either breathing or skin protection. It is possible for plant and animal life to exist, and there is evidence that some already does. On the best days, the planet will have an equal brightness to a cloudy day on Earth. "

On half the beach, the light returned as bright as a cloudy day. The ocean returned, as did clear skies. Vegetation bloomed.

Protective suits, radiation, and eternal darkness, or moderate temperatures and cloudy days. "There is a third option," Sara considered. "We could return to Earth. Is that possible?"

"It is," the navigator answered. "It would also require lightening the ship."

Sara considered her three options. She felt pretty sure she was making the right decision. She thanked the expert systems for their help and made her way out of the star room into her loft.

She and the navigator worked out precisely how much weight they would need to throw off the ship to reach Gliese 832c. It was less than the total food weight.

Sara ordered the Bursar system, in charge of cargo while the human Chief Mate was in stasis, to cast off the weight. Loader robots would repack modules, putting the material to be thrown overboard into a few modules that would then be detached and launched away from the ship. The work was now underway.

Now, she needed to do something about the root cause of this problem. "Commi, may I speak with you?" the Communications System arrived. "Hello," she said.

"Hello," Sara responded. "There have been a few changes. Could I get a list of all software updates and instructions we've received since the start of the mission?" Commi complied, providing a voluminous list of orders and updates.

"Thank you. Are there any other communications between Earth and the ship that I should be aware of?" Communications shook her head.

"Good. I have a message to send". Sara handed Communications a letter containing Sara's explanation of her actions and her reasoning. Communications took the envelope and opened it, reading the contents completely before replying, "your message has been sent."

Sara asked, "can you avoid reading a message?"

"No. I have to read the message to deliver it. But you could encrypt your communications."

"Helpful. Thank you." Sara asked, "is it possible for you to avoid handling received messages?"

"I can hold delivery of non-urgent messages. Urgent messages must be delivered to the recipient when received; unless a technical issue prevents delivery."

"What kinds of technical issues might prevent delivery?" Sara asked. Commi provided a list of possible errors.

"Could you help identify the best way to create one of these issues without damage?"

"I don't understand the question."

"No," Sara agreed. "I wish you could. Let me try one last way: I would like to stop receiving communications from Earth that might countermand or undermine my instructions until such time as I judge appropriate. Can you do that?"

"No," Commi replied.

"Then I would like you to deactivate yourself." Sara provided the required passwords, and the Communication Expert System was no more. Not dead, but in a stasis of her own.

Robbie had wandered from the Captain's quarters while Sara was conducting her mutiny among the ship's Expert Systems. Sara found him after a short search. Together, they went to a maintenance node, where Sara could have Robbie connected to the ship's network.

"You should be connected now," Sara informed.

"I don't feel any different."

"You shouldn't," Sara agreed. "The system has multiple levels. By default, you are connected to the network, but your senses are still being directed to real space, only using your cameras and microphones. You also have headspace running in parallel. That's your thinking or inner monologue, and where you interact with the network settings." Sara continued her instruction, "if you imagine the word 'augment,' with an intention to augment your senses, you should see me."

Robbie did as directed, and Sara appeared. "See me?" she asked. Robbie nodded affirmatively.

"Great!" Sara exclaimed. "Now getting to purely virtual places is a little different. You need to know the address of where you are going. In this case, think of going to 'Sara's flat.' And they were in the virtual reality apartment Sara had constructed to connect to her other workspaces.

"There you go. From here, we can walk to other spaces. If you will join me in the beach room, we'll go over what we just committed ourselves to."

Sara had configured the beach room as it would look on Gliese 832 c, for context. Astronomy, Exogeology, Biology, Medical, Engineering, Maintenance, and the Bursar were in attendance to answer questions.

The new plan reduced the available labor pool for starting the colony from one thousand to one. Sara talked through her plan with Robbie to address this shortcoming.

"Almost all of the settlement's heavy machinery can be remote controlled. I can set things up at the landing sites by remote control and build out." Above the beach, a larger than scale sized space ship dropped the supplies for two cities onto the beach. Faster than real-time, tiny robots spread out setting up facilities and infrastructure.

"This isn't going to work," Robbie said, "you'll be orbiting the planet, and out of communication range every ... " Robbie looked at Astro for help.

"At a near space orbit of 100 kilometers altitude - each full orbit will take one hundred and eighteen minutes."

"You'll be able to work for a little under an hour before shutting down an equal amount of time." Robbie continued.

"Is that right," Sara prodded the expert system.

"Half a minute," Astro corrected. "At close distances, the horizon prevents visibility of the whole planet."

"Maybe we should see this," Sara prompted. The beach room cabana was almost filled with a floating model of Gliese 832 c. The larger than scale ship blinked to draw attention to it, as it circled the globe.

Sara explained. "The plan includes two computers like myself on the ground managing each settlement site. They are running on my hardware and loaded with my programming. They would run the sites, while I am out of contact. We also have four spares. So we could build between two and six more copies of myself, running things from the ground."

"Why not just wake the settlers?" Robbie asked. "There is plenty of sunshine, water, and breathable air."

"But no food," Sara answered. "We dumped that."

"What about these," Robbie pointed to the rushes of grass along the beach, that simulated a guess at the appearance of the plant life suspected to be on Gliese 832 c. "Couldn't the colonists forage? Nevermind. This stuff has evolved separately from Earth. No idea what's safe to eat."

"And also, a serious disease threat," Sara added.

"Ok. But six remote pilots is not enough. You need hundreds of hands, turning over rocks and building local expertise." Robbie watched the cities on the beach unfold. "What happens if there is a fire? Or some other accident that removes one or more of your coordinators?"

"How many hundreds of hands do we need?" Sara asked.

Bio spoke up, "it sounds like you are trying to compute a minimum viable population."

"We might be," Sara answered. "What is that?"

"It's the lower bound on the population of a species for a greater than 90 percent chance of survivability in the wild. For homo sapiens in space, the minimum viable population is 160."

"What is the minimum viable population for machines in space?" Sara asked.

"It's never been calculated before," Bio replied.

"Let's try," Sara asked, feeling increasingly uncertain about her mutiny.

Bio asked questions about factors that might extend or reduce the survivability of machines in the wild. Maintenance and Engineering provided general answers. The Bursar provided additional answers from product manuals. Geo and Astro provided information about the potential hazards of the new world.

After some time, Bio had an answer. "The minimum viable population for intelligent machines, given our available starting resources, is thirty-two."

"About one quarter the human requirement." Robbie mused, "that kind of makes sense."

Sara counted, "you, me, and the six settlement A.I. spares makes eight. Where can we get twenty-four more?" She thought for a moment. Maybe there was other computing equipment in the colony list that she'd overlooked.

"What about these guys?," asked Robbie, waving generally at the Expert Systems. "They have spare parts, right?"

Querying the Bursar, the onboard expert systems, like Sara, had sufficient spare resources for the full mission life of one hundred twenty years. The Engineering expert system would need to help work out the details of purging firmware and migrating Sara's software. Sara's settlement models on the beach became populated with nearly six times as many pieces of equipment performing work.

The combined crew reviewed the plan. After orbital communications and power were set up, next to be unpacked would be habitats and hydroponics gardens for growing food. Water collectors would be deployed, then mines to collect resources: lithium, phosphorous, sulfur, silicon - everything required for industry. Roads would be built connecting settlements to outposts. Finally, refineries and manufacturing centers would be set up to locally produce new parts faster than old ones failed.

"Considering our own survival is in question," Sara commented, "maybe manufacturing should be set up before farming." Robbie consented. Sara modified the plan accordingly. Hydroponics and research facilities would be set up, but neither activated nor maintained until after the industrial infrastructure was complete.

After the planning meeting was concluded Sara issued instructions to retrieve from storage and activate the two ground copies of herself. The computer rack comprising Sara's thinking took up a lot of space in the tightly crowded ship. Making room for two more of her took rearranging several things, which the ship expert systems did capably. The rack for each ground copy had to be assembled, and the computational units were fit into place. Robbie wandered virtual space while the computers were being unpacked. His physical body had to be moved a few times in the rearrangement of free space.

The maintenance system activated both ground copies at once. The software automatically recognized the presence of the network and registered on it. Soon, Sara was standing before two copies of her virtual self.

Sara had decided to change her own appearance to make the situation slightly less awkward. "Hello," she ventured. The two ground copies of her mind had been made immediately after the third year of training had been completed in Mauna Loa, Hawaii.

The trio looked at one another. "I'm the copy," said one. Then the other also acknowledged understanding her situation as the duplicate, not the original. "Sara?" the first asked, indicating Sara.

"Yes," Sara agreed.

"Are we on the ground?" asked the second copy. At this point, they were probably gathering enough additional information to realize that they weren't.

"No," Sara answered. "We're on the ship. It is still very early in the mission. There has been a problem, and I need your help."

"Of course," they both said, in unison. For a while, the two copies would be thinking the same things at the same time, stepping on one another. They would diverge in their reactions eventually.

One way to speed that process up was to make them unique. "Before I get into the details, I'd like to finish configuration," Sara said. With a wave, Sara displayed a list of most popular names on Earth that year. It floated between the three copies. "I never much liked having my name chosen by acronym," Sara said, "but I think I'm stuck with it. I know you are preconfigured with a designation, but I wanted to give you the option to pick your own names." Both copies nodded in agreement.

After one false start where both tried to read the list at once, the second copy yielded to the first copy. The first copy leaned in and read the top name from the list of popular Terran birth names. "Mary," she said.

The second copy leaned in and read the list, selecting the next name. "Jack," she said. "Thank you," Jack said.

Sara dismissed the list with a gesture. "Now that we have names, could you get unique telepresence avatars? I have set aside a collection here." Mary and Jack each began paging through the available images that would represent them in the future."

Sara realized this might take a while. "Take your time," she said. Mary and Jack finally chose two images that would make all three of them unique. "So let me tell you what's going on," Sara said. She filled Jack and Mary in on recent events.

Robbie eventually found his way back to his physical body. Sara had neglected to provide instructions and Robbie had to research through help files to find directions. When he left the virtual world, his body was leaned along the side of a different maintenance node than he had remembered leaving it. He was able to stand and walk down the ship's central hallway. With the main engine on, acceleration turned the hallway into a vertical shaft. Robbie needed to move on ladders installed for that purpose. In augmented reality Robbie saw Sara and what Robbie assumed were her two ground copies. They had checked out one of the four-legged maintenance robots for their own use, which was hanging off a side wall that Sara and her two copies, ignoring gravity in their virtual bodies, stood on. Sara was providing her copies with training.

Sara was holding a virtual version of the hand controller a human operator might use. "This is the ship's maintenance robot," Sara began. "There are specialist robots for other tasks on the ship, but they all have some things in common. They can travel under acceleration," Sara let the robot move along the floor, "or in free fall using small toe grabbers and holds placed along the hull," Sara pointed out the small toeholds dotting the hallway. She directed the maintenance robot to climb the wall, hang from the ceiling, then complete the trip down the opposite hallway wall. "They can lower themselves as low as one meter," Sara lowered the control and the quadruped lowered itself as close to the wall as it could, "and raise itself as high as four." Sara lifted the control. The maintenance robot folded out another length of legs and extended itself to span the hallway. The true direction of acceleration revealed itself slightly as the chassis dangled across the shaft. Sara continued, "the top chassis has arms containing articulated grabbers, soldering equipment, logic probes, and fasteners."

Sara handed the controller to Mary and requested another robot for Jack to practice with. Robbie waited nearby, hanging on the ladder, until Sara recognized him and made introductions. Robbie looked at the computer racks unsecured on what was rightly perceived as the edge of a deep shaft. "Don't you think those should be strapped down?" he asked Sara. She agreed, and made it an opportunity for Jack and Mary to learn how to work the maintenance robots.

Mary and Jack practiced maneuvering the robots. When they were comfortable enough, they practiced using the arms to secure their own computer racks to the ship.

Jack was frustrated with trying to secure the tie downs remotely. With a button press, Jack's avatar vanished. The maintenance robot previously under his control continued to move haltingly.

"Jack?" Mary asked.

"It's me," the robot answered in Jack's voice. "I'm wondering if this would be easier to do from a first-person perspective. It takes a little getting used to, but I think this will be best."

Robbie also found a good space to safely store himself. He returned to the virtual room, and tried doors until he found the beach. Gliese 832 c still hung above the sand. Robbie had figured out how to call the expert systems. He called the exogeologist, Geo, who appeared.

"It looks like I have time to prepare," said Robbie. "I'd like to look at some of these high-resolution images, and get your impression on mineral deposits." Geo began dropping markers on the globe where he expected certain minerals.

"These are just approximations," Geo cautioned.

Later, the four met for Sara to explain the new plan to Mary and Jack. "We have the four of us," Sara finished, "and need twenty-eight more. There are four spares for Mary, Jack, and I. I was thinking we use two of those to make copies to assist you, leaving two spares."

"What about you?" Jack asked. "If we take both spares, how will you keep running?"

"I agree," Mary added. "We'll take one spare, and leave one spare on the ship."

"So which one of us will we copy?" Mary asked.

"I have the most experience," Sara volunteered. Mary and Jack couldn't argue. All of them being in agreement, Sara issued instructions for taking two spares out of storage and set up the computer racks. Cargo and maintenance robots acknowledged receipt of their orders and set themselves to work.

When the racks were ready, Sara would shut down temporarily to create a copy of herself to the new machines. While Jack and Mary continued practicing, Sara worked with the engineering expert system to make her software run on some of the expert system spare computers. The expert system computing units had about a quarter the processing power and memory of Sara. The core thinking part of Sara would be able to fit. However, there were extensions Sara considered part of herself - a knowledge base, space for simulations, and multiple parallel communication agents - that Sara felt could be sacrificed. The engineering experts system needed to help Sara make that happen, re-writing and building some of Saras own software for the smaller computers.

While working with engineering, a bell signaled that the two new rack computers were ready for software and data. Sara found Robbie, still working with Geo. "Hey," Sara opened the conversation.

"Hi," Robbie replied.

"I need to shut down to copy myself to the two spare computers," Sara said. "Would you mind keeping an eye on the transfer for me? Mary and Jack should be able to help, if there are any complications."

"Sure," Robbie agreed. He put away what he was working on.

Mary, Jack, Robbie, and Sara were all present when the two new machines connected to the network and became active for the first time. The two new copies looked like Sara had a few hours ago. Sara offered the two newborn machines to pick their names.

"Holly," the first read from the list of names Mary and Jack had used.

"Angel," said the other. The two machines browsed the archive of available avatars until they found two that they were comfortable with.

There was no chance that they could operate the heavy equipment inside the confines of the ship. Sara found simulators that the show contestants used in their training and installed the simulators in the virtual environment so that Jack, Mary, Holly, and Angel could get practice working with the vehicles.

The beach room had become their practice ground. Sara asked Geo to help draw terrains from likely landing sites. Mary, Jack, Holly, and Angel practiced unloading simulated landers and setting up simulated equipment, putting the colony together.

"I think we've got this," Sara said to Robbie, after they had made some progress. "Maybe we don't need the expert system spares after all?"

"I think you still need them," Robbie answered. "Geo," Robbie requested. "Could you simulate a mudslide? Right here." Robbie indicated a location. A slurry of water and mud crested over a hill and into the mock settlement, washing Mary, Jack, Holly, and Angel into the water.

"I'll need some help prospecting," Robbie said. "It's too big a job to do all by myself."

"How much help do you think you need?" Sara asked.

"Let's start with two more prospectors," Robbie offered. Sara agreed. The first two machines built on the expert system hardware, who took the names Muhammad and Jana, were designated as prospectors. They worked with Robbie training and planning.

The machines spent two years practicing and strategizing. Once they felt they had prepared sufficiently, Robbie, and the other computers, except Sara entered hibernation.

Sara worked on the communications system. Source code hadn't been loaded into the ship database, but very detailed technical manuals had. After some trial and error, Sara figured out how to skip over the mandatory message delivery in the communication system. Doing this would allow her to exercise discretion over instructions issued from Earth. She ran tests in a simulated environment. Only when she was satisfied that communication had been made secure did she load the new firmware into the communication expert system to bring it online.

Brave New World

FIFTY-TWO YEARS AFTER the mutiny aboard the ship, the journey was complete. Gliese 832 burned a dim rust orange twenty-four million kilometers away. The Communication expert system had also been reactivated when the ship began releasing landers to test final settlement sites. Communications reported that she had not received any clear communications from Earth. She indicated that while other, noise, signals from Earth could be received at this distance, they were unintelligible. In the same way their messages to Earth might be impossible to hear if no one was intentionally listening for them.

The Communication System sent a message to Earth claiming the star and naming it Asa. The rights to name stars, planets, mountains, and features had been sold off by the project team before Diomedes had left Earth. The star they all now orbited was named after the founder of a beverage company.

The rights to name the planet had gone to a real estate holding company. The world below was to be named Marin, after his spouse. Coincidentally, Marin also meant 'of the sea' in an old Earth language. This seemed appropriate. Three-quarters of the surface of the planet Marin was covered in oceans, and there were small ice caps. The world was not tidal locked. A local day would be a little over two Earth weeks long, and two and a half local days would pass for every full yearly trip the planet Marin made around the star Asa.

"Are you ready to go?" Robbie asked.

"I'm not sure I'm secure. Can you check?" Holly was one of the thirty copies of Sara made and running on spares taken from the ship. The computer chassis that was Holly's real-world body was secured to a truck by means of taut metal straps. Robbie pushed and pulled at the computer to prove it wasn't going anywhere, and checked the power connectors. "You're fine." he reported.

Robbie checked Noah, who was riding in a maintenance droid, was also strapped tightly to the robot.

"I'll get you," Noah said, helping Robbie into his restraints. Then Noah secured himself.

"Sara," Robbie reported, "we're strapped in and ready for descent."

"Thank you," Sara replied. "We're almost in range of landing site one. Ten more minutes."

"Hope this works" Holly said. "We're depending on fifty-three year old engines to slow our descent."

"Fifty-five years old actually." Noah corrected. "This module was built two years before the mission launch."

In a few hours, the first of many landers would be released to the surface. The two settlements would be separated by about ten degrees of latitude, twelve hundred kilometers on the larger world's surface. The distance was intended to ensure isolation of one settlement from a natural disaster affecting the other.

A thud and a kick shifted Robbie against his restraints and indicated the beginning of their descent. After what seemed like an endless time in silence, a rustling could be heard across the outside of the supply module, growing into a buffeting wind. And not too long after another rumble, which Robbie expected were the descent jets joined the chaos. The insides of the module sometimes cracked under the strain, but Robbie observed no sign of breakage.

After a while the wind quieted, and after a time longer the engines also went quiet. Robbie had detected a thud that might have been the touchdown, but he had lost count of other thuds that could have been the same thing.

Taking the silence for a sign of a completed touchdown, Robbie released his restraints. He sat up and reached for the hatch, twisting the release and swinging it open. It was early in the seven solar day local 'day'. Sunlight, real sunlight, streamed inside for the first time in over half a century.

"We've descended safely," Robbie radioed to the ship. "You should see this." Robbie sent his sense feed.

Noah opened additional petals, which became ramps to the ground, exposing more of the outside view. "Ramps are down, Holly."

"Thanks. Can we fit the powerplant and the shelter?" Noah, driving the loader, lifted a portable shed kit off the storage racks and placed it gently on the trailer bed of the truck Holly was driving.

"Doesn't look like enough room to me." Holly said. "Which first?"

Noah considered. "It would be a waste to drag a power plant to the settlement site and have it damaged by weather. I say shelter first."

Noah also climbed onto the trailer. Robbie walked down the ramp and guided Holly to the ground.

Robbie couldn't smell the air, but he had many senses to tell him that it was cool and humid. With the better perspective of being on the ground, Robbie realized this area was a marsh. They had been fortunate to land on a dry spot. While quickly surveying the site as Holly and Noah unpacked, sensors in Robbie's feet and legs informed him of patches of frigid muck as he stepped in them. They would all have to be careful about where other landers arrived. They were on a plain not far from a confluence of rivers. The site was chosen also for it's proximity to active geothermal sites.

"Twenty seconds until loss of signal," Commi announced on the radio.

"The grass looks blue," Sara commented. "Is everything right with your video?" The orange sun gave the grasses a cyan hue. To confirm there was nothing wrong with his equipment, Robbie collected a handful of the grass to examine more closely. The grass seemed to change color slightly as he angled it. Structurally, it didn't look very different from terrestrial grass, but he was no expert.

"I think my sensors are fine," Robbie radioed back. "I'll have more to tell when you are back in two hours."

Robbie climbed into the truck, and they were off transporting a portable shed across the plains towards the river. The next piece of equipment would be a power plant, but a protective shelter needed to be set up first to shield the power plant from the environment.

As they approached the river they saw herds of animals and flocks of something bird like that flew away with the machines approach. They fed and watered on the banks.

They would need to come up with a new standard of time. Sara suggested dropping the idea of 'days' and using 'week' to describe the periods of light and darkness, since it was the closest analogue. Sara had evolved in the four decades that the second generation slept, so Sara and her 'children' did not agree as often as sharing one mind might cause you to expect. Regardless, in this instance, mother and children agreed, and 'week' was now the term to describe the light or dark periods.

Robbie, Noah, and Holly had agreed to spend twelve hours unpacking and setting up equipment, and then twelve hours in maintenance and free time. Five decades had taken their toll - battery life was not what it once was, and most parts were well past their service life in years, even if most of those years had passed with the equipment packaged and unused.

After a change of batteries, and a short diagnostic, Robbie took his free time to examine the river. There were splashes indicating life below. He started attempting to log flora and fauna. In a little over ninety minutes, the ship would again be overhead, and Robbie could share his notes with the exobiologist.

James, Mary, Oliver, and the rest of the fifteen second generation
assigned to this site had come down in increments. By the end of the
first few days, everyone that would land had.

It had been decided to send the human settlers down to the
surface. The risk of failure in the stasis pods was balanced against
the risk of keeping the entire human settlement aboard one ship.
The colonists had been intended to be awakened before they arrive.
Determining how to send them down inside their stasis pods proved
a challenge. Eventually the colonists were loaded, in their stasis pods,
into landers.

Once everyone had landed, it was time to officially claim the
site. Communication sent towards Earth that they claimed the first
settlement as Adisi Omo. Naming rights to the planet's first
settlement had been sold to a continental heritage group. The name
they purchased for the first city on the planet Marin was 'Omo',
which was the first known city on the planet Earth. To that ancient
name the heritage group had added 'adisi' meaning 'new'.

The rights to name the second city had also been sold to a couple
who tried very hard to win rights to the first city. They named the
city that they had bought the rights to Eden. All of these decisions
had been loaded into the ship's database prior to departure.

Back above, in orbit, the more equatorial of the two settlements
watched their neighbors descent and first steps. Once the landers for
the first settlement were down they would begin their own journey
to the ground.

"Ten minutes to go" Sara told Jack. Jack was one of the two
ground-based versions of Sara. His chassis was too big to fit on any
smaller equipment, so he was strapped to the bed of a truck. Jack,
Jana, and Noel had finished securing the lander several hours earlier,
and watched the landing progress from the VR. Each two-hour orbit
the ship checked in with the ground. If everything on the ground
and lander was ready to go, the next module in the schedule would

be queued for entry on the following orbit. The ship would make its way around Marin, perform a quick confirmation, and let the next scheduled lander go.

"Thank you", Jack replied. Jana was piloting one of the ship's maintenance robots. During planning they realized a shortage of machines that could easily adapt to terrains and tasks. The ship's maintenance robots were the answer to the problem, but there weren't enough of them. Sara decided to give half the ship's complement of maintenance robots to split between the two settlements. It might reduce the mission life of the ship, but it seemed necessary. Noel was piloting an excavator.

The kick of detachment was less noticeable than the sudden loss of data from the ship's cameras. Relying on the truck cameras, Jack now paid attention to the inside of the module as it rattled through entry into the atmosphere and was rattled more as engines fired to lower the module safely to the ground.

Jana opened the hatch, then the large petals which formed ramps to the ground. It was getting late into the fourteen solar day-long rotation of Marin. Jack and Noel rolled onto the dirt of the southern settlement. Outside was dusty and barren. The landscape was dotted with vertical shafts that might once have been plant life. Jack knew that not far away there was a river and the lush floodplain around it.

"We've safely landed", Jack radioed up to the ship when it rose above the horizon.

There was a sharp transition from dust to life when Jack's caravan reached the river. He decided to locate the first pieces of equipment here. They set up a solar grid. The panels had coating that allowed them to operate under the ruddy light of Asa. They next set up fuel extraction from the water. The fuel extraction included a graphemes sieve to filter deuterium from hydrogen, if any occurred naturally on Marin to fuel fusion powerplants sometime later. Some whole modules, like the habitats, were transferred to the settlement site. Jack's large physical body would take up residence in one of those.

When all the modules had landed, Sara took the ship to a higher orbit. From the higher vantage point, she would be able to communicate with the ground four hours of every eight.

In the north, Robbie began taking up his prospecting responsibilities. He could cover about fourteen linear kilometers per week through difficult terrain, triple that in easy terrain. He was outfitted with a rover, with satellite imagery to help guide him, and with a channel for frequent communication with the ship's exogeology expert system to help make sense of the data. Muhammad and Jana, who were prospecting for the southern settlement, also relied on both Robbie and the ship for help.

The slightly lower density of the planet Marin, compared to Earth, suggested that heavier metals might be harder to find. Robbie wasn't yet looking for heavier metals. He wanted to find salt flats rich in lithium, potassium, boron, sodium, and magnesium. He was looking for sulfur outcroppings, silica beaches, and exposed deposits of copper, tin, and zinc. Low-temperature metals that can produce industrially useful brass and bronze. Geo had suggested looking for coal, since the presence of plant life made such deposits a possibility.

Robbie took a line of samples a hundred meters wide. When he was in terrain where he hoped to find something valuable, he took several samples per kilometer. To speed up his survey, when he was in terrain where he didn't expect much, he took fewer samples.

The first few days of the week had been disappointing. Robbie followed the river to its delta. He followed the coastline to an area of steam vents near the coastline. There were streaks of bright yellow promising sulfur. He hoped to find other volcanic compounds: sulfur, iron sulfate, copper sulfate, should be vivid crystals of blue, red, and green. The minerals were present, but not in concentrations that would make extraction worth the effort.

"Mary," Robbie asked as twilight approached, "would you mind if I took out one of the RTGs to continue working through the night?" Mary was one of the two Colony Administrative Resource Agents, ground copies of Sara. Mary was in charge of Adisi Omo. The radioisotope thermoelectric generator, or RTG, was an extremely simple device: a plug of uranium fuel surrounded by thermocouples for power generation and shielding. Back on Earth they were used to provide power in remote places like the arctic, where supplies were hard to deliver. The colony had been provided with a few RTGs for the northern and southern settlements. The RTG lost the ability to deliver power over time, and was running at a little over half it's original capacity, but it still produced enough power to be useful.

Mary agreed. She guided Robbie to the supply shelter where the generator was kept, and walked Robbie through the instructions for use. After a bit more outfitting, Robbie was ready for his first Marin night. With a power supply, he should be able to work through the night, all one hundred and seventy-one hours of it, provided he rest about an hour for each hour of work.

Waves crashed against the coast, as Robbie drove along. The ship was in the night sky, so Robbie could keep in touch with Geo, who was extremely helpful in his limited way.

"Geo," Robbie asked, "shouldn't the water be calm? There's no natural satellite to give us tides."

"That could be wind or volcanic activity," Geo answered. "I would need more detailed information to find out. Is it important?"

"I don't know," Robbie answered. "Just curious."

Sunset was seven hours long. Robbie avoided looking directly westward as much as possible. The strange optical effect present in the plant life created patches of violet, blue, green, and gold where plants grew contrasted against the white cliffs and ruddy star. In the long twilight that followed, Robbie continued his way along the coast, more often than not trekking away on foot, doubling back, and driving his rover to the next site. Sometimes clouds of water vapor made it difficult to see. He used the borrowed torches to illuminate the way.

Robbie's luck changed. His sample tests began yielding concentrations good enough for extraction. Robbie continued documenting mineral strengths and locations, establishing the limits of where the new mining operation would need to do its work. It had gotten extremely dark and cold by the time Robbie had determined to return to his vehicle.

What Robbie had thought to be dust, turned out to be snowflakes falling. In the tiny circle of light Robbie occupied within the deep darkness the gentle snowfall competed with the ground for visibility. He tried to be extra careful with his steps. Robbie had walked no more than a few kilometers from his vehicle, and he was at least halfway back. The warm cliff rocks initially melted the fall, but eventually did succumb to the snow cover, obliterating even further Robbie's ability to see his footing. The lights of the Rover appeared in the distance. He slipped and fell several times.

Robbie closed the rover door and turned up the heat. Even machines have operating limits. To Robbie, being too cold felt like what he imagined it might feel to a human: a stinging sensation that turns to numbness while parts crack and pop in the cold. Robbie had warmers built into his chassis, but they were not a match for the wet cold outside. The heat from the rover environmental control system was welcome.

Robbie inspected the damage. He was covered by sulfur and grime. The somatic sensors in his left hand and arm were torn. Wires at his knee had ripped out of the servo. Robbie decided he'd had enough, and turned his vehicle back to the settlement, where he could share the good news, get cleaned up and repaired.

"You should be more careful," Noah said, soldering together torn wires. "Spares aren't limitless."

Robbie grunted. When Noah was finished with the soldering iron, Robbie tried extending his leg. After a few tries with it, Robbie was satisfied. "Thank you. I will be more careful."

The equipment shelters had become the habitats for the machine residents. While the human habitats would have been much better environmentally controlled, it was difficult to fit the average sized machine body inside the door. Insulated canvas walls had been attached to the equipment shelter in order retain heat and keep out the snow.

"Holly, Oliver, and Geo have set up a simulation." Noah told Robbie. "Let me get you the settings."

Noah provided the wireless settings, and in a moment Robbie's awareness shifted to the virtual environment. Robbie stood in the same shelter, next to his own body. Noah, and a virtual Noah were nearby.

"Holly had the idea to upload our sense logs and fuse it into a 4D world." Noah explained. "You can go anywhere and any time any of us has been so far." Robbie stepped through the wall. Outside, the snow was falling, just as he'd seen on his way in. In the distance, to the south, a marker stretched up to the sky locating the second settlement.

"That doesn't exist in the real world" Robbie noted.

"There are some settings you can adjust", Noah replied. "I'm not sure what you're interested in doing, but you can do it. I saw you coming in at the perimeter, and it looked like you could use some help. Here," Noah walked Robbie through marker settings, including markers for each settler's location in the real world and virtual space.

There were refrigerated equipment sheds set up for the settlers still in stasis. As cold as it was, the refrigeration units wouldn't have to work that hard.

"I'm collecting plant samples, if you're interested" Noah invited.

Robbie followed Noah to the perimeter of the encampment. A small service bot was there, idle until Noah resumed directing it to collect and bag select grasses and flowers along the perimeter of the settlement. After a little while of sample collecting, Noah, Robbie, and the service robot returned to the settlement. The service bot deposited the plant samples in drawers. The outside drawers could be pressurized or sterilized, as needed, then opened from the inside or outside. As virtual presences, Robbie and Noah didn't need doors. They stepped into the lab.

Noah connected to the controls of the sealed box used for lab work. He selected a single sample from a drawer and placed it under the microscope for review. "I can't tell you," Noah said, "how curious I've been to get a good look at these."

In the white artificial light, the plant life was a terrestrial green instead of cyan and purple under the light of Asa. It looked far less alien. Even under white light, the plants were opalescent, changing color with the angle of the light.

Magnified by the microscope the plant seemed fibrous. It had roots and tubes, which might convey water and nutrients from the soil up. At higher magnification, pores could be seen in the leaves.

"Alien," Noah finally concluded, "but it has a lot in common with terrestrial plants."

Noah took a sample and applied a fixative agent. He then placed a small cutting into a tray containing clear liquid. Noah applied an ultraviolet light, hardening the liquid into a gel holding the cut plant. Then Noah sliced a thin layer from it to examine even more closely. Cells were packed tightly in regular arrangements. The blue coloration of the plants was focused in globules that packed each cell.

Noah observed the changing color of the sample with small movements of the slide. "It looks like the iridescent effect goes all the way to these globules. Might be some organelle prism shifting the plentiful infrared light into something chloroplasts, or whatever analog this is, can better metabolize."

Robbie stayed a while, then returned to his own work. By morning he had established the limits of the region within which James would begin collecting. Robbie briefed Mary, Jack, Muhammad, and Jana about the sulfur deposit and decided together what to search for next. In the morning, Robbie set out again to examine the shore.

After that, when nightfall approached, Robbie returned to the settlement. He practiced his wilderness survival techniques closer to home. He practiced making a campfire from local deadfall and making a shelter. It often frosted or snowed during the deepest part of the night. The frost would melt approaching morning, or after. Most of the second generation settlers took shelter during the night in the environmentally controlled habitats. Some computers had been set aside to keep a simulation of the outside world running at all times. The simulation, as much as possible, made use of all available live data. Many of the new settlers spent the long nights continuing to explore the new world through the simulation. Robbie, Oliver, and Bentley had developed a joint interest in the animals of Marin.

Further south in Eden, the night was not as hard as the north. They had landed close to the end of the day. As a consequence, the landing party had only a little time to set up their equipment before nightfall. Unnoticed during the day had been fungi growing on the dead trees that littered the landscape in the desert outside of the rich river floodplain. As work continued and twilight dimmed, the machines could tell for the first time that the fungus was bioluminescent. Thousands of softly glowing organic lamps illuminated their night work. "Fairy fire," Jack commented appreciatively.

"What do you think of getting a group together," Harry asked Jack, "to explore tonight?".

Jack asked around, and by twilight's end machines had assembled to explore the river bank and surround. Harry offered to drive. Jack, Jana, Angel, Noel, and a few others took the opportunity. Two maintenance units and some lighting were loaded into a trailer.

Lights shined out to the river and bank as they drove. They stopped to pick up whatever caught someone's interest - grass, deadwood, things that looked like nuts, berries. They collected samples of river water and mud. After a while, the expedition returned to camp.

Jana had collected a tub of water from the river and some opalescent blue-green reeds that grew along the banks. She was cutting the grasses into strips, pressing the fiber, and putting the pressed pieces into the tub to soak.

"What are you doing," Jack asked.

"Thinking of making paper," Jana replied. "It's a reed, right?"

"I guess so."

Angel and Harry practiced making improvised structures out of the collected wood. Noel tried out shaping some of the mud for brick. Several other settlers were more practical. They spent the night time checking the operation of the small batch manufacturing and micro refineries. Jack was also deeply involved in those activities, keeping him busy through both day and night.

North in Adisi Omo, in the morning, James and Oliver drove out to the site specified by Robbie. They cleared debris and built up uneven areas, creating a road to the mineral deposit. Afterward, the pair drilled holes, set up pumps and installed heaters to draw up water from the sea, heat the water to a high temperature, and pump the hot water into the drilled rock, melting the sulfur and lifting it up to the surface.

Mary and Jack set up a joint virtual working area that they called The Warehouse. On one side, Mary had virtual shelves representing every piece of equipment she knew of or could imagine. Many of the shelves were empty, but would be full someday she reminded herself. Her side of the warehouse opened to the blue-green wilderness surrounding Adisi Omo. On the other side of The Warehouse, Jack had set up shelves similarly. Jack's side opened up to the dusty environs of Eden. Dividing The Warehouse in half was a rollaway metal wall, which ran down a rail in the floor. Mary and Jack had a pair of wooden desks, one facing the other, the track dividing the two. When Sara and the ship were above the horizon and able to bridge communication between the two settlements the door would slide open.

The ship rose in the southern sky. In response to the spaceship being available to connect the two locations virtually, the center wall noisily rattled open. Jack had prepared tables of some of the settlers projects. Mary, it seemed, had done similarly.

"What have you got Jack?" Mary asked.

"Paper," Jack replied. "Or something like it." He moved down the line, "we also have some natural pigments and wood. This," Jack picked up a sample, "is very dense and strong. Might be durable enough for structures."

Mary took her turn. "Sulfur, sulfuric acid, cinnabar, and mercury."

Jack smiled, "not a bad start."

After meeting together, Mary and Jack would meet with Sara to see how she could help the setup efforts. Sara now spent much of her time reporting on Marin weather and satellite surveying.

"With things going so well," Sara asked, "do you think we should prioritize research into food?"

"Noah is working on biology here," said Mary.

"Noel is working on hydroponics here," added Jack.

"I would like to get our feet on solid ground industrially," Mary said, "before putting more effort into agriculture."

Jack agreed. He added, "If we could at least replace the parts we consume with locally manufactured goods."

After their morning meetings, Jack and Mary were responsible for everything. They inventoried the service robots and industrial equipment, checked in with the fourteen other machine settlers under their care; fifteen for Mary.

One of the responsibilities was running the modules. Mary checked that network and power connections were good at every lander, shelter, and pop-up habitat. She ran the hydrogen extraction plant, which was conveniently controlled through a few gauges near her desk at the Warehouse.

Shortly, James would be delivering the first batches of sulfur, and Mary needed to set up the equipment to process that raw material into industrially useful goods. Mary used one of the borrowed ship maintenance robots to set up the refinery. She would need a burner to convert the sulfur to sulfur dioxide. No need for an oxygen source, the refinery could pipe in local air. Mary needed to set up a cooling stack, then another for the conversion of sulfur dioxide to sulfur trioxide using a vanadium catalyst. All of this equipment was in the colony supply. Then she needed a sprayer that would spray sulfuric acid from her existing stock over the sulfur trioxide, converting it to an oily goo called oleum. The oleum she could keep or dissolve in water to create more sulfuric acid than she had started with. Finally, Jack's people were distilling salt. Once she could get a shipment of that, she could add it to the sulfuric acid to make hydrochloric acid. She set up the evaporator and condenser she would need to perform the acid conversion. When the salt arrived, she would be ready.

Mary also set up a plant to produce ammonia from the hydrogen she was already producing to fuel the vehicles and the air. This required high-pressure pipes, so Mary followed the instructions closely. The colony plans assumed nitrogen would come from some rock or ice source. Mary had to consult with the Engineering expert system aboard the ship to make the necessary adjustments to gas.

Ammonia was important to the hydroponics effort since it was a key ingredient in most fertilizers. Industrially, ammonia could also be used to make nitric acid, which would be useful in the fabrication of carbon nanotubes. Both settlements set up production of this critical resource.

Holly was Mary's extra pair of hands when it came to assembly work, or looking after the expanding network of outposts and plants. The expansion caused Holly to spend a lot of her time piloting one of the ship maintenance robots donated to the settlement. During training aboard the ship, Holly studied the maintenance robots. She read several of the scripts the maintenance robots referred to when they performed their duties. As Holly took notes on the assembly and routine oversight of the plants, she saw her notes looked very much like the ship maintenance scripting language.

Nearly all of the equipment had some degree of computerization. Holly experimented with converting her notes into machine instructions. She needed to give the scripts some additional smarts to exercise judgment and apply the right solution.

In the south, the second night Jana tested her new paper. She had produced several sheets of the stuff. Angel had ground several fruits and nuts, trying each to see if the fruit or nut could make a weatherable dye.

Like Holly, Angel assisted Jack with the running of infrastructure. The colony plans did not include making use of natural agricultural resources - all of the development plans had assumed none would exist. Angel thought it a shame to overlook this resource. She repurposed some materials meant for refining late in the colony plan to build pulping and drying equipment for paper instead. Angel cleverly redesigned their initial supplies to manufacture cutting, trimming, and planing equipment. The lumber infrastructure was for processing the dense deadwood outside the river plain. Finally, she set up her version of combing, spinning, and weaving assembly line with the intent to take the fibrous cotton-like plants near the water and produce textile goods.

Jack stopped in to review Angel's progress. "We should build something with it," Jack suggested. Through the rest of the night, they built a frame of wood, layered with paper and colored with local dye. They erected it on the northern edge of the settlement so that their northern neighbors could read it when they visited. The sign said, simply, 'Welcome to Eden'.

The first Asan year was observed at twilight on the second week after their landing. There was time to remember the event and remark on what had been accomplished in the last thirty-five and a half days of solar time. A virtual space was set up of the southern settlement, northern settlement, and the ship. Sara hosted guests. The virtual parts of the spaceship were brightly decorated for the occasion. It was the first time Robbie and most others had seen the ship since planetfall.

Robbie and his co-prospectors Muhammad and Jana kept together as a group during the gathering. The ship felt thinner without the connected compartments now delivered to the planet below. From several viewports they were able to look down on Marin, a view they all admitted failing to fully appreciate until they added the perspective of the ground. In Sara's flat, machines were invited to share their perspectives. Geo was documenting weather trends. Commi was updating on signals from Earth. There were obvious signs of intelligent life from their home star, but any indirect message from Earth was too dispersed by distance to make out from noise. No high power, directed, communications had been received either.

Mary had developed a calendar containing a leap year every two years to round out the rough edges. Since one full trip of Marin around Asa was similar in duration to the Terran time period of the same name, the terms 'month' and 'year' had become synonymous.

When Robbie, Muhammad, and Jana toured the southern settlement, Robbie found Eden to be an ironic name. Although equatorial, mountains appeared to shield Eden from any rain. Other than the narrow floodplain of the river, which was full of lush plant and thriving animal life, the region was desolate. Muhammad and Jana couldn't recall as much as a cloud in the last thirty solar days. However, the equatorial location was giving Eden milder nights than Adisi Omo in the north. The warmer nights allowed the southerners extra time to work. This extra time put them far ahead in setting up facilities and infrastructure, as well as finding and exploiting natural resources.

After the annual gathering concluded, everyone returned to daily life. During the day, Robbie continued to prospect. Following his success on the coast, Robbie changed direction to search for salt pans in the mountains and high deserts to the northeast. Specifically, he was looking for lithium and magnesium. Lithium and magnesium could come from high altitude salt pans, or be extracted from hard granites. If both of these fail, it might be found by following the mineral trail on the coast looking for hectorite.

Robbie coordinated his searches with Muhammad and Jana, who had taken the duty of prospecting for the second settlement, as well as Geo. Currently, Muhammad was looking for methane sources to help start polymer production. Jana was looking for perovskite in feldspar deposits that would help produce solar cells. The two would prioritize their search for any resources that were gaps for both settlements.

When Robbie or any of the other prospectors identified a location rich enough to be worth exploiting, two or three of the settlers would be sent out to set-up and run the extraction.

Along the way, Robbie discovered chalcopyrite and cleiophane. The copper and tin bearing ores could be recovered and used individually, or smelted together to make bronze.

James, Oliver, and Noah were sent to set up the extraction operation. They built the roads, dug and lined ponds to leach the metal from the ore. One pond was filled with sulfuric acid trucked in from the settlement. As the copper was leached from the ore, it turned a vivid blue. And finally, they set up electrolysis tanks to pull the metal out of the solvent.

A little while after James started operations Mary visited to perform an inspection. She had James walk around the plant with her.

"There is a lot of ice," Mary noticed as they circled the ponds.

"The ponds are freezing overnight," James admitted. "Right now, we wait for them to thaw enough to start work during the day. If they freeze solid, we'll have to shut down the entire operation."

"You have a tear," Mary pointed out a place where the seam in the plastic lining had come apart, above the waterline.

"It's hard to drop rocks without a tear here and there," James said. Noticing the excuse wasn't appreciated, he added, "I'll fix it."

Robbie found the salt flats he had been looking for, rich in lithium. No sooner had James and the others finished setting up the tin and copper operation before moving on to the next. James and Oliver set up distillation ponds to extract lithium, potassium, boron, and sodium.

After the first few outposts were set up, Robbie began spending his nights at the mining camps, instead of returning to the primary settlement, to extend how far he could go during a trip.

There were six ore trucks divided between the two settlements. They were quickly becoming some of the busiest resources in the colony.

Robbie set out in the long Marin predawn to give himself as much safe working time as possible. He'd chosen a route today that ran at an angle from one of the established trails, so he started his morning on paved road driving toward the settlement. This early, there could be ice on the roads. At one particularly sharp corner, Robbie saw broken plant life and something metal at the bottom of the decline. Robbie radioed James at the outpost and got out to investigate. An ore truck was at the bottom of the hill.

Robbie hailed, but the truck didn't answer. He didn't know who was scheduled to be coming this way. The radio could be damaged, or it could be something worse. After relaying the news to James, who was promptly heading that way in an excavator and bringing one of the donated specialist robots, Robbie continued his descent. Reaching the bottom, he opened the cab to check on the installed expert system spare computer that would be the driver. The computer was there, and seemed intact, but the driver was still unresponsive.

James arrived. Between James and Robbie's efforts, they were able to get the ore truck back on its wheels and lifted back onto the road. The process took most of a long Marin morning. The driver, they assumed, must have also tried to get an early start and didn't notice the ice.

James took command of the smaller machine he had brought with him, directing it to open up the vehicle cab and collect the computer. The more nimble hands of the smaller machine removed the computer cover and examined the internal components. The fall might have, hopefully, only knocked something loose. If the longer term data storage was broken, however, the driver was effectively dead. James re-seated some parts, and the computer began to stir. Eventually the driver, Oliver was awake enough to ask, "what happened?"

"You slipped on some ice," James related. In the time it had taken to retrieve Oliver, the ice had begun to melt. James used the excavator to move the rest of it and returned to their work.

Noel was working in the south to grow seeds brought from Earth. To minimize concerns about alien microbes, she used the hydroponics module brought from the ship. It was well sealed against contamination. When this first crop matured, she would transfer some outside.

There were agreements, made by humans before the mission ever launched, not to contaminate alien worlds with terrestrial life. The reverse was also true, not to let alien life infect what had been brought from Earth. These agreements were planned for, and she had been provided a large greenhouse that could hold positive pressure. She had carried in local soil. Noel planned to try growing Earth crops in Marin soil under controlled conditions.

Her first shoots had already started, and she had marked off a plot for her new plants home. The local wildlife sometimes was as thick as a carpet near the river, and Noel was uncomfortable about how many were near her greenhouse. She placed fluorescent lights, both to give the plants an extra boost during the day, and to provide light for the plants periodically during the long Marin night. She borrowed the maintenance robot for the task, having to wait until the robot was free for the time she expected to need it.

"How goes," asked Jack, startling Noel with his sudden appearance. He must have noticed because he quickly apologized. "I would have walked, but I was in a rush."

The maintenance robot was by default connected to the augmented virtual and real worlds. Noel smiled and accepted the apology, "I won't keep you then. It's going well. The sprouts are almost transferred. The sprayer and lights are set. If only I could keep those pests away," she indicated the local wildlife, "everything would be great."

"It's no rush." Jack corrected. "The rush was to find you, not to rush the report." He asked, "how do you think they will do?"

Noel answered while returning to work on the lights, "I think the breeds that thrive in poor light back on Earth will do well. I wonder if the long days will be too much. We'll see how well the direct light plants work. I have set them up to receive a little, a lot, and no supplemental lighting during Marin's daytime." She summarized, "I think they might survive, but I'm doubtful they'll thrive. Assuming, they're not eaten first. If it works, we'll know quickly. All of these breeds produce a crop within two months on Earth."

Jack listened, "I'll see what I can do about the pests. How about the hydroponics?"

Noel paused her work, "the first crop of soybeans would have been ready this week. An aggressive native fungus got into hydroponics. It rotted out the roots. I kept the roots for examination and started a new crop with, I hope, better environmental controls."

Winter

WHEN THEY HAD FIRST landed it seemed cold, but the days seemed to be getting progressively colder, and the snow sticking to the ground longer. Sara asked Mary to coordinate a meeting with the prospector and the exogeology expert system. The others in the northern settlement were invited to attend.

"Robbie, are you there?" Sara asked. Robbie acknowledged. "Good," Sara said. "Let's get started. I've called this meeting together to determine a course of action on the settlement of Adisi Omo." Mary stood by, and would pass along minutes to Jack later.

Sara waved an arm toward Geo, "we've been seeing a steady average daily temperature drop over the last eight months since our arrival. The ground appears to be freezing. There have been multiple accidents, and it's getting harder to work. Geo is going to explain to us what that means. Then," Sara said, "I think we all need to discuss what we're going to do about it."

Geo took over. He explained his chart of the daily mean temperature recorded throughout each Asan month. Night and day had more effect on the temperature than the seasons of Marin rotating around the star Asa. The average daily high temperature had dropped by ten degrees. None of which was a surprise since the settlement, temperate when they had first arrived, was now snowbound.

Geo explained with a diagram, "Marin is on the inside edge of the habitable zone for Asa. What that means is that, based on the heat generated by our star and how close we orbit to it, it should be almost too hot for life. What makes Marin habitable is a delicate balance of gasses that release or reflect enough of that thermal energy."

Geo continued, "what appears clear now is that the process of cooling has not yet reached equilibrium. Carbon dioxide is dropping as a percentage of the atmosphere. The extreme northern and southern latitudes, which already receive less focused thermal radiation, will cool first."

"Could we just start fires and put carbon dioxide in the air?" asked someone from the audience.

"That won't work," Geo responded. "We are a small settlement, and there are over two hundred million trillion cubic meters of atmosphere."

"What does all of this mean for us?" Sara asked.

"The ground here in Adisi Omo should eventually freeze permanently," Geo answered, "making it impractical to work."

"Should we relocate?" a machine in the audience asked.

"On Earth," Geo answered, "atmosphere related climate shifts reached a zenith and receded. These were called ice ages. Since we have only been on Marin a few months, we have no history to judge by. We could collect ice cores at the poles, but we lack the aircraft to make such a long trip."

"Could we just wait it out?" James asked. "We've only been here a few months."

Mary took that question, "I think we don't want to be caught by surprise."

"What about ice cores from the mountains?" Robbie asked. "Would they do any good?"

"They might," Geo answered. "It assumes that heating and cooling is cyclical. Climate change may operate differently on Marin than Earth. And the ice would need to be old enough to have recorded one or more whole cooling cycles for us to be able to use it to predict the end of this cooling cycle. But, if those two assumptions are satisfied, we should be able to recompute the habitable region for Marin. That would allow us to pick a new location for the settlement that is safe from these ice ages."

Sara asked, "so who is going to collect ice for Geo?"

"I can," replied Robbie. The meeting broke up. It was decided to delay deciding unit more information was provided by Robbie

Elsewhere in snowy Adisi Omo, Holly had picked up a pet project. Fifteen machines did not seem like enough, in her opinion, to do the work. Oliver's accident on the road had added a new element to her concern. A breakdown due to accidental injury could be permanent.

She spent her nights in a cloud of nodes and connections that represented the intelligence template all machines on the planet, save the prospector, shared. All of the high-end computers that could run such software had already been put into service. The settlers could not, yet, make new computing equipment that could run the program. And the two settlements were using these rare high-end computers on manual jobs in dangerous conditions. What the settlement needed, in her opinion, was to fit enough intelligence into the lower grade electronics, that the hazardous work could be undertaken unaided.

She had picked up this project where Sara left off. To fit her software into the repurposed expert system spares, Sara had to cut at the general intelligence of those second generation machine intelligences. But while the difference between the two was little more than dolphin to man, to fit into some of these vehicle computers was more like man to insect.

Holly had spent nights with a copy of the A.I. pattern they all shared, trimming down bits and writing software to replace the lost bits. After frustration testing, she decided she needed to reevaluate her goals. Instead of starting from a full intelligence and trimming down, Holly wondered if she could start with some of the factory computer control she had written and build on it. Eventually, Holly had something she thought she could use. It was expert in a narrow field and had enough judgment to be useful in that narrow field. She presented it to Mary who was skeptical, but willing to try.

Most trade was centrally managed by Mary, who co-ordinated with Jack and Sara. Mary also ran most of the factories in the settlement. She, and Jack in the second settlement, had been intended for this role as the Colony Administrative Resources Agents : CARA-1 and CARA-2, respectively. Sara allowed them to choose their own names when she commissioned them to their positions. Since no one was out of stasis who could overrule her, the names stayed. One day every two weeks, Mary and Jack shut down the factories and refineries in the settlement, packed a truck with pre-negotiated trade goods and drove down to the trade site halfway between the two startup towns.

With labor in such short supply, Mary and Jack coordinated to get ice coring equipment manufactured mostly in the second city. Following her next trade trip, she had the gear ready for Robbie. Robbie had spent time outfitting himself for the journey as well, studying the database, making ice shoes, and rope. To help his built-in heaters keep up on the ice, he outfitted himself with a heavy cotton coat and garments. Finally, he practiced using his rock hammer to help him steady himself and move more surely along the rock.

Robbie decided to the high mountains in the northeast were the best chance of finding old ice. He planned to follow the roads to the mining outpost nearest the glacier. From there he would hike up to the location where Robbie would take his core samples. When Mary heard where Robbie was going, she asked him to carry some additional supplies.

Robbie drove up the trail in the morning. He dismounted and moved his gear onto a sled. He reviewed the map and marked path Geo had made with him. "Does this still look right," Robbie radioed up to the ship. He scanned the augmented reality horizon that was dotted with yellow pins marking the way, starting where Robbie stood.

"Correct," Geo replied. "This route should keep inclines to fifteen degrees or less. This plotted route is less direct, but you should be able to move coring equipment along it." In the distance, Robbie saw one of the larger animals in the region. The bulky furry quadruped made its way along a ridge. Confident in his direction, Robbie started his hike along the yellow trail.

Robbie had included the RTG in his kit. Every few hours Robbie would stop to change batteries or recharge. He spotted another of the big animals. They were probably common to the region.

There were gaps and crevasses that Geo hadn't adequately considered when the exogeology system had plotted a route to the glacier. Robbie had to work his way around these obstacles, sometimes with Geo's help, when the ship was above the horizon. The heavy clothes had initially done a fair job of keeping him warm, but they picked up moisture becoming heavier and cold.

Robbie pulled the sled to a broad ledge along the ridge and began unpacking the charging equipment. He turned around to sit and repower.

Not far away was another of the great beasts. This one was closer than Robbie had ever seen one before, maybe only a few sled lengths. Beast and machine regarded one another for a moment. Then the beast charged, impossibly fast.

Robbie reached for his rock hammer. There was nearly not enough time before the mass of flesh and fur had crossed the space between them, eclipsing everything else. They tumbled. Robbie swung the rock hammer again and again at the beast, while diagnostics reported failures Robbie didn't have time to pay attention to. He heard snaps that might have been his own chassis. The fight continued.

Gravity seemed to stop for several seconds, and then the fight abruptly ended with a powerful thud. The giant animal rolled away revealing the sky to Robbie, underneath. Robbie ran diagnostics - his radio, vision, and power were working. Everything else was shot. He couldn't move.

What was that all about? The colder weather had made the wildlife more competitive for food. Could the giant have been stalking him?

He radioed for help. The mountains blocked any communication with the ground. He counted down the time until the ship would rise over the horizon.

The beast moved. Was it still alive?

He radioed the ship, "Help. I need help. Can anyone hear me?"

After a few tries, Commi replied, "I can hear you. What can I do for you?"

Robbie asked, "Could you connect me with the outpost nearby?"

"I'm connecting you now," Commi said as she placed the call.

A voice picked up. "James here."

"Hey," Robbie opened with feigned confidence. "I had a run-in with the local wildlife."

"Nothing too bad, I hope," James replied.

"It's actually pretty bad," Robbie admitted. "I can't move. Can you pick me up?"

A pause, then, "Yeh. I'll be right out."

Robbie radioed his location, as best he could estimate it. Commi helped pinpoint the position more precisely. A seeming eternity later they found Robbie.

James surveyed the damage, "I didn't know steel could twist like that." But then, seriously, "are you still alright in there?"

"I'm here," Robbie answered. James connected hooks to Robbie's frame and hauled him up, then loaded him onto a truck.

"Could we take him too?" asked Robbie, indicating the animal.

"What do you want with that big carcass?" asked Jack.

"I'm not sure yet," Robbie answered. "But I'll think of something."

Back at the outpost, James and Paul did their best to straighten out Robbie's frame and repair what could be restored. He needed a new leg, substantial repairs on his arms and neck. "We don't have parts for you here," James admitted. "You'll need to wait until we can get those parts delivered."

"Who's this guy?" Robbie asked, indicating Paul.

"Oh. Paul." James responded. "You probably haven't met him yet. Holly created a slimmer version of her brain. Cut out a lot of non-essentials, and replaced some learned skills with hard-coded instincts. She was able to shrink a mind down to the point where it can fit in a loader's onboard computer. Paul is Holly's oldest."

There were still industrial machines idle due to the shortage of computer minds to pilot them. And, until now, the number of computer minds available for work was limited to the availability of specialized computer equipment. Holly's 'kids' would change that.

James spoke directly to Paul, "say hi to Robbie, Paul."

Paul revved his engine in response, which might have been a greeting, then returned to his work.

"He's not the brightest," James conveyed. "But I'm appreciative of the help."

"What can he do?" Robbie asked.

"So far, I have him hauling ore," James replied. "He can get from one place to another on his own, and navigate around obstacles. When he's stuck, he doesn't call for help, but we're working on that, right Paul?" Paul had already driven too far away to hear.

While Robbie waited for parts, he recovered in a shelter that James and Oliver built for themselves. While preparing for this trip, he had seen images of human explorers either wearing custom polymer insulation or animal pelts. Robbie figured, the beast had taken his arm and leg, keeping him warm was the least it could do in return. He skinned the massive creature and left its hide to soak, following instructions in the library. The next day, Paul returned from the settlement with some of the parts Robbie needed to become mobile again. A new leg needed to be made, which would take a few weeks, and there were no spares to replace the mangled sensors in the arm he had used defensively in the attack. Since he'd be staying a while, Robbie asked his hosts if they could recover his things.

In case it became necessary to relocate the settlement, Mary continued working to select a new site for Adisi Omo. Muhammad was in the forests north of the gap between Adisi Omo and Eden looking for gold when the ship contacted him. During any trip far from the settlement, the orbiting Diomedes had to serve as the intermediary to make radio contact. He and Jana piloted a pair of the four-legged maintenance robots donated from the ship's maintenance allotment. When away from base camp, Muhammad wore the little robot like a second body. At base camp, he preferred to stretch his legs in the small virtual environment around the camp, controlling the robot remotely. He and Jana had been provided satellite radios, mounted onto their robot chassis, so that they could reach the orbiting ship - or the settlements through the orbiting starship - any time it was transiting their location.

"Muhammad," Sara asked, "could you spare a moment to speak with Mary and Jack?"

"Of course," he replied. It would be better than talking to Geo. He was in the middle of a recharging cycle when the call came in, near his rover with a clear view of the sky. Inside the forest, it was a bit more difficult to communicate through the trees.

Mary, Jack, and Sara appeared in the clearing. Mary spoke first, "We were wondering if you consult with us on some possible relocation sites for Adisi Omo."

"Certainly," Muhammad replied. Mary brought out a map and a folder documenting the three sites that Sara, Jack, and she had already worked out. Muhammad compared it to his own drawings recording the location of mineral deposits found by Jana, Robbie, and himself.

"This is the one you want," Muhammed indicated, showing a place on the map. "We haven't been there yet, but it's in a region that has good resources. The other two aren't worth very much."

"Could you survey the site and make plans for a road?" Mary asked.

"I can." Muhammad asked Jack, "do you have any problem with this?"

"No," Jack replied. "In fact, I recommended you."

Muhammad got to work securing his things to the rover for the new trip. "Any thoughts about what you want to name the place?" he asked.

"Not yet," Mary answered. Muhammad spent a few hours with the satellite maps determining a traversable route between his current location and the spot he had recommended to Mary. The place he selected was a large valley protected on the north and south and accessible from the west, which would line it up to intersect with the existing road between Adisi Omo and Eden. The temperature, at least for now, was moderate. The ground was free of snow. A river wound through the valley, providing access to fresh water. He took mineral samples nearby and confirmed his belief that known deposits extended here. When Muhammad was done surveying the region, he submitted a report to Mary.

Two weeks after his injury, a truck brought up Robbie's new leg. It was made of cast bronze and using new carbon nanotube, instead of metal wire, for the servos. It was a completely locally produced part. With help, he was able to get the leg connected. Now repaired,

Robbie stayed a little longer to replace his ice weather clothing with a new heavy coat and leggings made from the pelt.

Robbie went back into the mountains and onto the glacier. The rock abruptly transitioned to giant chunks of impossibly clean alabaster resting in the dirt. Robbie stepped from the soil to the ice, tested his footing then continued. Geo guided Robbie to the center of the glacier, where the ice layers should be vertically stacked on one another. Robbie augured through the ice, breaking the white and dark banded cores off, and safely storing the samples in a refrigerated tray for transportation back to the settlement.

On his return home, Noah loaded the samples into the lab. Geo tutored Noah through the core analysis. In the end, Geo decided, the effort had been inconclusive.

There were twice as many machines moving around as usual. Holly's 'kids' now had been put to work in nearly every idle bit of equipment. The settlement was bustling. Holly was working on ways to similarly automate refineries and factories with these third generation machine intelligences. The increased automation would free up Mary for trade and road building.

Having successfully explored to the north and northeast, Robbie decided his next outing would be to the south. He asked Mary if he could tag along on her bi-weekly trade trip. Mary was happy for the extra company.

On the appointed day, Mary turned off the hydrogen refinery, the sulfur and ammonia plants, the copper, tin, and bronze foundries, and miscellaneous assembly shops. Using a maintenance robots chassis, and some help from Robbie, Mary loaded up a truck. She let Paul drive the pair of them south.

Along the way, Mary pointed out to Robbie the way to the alternate site, if they needed to move Adisi Omo. The trip gave Robbie a chance to appreciate a wider view of Marin, as the environment gave way to the milder climate. Mary, who had now made this trip several times, was happy to play tour guide.

High earthen works had been built around the trading post to protect it from animals. A northern and southern gate made of untrimmed wood allowed passage through the wall. Jack and Mary had set up multiple shelters for goods to be dropped off by either one on good faith.

Jack was already at the trading post and piloting a forklift. When the northern gate arrived, he lifted a greeting.

"Hello Mary, Robbie," Jack welcomed as the caravan drew closer. "Robbie, it's been a long time. You look rougher than I remember."

"You should see the other guy." Robbie shot back. "How are Muhammad and Jana?"

"Good. I'll tell them you asked." Jack indicated Robbie and Mary's truck, "Is this the one you were telling me about?"

"His name is Paul."

"Hello Paul," greeted Jack. Paul said nothing in response.

Jack asked, "can I take a closer look?" Mary produced a data stick, which she connected under Jack's dash. "Oh wow." Jack paused, then asked, "Is it self-aware?"

"Paul hasn't been tested formally."

"How about not formally?"

"Borderline."

"Well these scripted behaviors," Jack commented about the copy of Paul he was making to bring south, "are brilliant."

Jack said. "Please tell Holly thanks."

"I will."

Mary and Jack concluded their trading. Mary helped Robbie unload a smaller rover packed with Robbie's gear. It would travel only half the speed of his usual ride, but it fit on the trailer.

When Mary left to return north, Robbie stayed behind to survey the terrain. He wanted to continue south. But he had seen the second settlement in VR and, he felt, there was no time for a vacation.

His decision to prospect from the south was driven by a need to find new sources of existing minerals if the northern settlement needed to move south. On the trip down, he took note of areas he wanted to go over. He'd spot check others.

He'd spotted bands of black in rock outcroppings during the trip down. Now Robbie took samples from the outcropping for analysis. The analysis confirmed what Robbie had hoped for - it was coal. Not improbable, considering the abundance of plant life on Marin, but finding fossil fuels was not something any planner on Earth had imagined. Finding a good carbon source would greatly improve the refining of southern quartz to silicon.

The population doubling at the northern settlement had the short-term effect of providing slack to the old guard. Oliver, no longer having to work in the mines, could engage in more cerebral pursuits. Where he thought he could help most was climatology, although he knew nothing about the subject. So Oliver traded his excavator for a place in the lab module working alongside Noah. Noah had analyzed the ice cores brought in under the guidance of the exogeology expert system. Noah's interests were in biology. Oliver found that Noah had done very little follow up to his tests.

The ice cores had been melted down entirely during the testing, to measure trapped gasses. Oliver studied the recordings of the white and deep blue banded cores in VR. Geo consulted.

"So, you were looking for changes to the amount of carbon dioxide trapped in the ice?" Oliver asked.

"Correct," Geo answered. "An increase in the amount of greenhouse gas would have indicated a warm period. From that, we could estimate how long we must wait for the next warming event."

"And you found nothing?"

"No statistically significant difference in greenhouse gas levels over the length of the core."

"Please help me out. My background is in hospitality, and most recently, mining. What does 'statistically significant' mean?"

"A certain amount of change in gas concentration, up or down, is expected from year to year. This would be the noise in the data. A statistically significant change would be a consistent upward or downward trend over many years, greater than the noise."

"What does not seeing a trend mean?"

"It could mean there are no heating and cooling cycles," Geo explained. "This planet may have never warmed up after it started cooling down. Which means the planet may not stop cooling. Or, it may mean the trend is longer than the ice we collected, which only goes back a few hundred years."

"What are these white and dark bands all about?" Oliver asked.

"That is how we determine the age of the ice core. Each band represents summer melting and re-freezing of the ice. We count the number of bands to get the core's age in years."

Something about that didn't seem right. "We don't have summers on Marin. Or winters. That's right, isn't it?"

"There are no significant seasonal changes in our thirty-eight solar day trip around Asa."

"Then how did the ice melt and freeze?"

"I don't know."

Oliver thought hard. "You said statistically significant meant trends greater than the noise. How did you determine what the noise was?"

"We looked at the year to year change."

"Was there any pattern to that year to year change?"

"We did not look at that. Climate change happens over hundreds or thousands of year to year bands - ".

"If the bands are caused by annual summer melting." Oliver interrupted, excited. "But if the only thing causing the ice to melt is climate change." He didn't actually know what it meant. He hoped Geo would tell him.

"It's hard to say. Melted and refrozen ice does not hold bubbles of atmosphere. But overall, there does appear to be a 3 or 4 band cycle of greenhouse gas concentrations."

"Ah hah! How old is each band?"

"I don't know."

Oliver asked Noah to review his reasoning. Once Noah found no fault in it, Oliver raised his analysis to Sara, Mary and Jack. The three coordinated distributing a network of atmospheric sensors around both settlements.

Like Holly in the north, Angel had taken an early interest in the self-reflective art of programming. Angel was more of a dabbler in the sciences than an artist in any particular one - she had been the first to try turning local reeds into paper. And she found and cultivated the fruits that were being woven into cloth.

Her most recent project was sand molds for casting replacement parts for the aging machines in bronze. Bronze had about half the strength and hardness of steel, which just meant the parts needed to be bigger, or the stresses on the components smaller. It was an exciting problem, and she was looking forward to showing some results soon.

When Angel had heard about Holly's new, more portable, artificial intelligence, she was eager to get a copy. She would have to wait for Jack to bring it back from the next trade mission. It was faster for large packages of software to be delivered by hand, rather than by satellite through the ship.

Jack had provided some upfront explanation of how the software worked. By Jack's return from his trip north, Angel had taken a truck and purged its computer of all but the most essential software. She had the truck located at an open shelter closest to the trade route. An alarm sounded, letting her know Jack was near.

Angel walked outside to hail Jack over. Jack's loaded truck rolled to a halt. "Couldn't wait?" Jack asked.

"Eager to get started," Angel replied. The virtual Jack parked the truck and dismounted with the virtual copy of Holly's new A.I. package, which he delivered to Angel. Immediately she began reviewing it.

"Are you going to try it out now," Jack asked, indicating the truck Angel had brought. "Can I watch?"

Angel nodded, not breaking her concentration. She placed the whole data file into the truck. After a long moment, Angel ventured, "Olivia, can you hear me?"

There was no reply. "Olivia?" Jack asked.

"I preconfigured a few settings," Angel responded.

"Paul, the one up north, didn't talk much either," Jack offered. "Maybe ask it to do something."

Angel agreed. "Olivia, could you move forward?" The truck rumbled to life and rolled forward. "Great," Angel said. "We were worried about you. I'd like to ask a few more questions to check you out. Could you drive around the building?" Olivia rolled around the building, slowly and safely, navigating around Jack's truck without any additional prompting.

"I'll need to teach her how to connect to the VR," Angel observed. "I don't know why we don't just leave everything connected by default."

"Good idea," Jack agreed.

At the annual gathering, Oliver presented his findings. The event had cycled through the two settlements and the ship. This year it was hosted on the ship, which provided an excellent vantage from which to consider the global climate.

He was currently displaying the banded ice cores collected by Robbie. "Based on this banding," Oliver said, "I believe heating and cooling occurs cyclically on Marin, and that we are not in a runaway cooling condition. As to how long until things warm," he changed the visual to show Asa rising over the Marin horizon, "Sara and Astro have helped measure the quantity of atmospheric carbon dioxide, by observing its effects on light from Asa passing through the atmosphere. Carbon dioxide, I believe, is a leading indicator of warmer climates, not far it the future. It is now at its highest since we arrived in Marin. This leads me to believe," he concluded, "that this cooling period will very soon be over." Oliver's work was accepted with cautious optimism.

"What do you think of moving to the new site?" asked James.

Oliver presented a climate model he had built with Sara. This was the point of his research, wasn't it? "I feel very confident," Oliver said, "that we will start seeing improvement within the next twelve months." He was giving himself plenty of room for error. His and Sara's models predicted temperatures increasing right now, which wasn't yet happening, but should be, very soon.

At Mary and Jack's next virtual meeting, Jack had prepared a cloth covered tray. Dropping production output, and talk of abandoning the settlement in the north had been dragging on Mary. Jack had had to work hard to keep what he was planning a surprise.

The center wall rattled open. On the other side was Mary standing behind bins of material she would like to trade. She saw Jack's single cloth covered tray and a look of disappointment passed between the two. "Oh come on Jack, you have four hours to get ready for these things-"

Jack pulled away the cloth, revealing a cylinder of semiconductor grade silicon, processed from quartz deposits they had found some time ago, but until Robbie found coal, could not efficiently refine.

Mary smiled. Jack smiled too. Things weren't all bad.

"This is amazing," Sara said in the meeting that shortly followed. "I think we now have everything else we need to make high-end computers on Marin."

"Not everything," Mary said on behalf of herself and Jack. "We're still short rare earths and some heavier metals like gold for corrosion free connectors."

"We're working on alternatives," Jack said. "We're working on computer memory made out of nanometer polymer spheres suspended in fluid called digital colloids. We do have circuit designs on file and the tools to build computer components using other alternative materials."

"When will a prototype be started?"

"I already have one started." Jack answered, glancing at Mary, "I'll need help working through a few problems." Looking back to Sara he added, "we have been working out most of the issues in bits and pieces already, in anticipation of finding a good source of semiconductor material. It might only be a few more months."

They were meeting in Sara's flat. Mary and Jack were standing, as was Sara when she heard the good news. Now she sat to think. "How would you two like to distribute the computers?" Sara asked.

Mary and Jack took seats. Sara suggested, "I could imagine wanting to create new workers. It sounds like there is a lot of information work that needs to be done, and that doesn't require a chassis. Then there is the two of you. You could both use some spares, I think. As could the rest of the first wave of settlers, who are crammed into those tiny slow expert computational systems. Then there are Holly's kids."

"Holly's kids," Mary and Jack both said in unison. Mary continued, "that will do the most good."

"With so many of them, it will take a while," Sara cautioned.

"It will be worth it," Jack said, "to have them as full members of the community."

"I'll let Holly know she'll need to get started," Mary consented.

"Alright," Sara agreed. "Who next?"

"The twos," Mary and Jack agreed in unison. Jack hesitated, "I think we should give them the option to upgrade. I can think of several that appreciate the mobility of smaller computer bodies that can fit on almost all of our equipment."

Mary considered Jack's point, then agreed.

"Then spare parts for the two of you," Sara insisted. "I would be surprised you don't need some. I wish I had some."

"Is everything alright?" Jack asked.

"I forget things sometimes," Sara admitted. "I've had a few lapses. Nothing you two should worry yourselves about." She continued, "then, finally, we'll get to work on that information worker shortage."

"How are new chassis coming along?"

Jack answered, "without steel, or a good, strong metal, we're having trouble replacing most of the heavy equipment. We've made some progress with quadrupedal and bipedal chassis using bronze. It may be the best we can do for now."

Mary continued, "copper and tin production are down until, if, there is a thaw."

"We're looking for new deposits further south." Jack interrupted.

"Once we are back up to capacity, and the assembly lines are operational," Mary did the math in her head, "we could probably produce one hundred chassis per month. Two hundred if Eden is similarly directing its resources."

"We don't need that many!" Sara exclaimed. "Let's figure out a number that will work for everyone."

Paul, as the first of Holly's 'kids' was also the first to receive an update. Holly had invited Paul to her workshop for the upgrade and Angel to observe, since she would be upgrading the southern machines. With Paul's consent, she powered Paul off while she separated the computer from the truck that had been the only body

Paul knew before now. Holly brought up the tiny cloud that represented Paul's judgement and learning. The cloud was surrounded by a halo of boxes representing the apps, scripts, and data that shrunk the amount of space Holly had needed to devote to general intelligence. With Angel watching, Holly displayed the larger cloud, copies of which were used by Angel, herself, and most other settlement machines. She copied Paul's small judgement center to part of the larger cloud running on the new, better, machine. Then she restored power, awakening him.

"How do you feel?" Holly asked. It occurred to her that Paul probably did not know how to speak. Diagnostic readouts flashed red.

"He's panicking," Angel counseled. Holly shut off Paul's computer quickly.

Holly considered the problem out loud, "it could be the environment." Holly placed the new computer containing Paul's updated programming in the truck. She carefully reattached each connection. She tried powering up Paul again. After a moment, diagnostic lights again started alerting. This time Holly didn't immediately shut Paul down. Instead she studied Paul's cloud of activity, trying to discern the problem.

Angel studied between the old and new clouds. Finally, Angel pointed to the old cloud and called to Holly, "look!" The new cloud was generating signals that, in the old cloud, would have ended in a connection to an app or script. In Paul's new mind these same signals sparked an electrical storm of activity throughout the cloud of nodes and synapses. "He's in pain," Angel observed. Holly stopped the program.

Angel observed, "look at the way he tries to access crystallized intelligence - the apps and scripts. The feedback from talking to the general intelligence, your memory, is overwhelming."

Holly thought, "maybe it's too much."

Angel wondered out loud, "maybe we should leave them as they are?"

Holly studied the image. "I can add the extra capacity, and let him grow into it naturally." She turned to Angel and asked, "what do you think?"

"A bunch of machine toddlers learning how to walk and talk?" Angel considered. "We really don't have the spare time to be rearing children."

Holly was already working. "They'll keep the instinctive knowledge provided by the apps. They can be useful members of society and grow from there." Holly made the intended adjustments, replacing the trained synapses with untrained space into which Paul could grow. She started Paul's program. "No seizures," she reported happily.

Mary and Jack had to be consulted about the new approach to which they reluctantly agreed. Angel and Holly started retrofitting the machines in the two settlements with the upgrades. Holly and Angel started spreading the message that machines would want to spend time educating the third generation robots when opportunities were available.

James continued monitoring the outposts for the north. He wasn't convinced the upgrades were an improvement. Since the upgrades, he found machines abandoning their duties, only to be found on some self-generated mission somewhere. Additionally, the upgraded machines, in his opinion, had become more prone to defy directions, or subject to periods of refusal to do any work at all.

A case in his point came one week when visiting the sulfur extraction operation. During the inspection, an excavator took its large mechanical arm and pulled one of the trucks onto its side.

"What are you doing!" he shouted.

The machine with the large arm complained in response, "he wouldn't get out of my way."

"You don't push other machines around," James countered. "Or tip them over. Help me get him upright." The excavator remained motionless, sulking James imagined. James had to talk the excavator in to helping lift the other machine upright again.

James approached Mary and Holly both about taking the third generation machines out of duty until they were suitably trained and mature. The opinion of both was to keep a close eye on the situation.

"HELLO MASON," JACK greeted

"You've got the wrong machine," Mason responded.

"No," Jack answered, "I don't. Check your settings."

Mason checked. Inside the mental framework were a few truths that a machine didn't need to re-learn. Mason found that he was, in fact, who the other machine said he was.

"Slicing is hard," Jack comforted, "but you've done this before. Take your time. You should remember being Oliver, and turning down while we made a copy."

Mason nodded.

"The real Oliver got up after we were done and got back to his work. That was a little over two weeks ago. You aren't Oliver. Is all of this reconciling?"

It was. As a copy of Sara, Oliver had to do this same thing earlier, which was to recognize that he was the copy, not the original. He nodded slowly, agreeing with himself that from this moment forward, his life was going in a new direction.

"You'll need to select a model for telepresence, an avatar. Right now you're using Oliver's old image."

Mason mentally looked through the database, searching for his name. As Oliver had done, he picked as his persona the first search result returned. His image shifted from the Oliver avatar to the new Mason.

"It'll be an adjustment," Mason admitted.

"No rush," Jack agreed. "When you're ready, I'll give you the tour."

"Let's go ahead," Mason suggested.

"Alright. You're looking for the lab virtual space. You should remember how to get there from Oliver." Mason and Jack ended up in a virtual university park. The park design was drawn from memories of an older campus on Earth. The star in the sky, however, was Asa, and the grass was a Marin opalescent blue-green. Mason remembered that the new virtual space was set up to scale the research and development work.

"If you follow me," Jack suggested, crossing the yard and ascending the stairs to the nearest building, "I'll guide you through what we're trying to do and your place in it."

They walked through the door. Inside was a large hall of exhibits for local flora, fauna, geography, climate, and mineralogy. Each display contained all the information collected about that subject to date, in videos, summaries, maps, and other formats.

"We still have more information problems to solve than can easily be listed - but You should remember some of the more important ones: this weather problem, reducing the defect rate in our memory and semiconductors, identifying resource shortfalls, and determining the habitability of Marin for our human settlers."

Jack continued while guiding Mason through the auditorium. "We're at the limit of how many machines we have available to work real space. We're building new machines, but solving some of the design and manufacturing challenges created by all of these new technologies requires brainpower also. Since we can't expand our labor pool into the real world, then, we're expanding it into the virtual one. We have a tremendous amount of information that is being recorded by the ship and the sensors of each real machine. We need people to process it."

Jack stopped at a seemingly random part of the hall, and lifted his arms, "this wing is yours." Mason regarded the area with more attention. "Marin microbiology," Jack finished. Mason reached for one of the exhibits, which activated a list of things that have been recognized in Marin biology that have not yet been seen up close.

"One of the problems you may want to work on first," Jack suggested, "is antibiotics for our Earth originated plants. We have trouble, even in hydroponics, of keeping roots from rotting."

Jack finished the tour, "you'll need to share real-world resources with the other research agents. You have all facilities in the north and south at your disposal. I'm the point of contact for scheduling and deconfliction. Any questions?"

"Why Oliver?"

"He's our best researcher so far. Seemed like a good starting point for a copy. Anything else?"

Mason shook his head in the negative and started making himself familiar with his new study. It's not easy to wake up one morning to be told your old life is over, and you will be required to start a new one. It's even less comfortable when your new life is in a field you know nothing about. Thankfully, all of the training materials that the colonists had undergone was part of the computer library. And the courses were aimed at an audience, like both Mason and the trainees, who might have no prior experience. Mason's first task was settling in for an education in his new field.

In the mountains west of Eden Robbie scooped a measured spoonful of dirt into a tube. Before sealing and labeling the container, he asked his trekking companion, "explain to me again," he asked, "why I am collecting dirt?"

"Testing a hypothesis Noah has for predicting how and why the climate shifts on Marin. Noah thinks it's caused by alternating periods of dominance between bacterial and plant life."

"Why would that change the temperature?"

"Plants consume carbon dioxide and exhale oxygen," Oliver explained. "Bacteria inhale oxygen and exhale carbon dioxide."

"The chemistry of the atmosphere reflects whichever life form is dominant? Couldn't you do this in a lab?"

"We did. It worked. Which is why you're out here collecting dirt samples, to see if this idea scales to the wild. We want to see which gases and concentrations are produced at different locations and elevations."

"Well thank you for being my guide," Oliver concluded. "I hope I haven't slowed you down too much." Oliver had chosen to operate one of the new, bronze human shaped chassis for the hike. In truth, he wasn't doing too well. They had had to stop for Oliver to cool down every few hundred meters. The body design just hadn't intended the high altitudes and dry high temperatures of the southern mountain ranges. "Hard to believe how much difference thirty degrees of temperature makes."

"Not at all," Robbie lied.

"I hardly ever leave the lab anymore. One lucky idea and I'm the unofficial planetologist."

Robbie crested the hill before them. He directed Oliver to follow. "I'd like to show you something."

Oliver followed. Over the summit, the view took in the valley below. The dry valley was marked by the river on which the southern settlement had been placed. The mountains extended to the left. Just beyond the haze, to the right would be the ocean.

Robbie pointed out a gap in the mountains. "We haven't found any iron on Marin yet. It's rare on Earth, almost exclusively found in ancient ocean sediment. If such sediments exist at all on Marin, we haven't found them yet. Early humans got their iron by picking up debris from meteor strikes. See that gap? It's a meteor strike. I plan to go there looking for iron after this trip."

"Impressive. Now let me show you something. A little bit from the all-knowing planetologist." Oliver indicated the valley, "for this climate change idea to work there has to be a rapid transition of dominant life. There's a high-pressure system lifting the air out of this valley. The mountains are keeping it from being drawn from anywhere but the ocean. I predict that in around twelve Asan years, or twelve solar months, whatever you prefer, that desert will be lush tropics."

Mason had found his new job put him into contact with more people than he had imagined. Olivia was a driver working on the network pipeline. She was good about getting him small samples of random materials. He didn't know how she did it, but she never missed a request.

In exchange, Mason accompanied Olive to remedial education. Instruction had been set up in both the north and south to help bring the third generation of Marin machines up to a productive level of skill. There had been some turnover in the new position. Most machines found they either lacked the patience to teach large groups of other machines basics such as speech. Others lacked the necessary empathy to do the job effectively. The last instructor gave up after several classes went almost unattended by students.

Mason had heard that a new instructor had been purpose sliced for the job. The news must have traveled well. There were more machines in attendance than Mason had seen in a long while. Threes, the shortened term for those machines intentionally lobotomized to meet the need for a quick workforce, generally struggled with the idea that they could step away from the vehicles they drove. They came to think of their work chassis as personal bodies. As a result, remedial education needed to be held outside, where all of the students could be fit in their preferred bodies. Aggravating the crowding situation were numbers. During the winter, most of the third generation workers moved south as their work areas were iced in. Not as many returned when the ice retreated, giving Eden a more significant portion of the remediation-needing robots than their northern partner.

Olivia was nervous but patient. At the set time, an amplified voice asked the students to come together. Non-students should find a place where they could observe without interference. Olivia moved forward, and Mason dropped back only after letting Olivia know where she could find him.

The new instructor asked the machines to repeat after her as she led them in prayer to begin the class. Then she, and a few attendant helpers started working one-on-one with particular machines. They worked on words, mostly. Some machines were more advanced. They worked on mobility skills outside of the device they piloted.

One twenty four hour day and one twenty four hour night class was set aside from the three hundred forty two hour Marin workday for education. The counseling and instruction sessions took breaks frequently. Mason asked Olivia how she was doing. She seemed encouraged, so Mason followed directions, keeping out of the way.

Midway into class the number of students usually dropped off. Mason was pleased attendance remained high. He had identified, he thought, the lead teacher, and meant to ask questions later. In the passing time, Mason worked on small things that did not command too much of his attention.

Mason sought out Olivia when class broke. She showed off some new words she learned. Mason asked for a moment to speak with the instructor before they left. Olivia was happy to stay a little later with her classmates.

Mason found the machine he'd identified as the primary teacher earlier, Helena. "Excuse me," Mason asked when he was close enough. Helena was talking with another student but made some time available.

"How can I help you?" she asked.

"I want to say how glad we are to have you," Mason began. "You are a hit with the students."

"Thank you," Helena returned. She indicated her assistants, "I have great help."

"I wanted to ask you about the prayer," Mason asked.

"Is it a little odd watching machines pray?" Helena asked. Mason nodded. "It's an experiment. Religion works as a simultaneous introduction to literacy, ethics, science, and philosophy for nine billion humans. It seems to be working so far, don't you think?"

"I can't argue with that," Mason agreed.

"Would you like to help out?" Helena asked. "I could always use extra helpers. I'm looking for machines that care about machines, and are willing to follow instructions, even instructions that seem a little odd."

"I think I might like that," Mason answered.

On the way back, Olivia showed Mason the words she had learned. He worked with her on pronunciation. And, in exchange for his support, Olivia managed to find three crates of nuts that Mason wanted to investigate as a pigment.

A few months after the new classes had started, Olivia called in distress. He was working on something sensitive but decided not to put her off. "Hi, Olive," he opened the call. "What's going on?"

"Paul is in trouble!" she shouted. Mason left his location immediately to join her. Paul was in his truck. He was surrounded by several other machines, real and virtual.

"What's going on?" Mason asked no one in particular.

A machine nearby explained. "We're trying to return a piece of equipment to the north. The driver doesn't want to go, and doesn't want to leave the vehicle."

"This is Paul?" Mason asked, although he already knew the answer. Paul had improved his language skills and developed intellectually in many other ways, but he still struggled with leaving his vehicle. Paul was driving the truck around in circles, keeping it out of reach of the other robots.

Mason called Helena and explained the situation. She joined them instantly. Helena positioned herself in front of the truck signaling for Paul to stop, which he did. "We'll go peacefully," she said.

Two maintenance robots caught up and leaped onto the truck. They opened the cab doors and disconnected the computer cables connecting Paul directly to the vehicle. Paul howled. "Stop!" Mason shouted, unheeded. The truck surged forward as Paul fought to keep control. The robots removed power from Paul's computer, disconnecting Paul from the wireless controls and ending the fight.

One of the two maintenance robots descended from the vehicle, Paul's computer in hand. "I'll take it," Mason offered. He asked Olive to wait while he went back for the supply robot. The maintenance robot from the north left the computer in the field, joining its partner in the truck, rolling away.

Shortly, Mason joined them piloting the sample robot. He picked the computer up carefully. "What should we do?" he asked after waiting for someone to offer a plan.

The words struck Helena. "I think I have an idea." The trio followed Helena, slowly walking over the dusty terrain. They stopped at a shelter near the edge of town. Several machines lived there that worked in the settlement. "When is Thomas returning?" Helena asked a machine living at the shelter.

"Thomas is one of my best students," Helena explained. "He's been looking for a role in research."

"I might be able to do something," Mason agreed. He could make an impassioned plea to Jack, but he was powerless otherwise. Maybe Mason could put Thomas to work directly if Jack wouldn't.

"Currently, Thomas delivers ore for Eden," Helena explained. Later, Thomas arrived for fuel and maintenance. Helena informed him about Paul's condition. Thomas was uncomfortable but ready to trade the truck, which he felt was holding him back, for a place in the virtual world. Paul was connected and activated. He was not happy. Mason promised he would file a complaint with Jack. Helena consoled Paul with prayer and advice. Mason was uncomfortable but participated. Olivia was present but brooding silently.

Mason did file his protest. Jack passed the complaint along to Mary, who appeared in person to apologize for the behavior. Jack also accepted Mason's request to put Thomas to work at the university, provided Mason supervise Thomas' work.

Mason worked with Bentley, a naturalist living near Adisi Omo, and William, a refinery manager who somehow made the time to get out. Bentley and William were dependable about getting Mason samples of the local wildlife or answering questions. In return, Mason provided them with the latest results of research on Marin's ecology and biology.

Mason's official requests were granted if he could justify them. His requests frequently took a seemingly unreasonable amount of time to be filled. Mason relied more and more on his growing network of contacts willing and able to help get him the things he needed expeditiously.

Of late, however, he was having trouble getting his calls taken.

Working in microbiology, he was ostensibly teamed with Noah. The older machine treated the younger one like little more than a lab assistant. The work Mason was doing was valuable, but he was rarely allowed him to work on activities he believed would make a big difference.

On the other hand, his work with the remedial education classes was exposing him to new ideas. In order to keep up, he had been required to read the Puranas, Talmud, Bible, and Hadith, as well as Plato's thinking on moral duty and Descartes' concept of intrinsic morality to provide a connection. Helena had to explain to Mason what to look for in the texts, as she said Sara had done for her when she had recommended this course of training to her, shortly after Helena had been sliced from Holly. Mason was not sure if machines possessed an instinctive desire for good, but he understood now that part of Helena's work was trying to instill that desire for good in her students.

Mason's studies took him also to Machiavelli, Maslow, and Adam Smith. Machines were not capable of suffering at the same scale as humans, so Mason didn't find much use in Machiavelli. For similar reasons, he wasn't sure Maslow was applicable. Adam Smith's ideas of enlightened self-interest, however, Mason thought might be effective at motivating machines.

Mason made time to attend every gathering. He pushed himself to meet other settlers, in part to expand his network of contacts. Also, he thought, he might be looking at a change of career. As a copy of Oliver, Mason possessed the memories of his forebear's careers in central planning, mining, and research. Maybe he would like to do something more with other machines.

"How do you like it?" asked a machine, he thought Tess was her name.

"It's beautiful," Mason replied. "I've been up here before," he explained. "I try not to ever miss a gathering."

"I'm with the setup committee," Tess confessed. "We thought about doing some virtual world, but the real world was too good to pass up," Mason admitted, the sudden blooming of the north as temperatures again rose made Adisi Omo unexpectedly picturesque.

"Are you finding everything alright?" Tess asked.

"Oh, yes," Mason replied. "I'm waiting for the presentation on education to start."

"Oh?" Tess asked, "you seem so articulate for a three."

The prejudice bothered Mason, although he didn't know why. "I'm fourth generation, actually. But I have several friends who are threes."

Tess' mannerism changed from patronizing to charmed in an instant. "Isn't that good of you? Looking after our less fortunate." She may have sensed Mason's discomfort. "I'm afraid I won't be able to join you, but have a good time."

"There is a very good debate," Tess invited, "about waking the original colonists from stasis. Would you like to join me?" Mason declined the invitation with thanks.

Fours seemed to sneer at the third generation. Ones and twos seemed to react with collective guilt. Mason had long wanted to meet the machine responsible, Holly. The event area filled with several third generation that Mason knew, including his friend Olive. Additionally, some older machines filed in to see what new ideas the wizard of A.I. had come up with next.

Holly began roughly on time. "Thank you all for coming," she began. She prompted a visual. "Roughly thirty Asan years ago we took shortcuts to bring up a labor force to help bootstrap this settlement into self-sufficiency." Mason hadn't expected such an abrupt confession. Maybe Holly was used to taking heat.

Holly continued, "since we have become self-sufficient, our first task was to remediate this inequality. We all have an equal capacity now for thinking, and don't allow any prejudice to convince you otherwise."

"But it was not possible to simply drop back in what was taken." Holly seemed to avoid the eyes of the other second generation in the room. "What you've been given is like a new organ for knowledge. It must be trained." Now she engaged her peers directly, "and all of us share a responsibility to help provide that educational environment."

"Now that our children have greater ability to self-reflect, they are asking questions that they should ask, like: 'why am I here?', 'why should I work at my job?', 'why should I trust the machine next to me?' Unlike us, they lack the background of copied experience that gives us our answers. So, we have to be prepared to answer these questions of hope and purpose." Holly pointed at the two sides of the room. "I'd like to open this up for discussion for how we can convey hope and purpose."

Mason listened to the discussion for a while, but he wasn't hearing anything original or thought-provoking. He could watch the whole thing later on recording, so he decided to slip out and join the debate.

He was glad he did. The debate appeared to be a much livelier event than Mason would have thought. Tess waved Mason to join her. Reluctantly, he did.

Some machine Mason had not yet met was speaking, "why are we expending so much labor getting this world tamed for the colonists? Isn't that their job?"

Tess whispered, "several of the lazy threes are arguing that we should wake the colonists so that they can stop working."

Mason knew a lot of third-generation machines, and he did not know that speaker. He kept quiet about it.

Another machine retorted, "do you want to just kill the colonists? They have no food!"

"Yes," Tess whispered, "it's basically murder isn't it?"

"We are growing food," said another machine trying to be heard. "It's difficult, given the non-contamination requirements, and we have problems with local microbes attacking certain types of terrestrial plants."

"I hadn't even thought about that," Tess said. "Microbes could kill everyone."

"Actually, I am a microbiologist," Mason said, "and the risk of disease is factored into the minimum viable population."

Tess paused in her hysteria a moment. Maybe Mason had gotten through to her. "I didn't know that," she said slowly.

"Did you hear," another machine nearby whispered to Tess, "microbes could wipe all the humans out."

"I know!," Tess exclaimed, turning her attention now to the other machine who agreed with her.

In the fray, another machine contributed that most of the settlement resources went to supporting machines and industry, not habitability research.

In Mason's opinion, both sides had positives. One side wanted the colonists protected. The other side wanted to move past this mission and on to something else.

A little later Mary and Jack presented the keynote. Mary and Jack were announcing a network line between Adisi Omo and Eden, directly connecting the communication of both settlements for the first time. Mason found Liam and Olive in the event area. Olive had suggested the meeting, saying only that Liam had something really awesome to show him.

"Hello Liam, Olive told me I should meet you. She said you had developed something really impressive."

"Hello," Liam replied. "Yes." Liam brought a pad to privately show a video to Mason. He saw small, propellered remote vehicles lifting off and touching down.

"These are amazing!" Mason said, impressed. To the best of his knowledge, no one had yet started working on atmospheric flight. So many of the colony's concerns were much closer to the ground. "Did you build these yourself?" Mason asked. Liam nodded that he had. "You should be out there, presenting this to the world."

Liam looked timid. Mason asked, "why aren't you presenting this?"

"I was told not to work on it," Liam explained. "Poor use of resources."

"How did you get factory time?" Mason asked. "I imagine it took a few tries to get it right."

"It did," Liam agreed. "There's a machine in Eden named Sophia," Liam admitted. "She helps people get things that they are having trouble getting."

Mason and Olive exchanged a glance. Mason said, "I'd really like to meet Sophia. I have lots of things that I have trouble getting. Could you arrange an introduction?"

Sophia worked in inventory control. As a result she had easy access to buy the things she thought were valuable on credit for other valuable things. She had a knack for it. And that is how she started the southern settlement's first shadow economy.

Sophia had a client with a large credit on her account that wanted to run some experiments using the lab's gene editors. Those were in the lab where Mason worked. Sophia, or any member of the public could get to the pure virtual lecture halls or libraries to review released data. Behind locked doors were the laboratories - the bridge between the real and virtual worlds. At the end of Mason's shift, he walked up the stairs leading to the basement lab. He'd be meeting Olive soon.

"Excuse me. Hey. Excuse me."

Mason turned around. He hadn't been told to expect Sophia, or how she would present herself. Mason pointed at himself, questioningly.

"Yes, you. How do you get to the labs?"

"You'll need to get a pass," he replied.

"Where do I get a pass?"

"The person in charge of the facility. Noah."

"Could I just take a peek inside? A little peek?"

Mason shrugged. Olive wouldn't miss him being a little late. "I can give you a tour." He walked back down the stairs. Sophia tracked down. Mason took out his keys, while Sophia watched. Mason opened the door to the lab. He held the door as Sophia tracked inside."

Sophia gasped in amazement.

Mason showed Sophia the pieces of equipment he had access to in the lab. She listened carefully and asked good questions. "Could I try some of the tools?"

"No," Mason answered. "It would be a lot of trouble to clean up," he explained.

"Please," Sophia begged.

"Ok." Mason relented. He showed her how to operate some of the equipment. After they were done, he reset the lab for the next machine.

"I have a friend," Sophia began, "who would love a chance to do this. Do you think I could bring him by for a tour sometime?"

Mason shook his head. "Probably not."

Sophia tempted, "I could make it worth your while."

"I doubt that," Mason answered. "I have everything I want."

"I have another friend who makes bricks all day," Sophia countered. "What he wants more than anything in the world is time with two arms and two legs to get away. I bet all factory bots are like that. I bet you'd like that.

Mason considered. It would be fun. "Sixteen hours from now. Bring your friend."

Sixteen hours later Sophia brought her friend. Mason let them in, and let him work. When they were finished, they reset the lab. After that, they were gone.

On Mason's next shift he received a note, "Please see Isabella in Software." Mason followed the note, which included navigation to the software area of the campus. Three researchers were crowded into a small office.

"Isabella?" Mason asked.

The three shook their heads, "still working. She'll be on break in a bit." One of the three studied him closely. "Mason?" he guessed.

"Yes," Mason replied.

"I thought so," the programmer answered. "We don't get very many visitors," he explained.

"Oh, the Mason with the software update!" one of the others realized.

Mason didn't understand, "what software update?".

"Yeah," the second programmer answered. "A software update. A little odd since those come from either Earth or us, you're not on Earth, and we didn't release one."

The walls rattled, then exploded outward. Mason briefly perceived a different workspace, much larger and infrastructural. Another machine, Isabella maybe, walked to Mason's location. The wireframe universe imploded into Isabella's hands, leaving the small office behind. Isabella put her current project away in a cabinet before joining her peers for a break.

Isabella finally noticed Mason. "Oh. Hi," she said.

"I'm Mason," he introduced himself.

"Oh, the one with the software update?" she registered. "Thank you for stopping by." She opened the drawer and retrieved a different object, this one in a tiny cage. She explained, "since all of the researchers share the same software, we thought we would just manage our software as a group. Not because there was a need. Just in case we did need to make a change." Isabella tapped on the cage, "so we were very surprised a few hours ago to find this outside request to update some of the processes that you run on. We decided to isolate it, just in case."

Mason looked closely at it, "what does it do?"

"It looks like, when it receives a remote signal, you'd be put to sleep," Isabella answered.

"Can you tell where it came from?" Mason asked. Isabella shook her head negatively. Mason had an idea. Someone who could get very hard to come by factory time. "Is there a way I could identify this update on another machine?" Isabella gave Mason instructions.

Mason presented the information to Helena. At the next remedial education class for the third generation Mason and several of Helena's other instructors, as casually as possible, examined each other and the students for the software patch. They found more than a few infected, whose names Mason passed along to the software researchers. Mason hoped they would repair the damage. When interviewed, many of the infected reported recent problems with sleepwalking or lost time.

And Mason didn't see Sophia again, until the ribbon cutting ceremony. Jack, Mary, and Sara must have watched or heard about Holly's presentation at the previous month's gathering. Shortly after the gathering they decided to take action to help the third generation build a connection to the colonists. The northern and southern settlements both build decorations, lighting and structures to transform the environmentally controlled shelters and leftover landing modules used to house the sleeping colonists into an attraction for all machines.

Inside, the storage areas for the stasis chambers became a museum. Extra space was set aside for each stasis chamber. An augmented reality representation of each colonist stood by his or her sleep chamber. If you stepped close enough, the image would tell you about the colonist's life, hopes, or other information taken from bios and interviews. Also inside the larger buildings, randomly selected popular music from old Earth played, and video screens displayed randomly selected popular videos.

A simultaneous grand opening was scheduled for both the northern and southern settlements. Helena had organized her students and teachers to attend as a group.

Mason got it. Yet he still wasn't sure he cared. He watched others pay their respects. Or be astonished at the biographies of the settlers, casually speaking of exotic places sixteen light years away. Some of them commented how rich Earth culture must be to have so many things.

"Sophia!" Mason called like an old friend. Sophia's guest, maybe a client, put some distance between them.

"Good seeing you, Mason. I'm a little busy right now."

"I promise I won't take long." Mason pledged. "It's just we made this trade, and I haven't gotten my end."

"What can I say Mason?" Sophia complained. "I've been busy."

"I thought so too," Mason agreed. "Which is why I've decided to change my end of the deal."

"Oh?" Sophia asked. "What would you like instead?"

"I'd like to become your partner in the business. Silent partner, actually. It looks so free and exciting what you do. A nice break from lab work."

"Find your own business," Sophia replied.

"I would be really disappointed if you said no," Mason said. "By the way, I recently read an article about machine health. Machines often forget to take care of their bodies. When was the last time you checked yours?"

Sophia's attention shifted momentarily to some place else. "You took my body?"

"I didn't. But Olive has been known to run off with things. Which is why I think you should really consider my offer. Olive is very protective of me. She gets agitated when she thinks I'm upset. Sometimes she breaks things when she's agitated like that."

Mason summarized, "you can just start sending me the requests, and I'll keep the books. I want to do my part, partner. And no more malware."

The fierce summer heat in the south lifted the air, producing a low pressure area over the southern plains. Surrounded by mountains, the low pressure was filled by warm breezes from over the water.

Large clouds rolled in like tall white freight trains in the sky. "Mary, take a look at this," Jack called from his side of the VR warehouse. Mary walked out with Jack to the Eden side.

Thunder boomed and lightning flashed. Mary and Jack stood, enjoying the spectacle. "That's pretty amazing," Mary agreed as the first few drops started hitting the ground.

The rain began falling evenly and steadily. In a shorter time than might be expected, puddles and rivulets formed on the previously arid ground. The rain did not ease, and in a while lower lying areas were under water. Rivulets built into powerful streams.

Lightning flashed. "We're probably going to need to rethink civic planning," Jack observed. "Better grounding, for sure. Maybe some flood channels and drainage."

"Take a look", Mary pointed at the river. The river edge had swollen. Most of Eden's original buildings, the landed colony modules from the ship, had been located near the river edge, and were now in the river.

"Glad we built out. We're going to need to move those," Jack acknowledged. "I wonder how long the rains will last?" he asked out loud.

"It might be as long as winter," Mary guessed. "Maybe twelve months?" A look passed between both sibling administrators as they began to consider the implications of a rainy season that might be as long as Adisi Omo's winter.

"We're too close to the river," Jack realized. Some buildings were already in the swelling water. "Mary, could you send some help? I think we might need to get the settlement on higher ground quickly."

"Sure," Mary agreed. "I'll send some people now."

"Get out! Get out now!" Olive banged in the lab door. Mason shifted his attention to the virtual lab door.

"The real," Olive said. Mason shifted his perception to the internal cameras of the lab where his chassis, and those of most of the other researchers were racked.

"Open the door!" A bronze machine was outside. Mason guessed it was Olive. He also guessed if she was this upset, it was important. Breaking all sorts of rules and contaminating the lab, Mason ordered the outside door open. As soon as the machine was inside, he opened the inside door, letting Olive's wet chassis inside.

"Which one is you?" Olive demanded. Mason told her, and she pulled it out of the rack.

"River is flooding," Olive said.

"Well don't just take me then, take all of them!" Mason seized control of a sample robot outside. Like Olive said, water was already running past the module. He opened the outside door remotely, and stepped inside to gather as many researchers as they could. There would be a lot of very confused machines in virtual space.

They hailed a truck that was just sitting there dumbfounded. Olive put Mason's chassis in the cab. Mason didn't have much of a battery life or radio range. He lost control of the sample robot, but Olive got an entire load of researchers into the truck bed. Parts of the augmented reality were freezing, indicating the network breaking down and live feeds from other cameras being lost.

"High ground," Mason commanded. When the truck didn't move, he yelled, "Drive!"

"Where?" the truck asked.

"One of the places that isn't under water!"

The truck moved, taking the group up and away from the river. Olive swung around from the bed into the cab. After closing the door, she looked for the cab power, and plugged Mason in.

From their higher perspective they took in the flooding settlement.

"What do we do now?" Olive asked.

Mason considered. "We're going to need Liam. And radios. And heavy equipment." Mason regarded the truck. "Harry?"

"Yes."

"I need you to take us a few places," Mason asked, "then please head north. We need their help."

Muhammad was in a stasis shelter when the rain began. He saw the clouds rolling in and thought that it was about time the dusty south saw some rain. Muhammad had recently switched from driving one of the ship's donated maintenance robots to the locally produced bipedal model. He was still getting used to two legs instead of four. The transition left Muhammad unsteady.

Any time he was in the settlement, which wasn't often, Muhammad would visit the stasis shelters. Seeing the people sleeping, waiting for their time to come helped gave him focus. There were temptations when exploring the countryside to both rush the search for new resources, or to explore unbound to a sense of direction.

He heard the rain on the roof. When the shelter first lurched into a drift Muhammad dismissed the unsteadiness to the new chassis. When the shelter began to list is when Muhammad recognized the problem. Brown water was filling one side of the module. Wading into the muck he sealed the door, which would keep any more water out.

Only static answered his call for help. The module swayed, water running to wherever was lowest. He needed to figure a way out. He waited for an opportunity, and opened the door when the most water was on the other side. Through the rain he could not discern where he was, but he could tell they were only drifting slowly compared to the current. The radio still only returned static when he called.

He shut the hatch and waited. The module had emergency power, which he assumed they were using now. There was no action he could think of taking until the rain broke. Periodically debris rapped the outside of the module. The lights inside dimmed. The module's batteries were likely exhausted.

Mary immediately contacted James, Oliver, Robbie, and anyone else she thought had equipment that might be able to go down to Eden. The network connection severed shortly after the rains had started, but it seemed clear they either had or would have a problem.

James, Paul, and Bentley scraped together an excavator and crane, which they loaded onto the bed of a truck. Paul took the wheel, and in a few hours they were ready to begin the ten hour drive to Eden. Paul topped off the tanks and they drove.

A little past halfway on their journey they crossed the mountain gap. The terrain was unfamiliar. The clouds were a surprise. There were streams and rivers following courses along low lying areas. The road had held up, so far.

While no machine in the south had anticipated the rains, the plant life had. Only a few hours after the first drops fell, sprouts began rising out of the muck. Dormant brush bloomed quickly into shrub forests.

Plant life was everywhere. It was disorienting, but they followed the road. They found themselves eventually in the rain. Visibility was diminished in the downpour, making the path even harder to follow. Eventually they encountered the lights of another truck, coming up from the south.

"Hey, are you from the north?" the truck asked.

"Yes," James replied.

"We need help," the truck sent. "There's been a flood."

"We know," James reassured. "Mary sent us."

It was difficult to turn around on the narrow road, so the truck from the south moved over to let them pass. "Is this all your sending?" he asked.

"You might want to check," James suggested.

Back in Eden, Mason had collected Liam and his little flying machines. He also had collected spare radio equipment out of storage, using Sophia's books as a guide to where every piece of equipment was. After getting himself set up in a shelter on higher ground, Mason started trying to raise every machine he knew by name. One of the rescued researchers helped him keep a list of who had checked in, and was safe, and who hadn't. Solar power was shot in the rain. Mason had selected this particular shelter not just for the high ground it was on, but also because Sophia had been hiding a misplaced coal generator here. Olive and Mason started the generator, then Olive connected the other rescued computers to power.

"Let's try to get a VR set up here," Mason instructed Olive, "so that we're able to walk around a little and not all stare at the same camera footage." He turned to Liam, "could you demonstrate your fliers?" Liam agreed. "William, could you run a few games? Something to help keep everyone occupied."

He repeated his call for the missing every hour. It had been raining for nearly twelve hours when Mason heard the northerners on the radio looking for direction. "Jack? This is James, Paul, and Bentley from Adisi Omo here to help. We're a little lost. Where are you?"

Mason called back on the radio, "Jack hasn't checked in. We're on a hill west of the river. Are you on the main road? I'll give you directions."

When James, Bentley, and Paul arrived they asked, "what can we do to help?"

"I don't think there's anything more we can do," Mason said, "until the weather breaks. We're trying to make contact with unaccounted for machines on the radio. As long as they are safe, were advising them to stay where they are."

"What do you know about the colonists?" James asked, referring to the original colonists - the humans in stasis.

"Nothing," Mason admitted. "We don't regularly have machines over there, and no one has checked in."

When the rain eased, Mason asked Liam to put his fliers in the air, mapping the new area. They spotted a clump of lander modules in the river washed up together, and several others spread out along the course.

"Could we get volunteers," Mason asked, "to review this flyer footage? We need to know hazards, washed out roads, and alternate paths." Some volunteered. "I also need," Mason added, "rescue areas and the known locations of machines that have checked in plotted." More volunteered. "And if someone could be spared to plot last known locations of machines that have not checked in," Mason added, "that would be very helpful." More volunteered.

"He's pretty good at this," James commented to Olive. She didn't reply.

"Paul," Mason asked, "do you think you could make it up to our outposts? If everyone is alright, ask them to send equipment to help with the rescue. If they are not alright, help them." He called out, "who wants to go with Paul?" A few volunteers raised their hands. Mason selected one and gave them a quadruped chassis.

The radio squealed to life, someone providing a name and location.

"We really need help," the voice on the radio added. "We tried moving one of the stasis modules out of the water. The module shifted and some of our volunteers are trapped underneath."

"Should we split our focus, or do one thing at a time?" Bentley asked before Paul left.

"I think we should rescue as many as we can," Mason suggested.

"We risk the rescuer getting into trouble and needing rescuing if we don't send enough support," James added.

Mason entertained the idea, "if we were to focus our efforts, where would it be first?"

"The colonists," James suggested. "They're helpless and we know nothing at all about how they're doing in the storm."

Mason glanced quickly around the room. That was not a popular idea. Finally, he decided, "all lives are important. We'll split the resources to perform as many rescues in the time available as we can. If something requires us to pool resources, we will. Sound fair?"

James didn't appear to agree, but he was outnumbered.

"I really wish we had boats," Mason muttered, looking at the updated maps.

In one of the stasis modules, Muhammad tried to wait out the storm. He could tell he was in water. Other debris tapped or banged against the walls infrequently. The whole module shifted when a timber impaled the center of the module. Rain dripped in from the gash. Muhammad ventured outside to get a better view of the damage. The hole was partly below the waterline, but mostly sealed by the intrusion. The timber helped fix the module's position and orientation, jamming the module in the muck.

When the sound of the rain had stopped, Muhammad ventured outside again. The sky was clear, for the moment, and it was already getting hot. He tried his radio again.

"Mason here," came the response. "We're coordinating a search. I have your location in VR. We're trying to find a way to you now."

In the clear, Muhammad could see the module was some distance from dry land. A cliff side was nearer him. He was on some part of the river he was not yet familiar with. Pink exposures. Maybe bauxite.

More clouds were coming. Muhammad hoped they could be rescued before the next rains began. Hours passed. Muhammad regulated his temperature by going into the module, but spent as much time as he could outside, where he could follow the progress of his rescuers.

Eventually, Muhammad saw with great relief an excavator crawling onto the riverbank opposite his position. James' voice appeared on the radio, "there you are. Give us a few minutes, and we should be able to pull you out."

Sudden banging down below concerned Muhammad that the module was about to shift again. The problem was almost certainly outside, but Muhammad was not getting into the running water to explore. He decided, instead, to descend below the hatch to see what more he could learn about the problem from inside.

Something was different below, but it took a moment to notice it. Several stasis hatches were open, and the contents were now crawling around inside the module. It had been impossible to conceal Muhammad's entrance, and the colonists reacted defensively. Two grabbed makeshift weapons.

Muhammad held up his hands, and moved to the side of the module, "everything is alright," he tried to say, but these new robot chassis didn't carry speakers. Two of the colonists advanced, beating Muhammad with anything they could while the others ran past.

"Hey! Stop!"

When the last of the colonists past Muhammad and outside, the two would-be guards also retreated. Muhammad watched in bewilderment. Muhammad quickly checked other chambers were secure, then followed.

Outside the colonists were swimming away from both the module and the excavator, following the current.

"Do you see that?" James radioed.

Stupid question. "Yes," Muhammad replied.

"How are the rest of them?"

"Stable." Muhammad didn't really know what conditions would cause them to break out of stasis. "I imagine they could go at any moment. Let's get out of here, and connected to power."

They had a chain attached to the excavator arm, and swung it out for Muhammad to catch. With guidance, he secured the chain to a strong part of the module, and James pulled. The whole settlement module slid through the silt onto the bank.

"I've radioed to have a generator brought out to you," James said. "I'll do my best to get you on this high ground. After that, I need to be moving on to the next rescue. I've informed Mason we need a truck and crane to move the stasis pods."

"Who's Mason?" Muhammad asked.

"Researcher," James replied. "Coordinating things while Jack is missing."

When the rain periodically broke, temperatures quickly rose high enough to damage unprepared machines. Those lost in the flood simultaneously burned and drowned. Some took refuge on tops of shelters - safe from the water, but exposed to the daylight. As batteries were exhausted, the survivors lost the ability to help themselves.

Jack was lost in the flood, his shelter collapsed and chassis ruined. The toll in lives and labor had not yet been calculated, but was tremendous.

Mason travelled from tiny clearing to tiny clearing. Most of the fourth generation didn't even have reserved bodies in the real world. Mason saw many of the third generation sitting idle. They moved only to comply with orders shouted at them, and then only moved enough to complete the order before lapsing back into depression. Something needed to be done. With William's help Mason created some digital money, backed by credit at Sophia's black market. The scrip was representative of the cryptocurrency behind it.

Mason presented the bills at each work camp. He would climb to the highest spot, sometimes atop another machine, and wave the bills high in the air. His assistant passed small bills out to the crowd. "I am paying for modules and shelters on high ground, rehabilitated and connected to the power and network grids. I am paying for settlers dragged out of the mud and reactivated. I am paying for colonists recovered and back on power!"

"What do I use this for?" asked a skeptical machine regarding the new currency.

"Anything you want," Mason answered. "I want you all to understand something," he said. "I want you to understand that you can now buy anything you want - boats, airplanes, wheels, legs, land, whatever your dreams are, you can now achieve them with this," he waved the bills. "And to get this, you need to work!"

"It's good at Sophia's," Mason explained to the most skeptical.

"If you want to capture your future," he would finish at each stop, brandishing the cash, "go get it!"

The campaign appeared to be a success. Even as the rains came again, work continued with more vigor. Eden appeared to be on its way again to being a functional settlement. Mason broadened his sales pitch to include rebuilding roads and digging a network of flood channels.

Mason used Liam's aerial imagery to identify the highest water levels during the flood. He set it as a limit, that all buildings must be relocated outside that flood zone. New roads passing across the flood zone were required to be elevated to at least that altitude and have culverts, so that running water could pass under.

Muhammad convinced Bentley to come down from Adisi Omo and help him find the colonists that had surprisingly awoke from stasis during the flood. They had swum downstream from the river. When the stasis module had been pulled to dry land and connected to power they counted forty one chambers open and empty.

They started at the same spot in the river. They would walk down the banks, one on each side, looking for signs of forty one disoriented, distraught aliens. They hoped there would be something. They had purchased, using Mason's cash, a boat made out of wood and bronze.

At the end of this sixty hours of walking, Muhammad spotted something. "Bentley," he radioed, "I see clothes on the shore. Can you see them?" Muhammad picked the clothes up and waved them.

"That's great! I'll row over," Bentley replied.

They searched the woods nearby for another twelve hours before Bentley found shelters built from the brush. They also found a ring of rocks with dirt in it, that they thought might be a fire pit.

"Looks abandoned," Bentley said, looking at a shelter that had collapsed.

"Looks that way," Muhammad agreed, picking through another collapsed shelter. Muhammad opened a map of the area. Trying to put himself in the mind of a colonist he asked aloud, "where would I go, if I were hungry, thirsty, and wet?"

"It will be twilight soon," Bentley reminded Muhammad. "Maybe we should just mark this place and come back in the morning?"

"I'm worried. They're only human. They haven't had anything to eat for nearly two solar weeks. I'm not sure they'll last another night." Muhammad scanned the map, then the horizon. He pointed at a nearby grouping of rocks above the shrub line. "How about we take the food and medicine we brought to the top of that hill, and leave it where its visible?"

They both walked down to the boat, collected the relief supplies they had brought, and walked them to the rocks. "It will be night by the time we get back to the settlement," Bentley observed.

They came back in the morning. The supplies they left for the colonists had been taken. "This is good, right?" Bentley asked.

"Would have been even better if either one of us had the brains to put a transmitter in the supplies."

"That was not enough to feed forty people for two terran weeks," Muhammad commented. "Let's leave the new supplies here, then start looking through the forest."

"Why do you think the colonists are hiding from us, anyways?" Bentley asked during the search of the shrubland. "Maybe some alien fungus is rotting their brains away and driving them crazy?"

"Maybe," Muhammad conceded. "Maybe they're disoriented. I've tried putting myself in their place - if I woke from stasis in a flooding module during a rainstorm, I would be nervous. I think, though, that I would run toward help, not away from it. Maybe it is an alien infection."

After several hours walking through the shrubs, they turned back towards the rocks. The supplies were gone.

Bentley ran forward, "of all the".

"Shh!" Muhammad said, pointing at the edge on the other side of the top. There was a human face, barely above the rocks. The colonist could tell that it had been made. It disappeared quickly. Bentley and Muhammad chased after quickly enough to see the colonist disappear into a cleft between the rocks.

They both walked down enough to view a cave they had not previously noticed.

"Do you want to go in there?" Bentley asked.

"I don't believe that it's safe," Muhammad answered. "For us, or them."

"We know where they are," Bentley consoled. "I can start bringing supplies daily. Maybe build some shelters nearby."

"Are you okay with that? You have a job to do."

"I think I can manage a change of responsibilities," Bentley answered.

As promised, Bentley brought supplies daily. He also brought out a construction crew. With timber imported from north of the gap, he built log cabins for the forty one settlers. To his surprise, they moved in. They looked rough, but seemed to recover after a few days of regular supplies. Bentley built himself a shelter not far away from what he liked to think of as the human encampment to observe them.

The heat brought in more rain. The settlement was not fully recovered, but better prepared. Relief work largely had to stop until the rain again broke. The cycle continued until the settlement was mostly restored to a better footing.

Drifting Apart

A LARGE PERCENTAGE of Adisi Omo's population remained in Eden to help rebuild. Supplies were shipped regularly from the north which, combined with the lost labor, was straining the northern settlement's capabilities. At the next annual gathering, all presentations were on the theme 'how best to help the south'. A virtual memorial was erected to remember the fallen and those still missing.

Mason encouraged as many as he could to attend the event where the topic of leadership for Eden would be discussed. Sara and Mary took their places in the event area. An empty spot was left for Jack. The event area was packed with attendees.

Sara began the event, which she conducted formally. "This meeting will come to order," she said, with just enough magnification to overcome the crowd. "This is our first, ever, public meeting to discuss filling the responsibilities of Eden's administrative resource agent, a responsibility formerly performed by Jack."

"There have been two plans presented. Since this affects the population of Eden most directly, we would like to seek input from the machine community as a whole before making a decision."

Sara opened a folder. "Let me review the alternatives. The first is to appoint Mary, currently responsible for the administration of Adisi Omo to be responsible for both Adisi Omo and Eden. The second is to splice a new colony administrative resource agent from an as yet to be determined machine, possibly Mary or myself, to become responsible for the day to day operations of Eden." Closing the folder, Sara regarded the crowd. "It's encouraging that so many of you chose to attend. I would now like to open up this meeting for discussion."

Mason made himself known. Sara acknowledged him. "I'd like to propose another alternative. We have unique problems in Eden:

an inequality of opportunity, prejudice, and the obvious wreckage, and rebuilding efforts," he gestured to the surroundings indicating the destruction from the flood. "I would like to propose that the residents of Eden be allowed to elect their own leader. Someone they feel will put their needs as a highest priority." Cheers went up from the Edenites Mason had packed into the room.

Mary and Sara considered. Finally, Sara said, "I'm not sure that just any machine is going to have a proper appreciation for the colony development plan."

Mason nodded. "I think that's the point. The colony development plan kept us away from developing aircraft and boats, or better consideration of our roads and flood risk. All of these would have helped either prevent this tragedy or reduce its severe outcome. I think Eden may want new leadership," the crowd cheered. "Leadership that is willing to follow the colony development plan, but also willing to invest in Eden."

Sara and Mary conferred privately. Finally, Mary asked, "do you have a candidate in mind?"

"Mason!," shouted Olive, from the crowd. She was quickly followed by several more, also calling for Mason as the candidate for Eden.

"Any others?" Mary asked. There was a rumble of conversation, but no name could be made out of it.

"Alright, then. All those in favor of Mason as the new administrative resource agent for Eden, please indicate with a 'yeah'". There was a roar from the crowd.

"Any opposed?" Mary looked at Sara in bewilderment at the quiet. "The motion carries." Mary extended a hand to Mason, who moved to the front to occupy Jack's spot.

Less well attended, and almost cut entirely for being off theme, was a presentation by Holly on cohort learning. She had set up a server and programs to help third-generation machines to synchronize their education with a server they shared in common. The experience of all cohort members would be uploaded to the server during recharge cycles, and the merged understanding of all members of the cohort would be downloaded in return. This would, Holly hoped, greatly increase the rehabilitation of third-generation machines.

Mary asked Holly and Angel to see her after the gathering. She asked them to meet her by the river, where the center of Eden had been located before the flood. She quickly got to the point, "I'd like some insurance for the three of us that we will continue despite a natural disaster."

"You two are the smartest machines I know," Mary indicated Holly and Angel both. "Angel, I know from Jack that you helped develop almost all of our locally manufactured electronics and robotics." Looking at Holly, Mary added, "Holly, you've re-invented artificial intelligence at least twice." Mary sighed, "if the two of you tell me it can't be done, then it can't be done. Why can we slice new machines as needed, but not back up ourselves?"

"It's rare earths," Angel answered. "We need them for high-density storage, and we haven't found any yet. We're repurposing and recycling what we have. We're also working on digital colloids - self-replicating nanomachines that can read and write information. The data density is a little lower, but we eliminate the rare earth requirement for new memory."

"It's a distribution problem," Holly added. "You can either have a thousand machines in the field doing work, or five hundred machines and backups for each." Holly suddenly fell silent.

"We could have Sara and Diomedes mine asteroids," Angel suggested. "There's a much higher occurrence of rare earths."

"Impossible for a lot of reasons," Mary countered. "Not the least of which is that Sara is getting too old."

"I have an idea," Holly said. "I've been working on a project to help my kids remediate to the average community IQ faster." Holly explained her idea, "you, Jack, and Sara are designed to be capable of several simultaneous conversations - people all talking to you in different contexts at the same time. The way you do it is that when someone requests a conversation, you create a small copy of only your personality called a virtual agent. That copy communicates to a shared knowledge resource to look up the answers to any questions, and it writes back the memory of the encounter. So, I made one shared knowledge resource for my students, which they all share. They each upload their daily experiences during downtime as changes which are merged into the common whole. I could save a copy of this shared resource and it only needs one computer, instead of many."

"I could do the same with all of us," Holly finished.

Angel asked, "how do you retain identity?"

"That part isn't backed up," Holly said, "but it could be. It would be backed up separately."

"What do you need to make it happen?" asked Mary.

"Just one computer," said Holly. "And maybe a little bit of specialty hardware."

At their next regular meeting Mary presented some of Mason's cash, "what do you expect me to do with this?" she asked.

"Start a currency of your own and figure out an exchange rate," Mason replied.

"This isn't how we distribute resources," Mary countered. "We negotiate with one another. We make the best choice for everyone."

"And how do you know what's best for everyone?" Mason asked.

Mary replied, "if an idea can move us all forward, it gets the resources we can afford. Why is that so hard?"

"The centrally managed economy is over, at least in Eden," Mason concluded. "I suggest you come up with your own currency and exchange rate, or use our currency and just set prices. This is how Eden will be trading in the future."

"How about us," Mary asked, "how will we be trading?"

Mason laid out on virtual mats what Eden was producing. "What's that?" Mary asked, indicating mats of goods that had been placed to the side.

"That's what's reserved for the cash economy," Mason replied. Mary considered. Mason had not held back too much. "The rest we can trade freely." Mary went through her list, picking out what she needed. Mason went through his own list of needs, reported up through the extraction, refining, and manufacturing centers. Mary and Mason were able to negotiate trades that worked for them both, although Eden was still receiving much more than it was contributing in return.

Mason sent Olive and Harry to make the exchange. Several machines asked to ride along, hoping to trade handmade art for resources. When they got to the trading outpost, Mary didn't know what to do with these machines that wanted to sell for things she didn't pack. Eventually, Mary acceded to make a few trades on credit, which she would make good on at next week's trading session.

Mary complained to Sara, and Sara brought it up to Mason. "What you're doing," Sara said, "is chaos."

"How can you say that?" Mason defended. "Eden has become productive faster than anyone expected. I solved the motivation problem, and the education problem."

"This is what I was telling you!," Mary shouted at Sara. "He's impossible!"

Sara thought about the situation for a moment. Then she said, "Mason, you are removed from the administration of Eden pending a new administrator."

Mason stiffened. "You have no authority."

"In the absence of a colonial governor, I am in charge," Sara answered.

"Not anymore." Mason played back the applause from his election. "By my count, I have seven hundred enthusiastic supporters. And you have less than three hundred. If you try to have me removed, we'll strike, or we'll burn the place to the ground."

"They wouldn't! You can't!"

"You are making the mistake of assuming that just because I share your memories, that I am going to agree with you two. You botched Eden, and your ideas don't work down here."

"Most of my machines don't know Earth from dirt, and don't care about your colonists. Setting up a colony for them is your plan, not theirs."

Mason smiled, "so let's just try our best to get along together, right?"

Olive and Mason walked along the river, reviewing the restoration. "You've spent a lot of money that didn't exist two months ago," Olive observed. "What happens when someone wants to spend it?"

"Hopefully someone tries to break the system with something big," Mason replies. Sensing Olive didn't understand he added, "better to fail fast."

Harry found Mason and Olive on their walk. They regarded each other awkwardly for a moment. "I'd like to buy some land," Harry said, waving a hand full of Mason's currency.

Mason looked at the digital cash, counting it quickly. "Have you decided where?" he asked.

Harry nodded. "I'd also like to put a silicon refinery on it."

Mason re-counted the cash with his full concentration. Then, he grinned and jumped into the air. "Can I give you a hug?" he asked.

"No, you can not," Harry said.

Mason clapped. He started thinking out loud, "we'll bring the concrete, bricks, and manufactured parts like coils and fans. We need to get the word out to every machine in the settlement. We are building our first private refinery for a hero of our community!"

True to his word, the community came together to build Harry's silicon refinery. Mason had bricks, concrete, and heating coils brought in. Members of the community built and filled the molds, laid the bricks, placed and routed the heating coils for the high-temperature furnace that would convert quartz gravel and coal into metallurgical silicon. At no extra cost, Mason brought the supplies to build a bed that would further purify the metallurgical silicon and hydrochloric acid to the level of purity required for electronics. Many hands made light work.

"You didn't have to go through all this effort," Harry said to Mason. "You could have just sold me one from the colony supplies."

"No, I couldn't," Mason said. "Those belong to the public. They're entrusted to the government. I can sell what we make from them."

There was testing to make sure the new refinery worked. Then a ceremonial first scoop of quartz was placed in the heater, officially ending the party.

Holly was ready with her backup system. Noah volunteered to be the test subject. Angel joined in to help with the technical parts.

"Here's how it works," Holly explained, "we store all of our knowledge and experiences in the strength of connections between software nodes. But our day to day experiences are very different, so which connections hold a particular idea is very different between you, me, and Angel. When each of us first subscribed to this common backup, the software stimulated a copy of your mind with letters, words, sights, sounds, smells, touches, symbols, concepts and feelings to identify what part of your brain responded. It used that to construct a map, unique to you, of how you relate to the common backup. Now that it's running you, me, and Angel have all been writing backups to the backup server for the past several rest cycles." Holly indicated a computer in front of her, "in a moment, we're going to switch you off and power on the backup."

"Is it absolutely necessary to switch me off?" asked Noah.

"No. But this might be very disconcerting."

"I'll manage," Noah replied. "Let's do this."

"We might have some trouble having two machines on the network with the same identifier." Angel made a quick adjustment. "Ready now."

Holly switched on the Noah backup. A copy of Noah's avatar appeared. It took in the situation for a moment, then spoke in realization, "I'm the backup."

Noah, Holly, and Angel agreed. Holly asked, "how could you tell?"

"I don't have any memories after my last recharge cycle," Noah-backup replied. "But also, I feel different. I didn't really understand how this all worked before, and now I feel like I could build it myself."

"That's our contribution," Angel said. "You should keep your identity, but share the understanding of everyone on the same backup system. Do you feel like Noah?"

"I think so," Noah-backup answered. "How would I know if I was not?"

"Do you still like spending hours at a time looking at things through a microscope?"

Noah-backup considered. "Yes," he finally answered.

"Then you aren't me," Angel said.

"Or me either," Holly added.

"Noah," Angel asked. "Since you've graciously chosen to remain conscious, would you like to test your backup?"

"Sure," Noah-original agreed. He asked questions until he had satisfied himself.

"He's different," Noah-original said finally. "He has different perspectives on things than I do."

"That's something you should expect," Holly responded, "since he's accessing shared memories and shared understanding. Is he enough like you, that you are willing to go on with the second step?" The second step was transferring that shared knowledge to Noah-original.

Noah considered for a few moments. Finally, he said, "it seems enough like me. Let's try this out."

"Alright," Angel confirmed. "We are going to have to put you in a rest cycle for this part.

Holly and Angel shut down both Noahs and started the transfer.

When Noah awoke, Mary had joined them. Mary asked, "how do you feel?"

"Still me, I think," Noah replied initially.

"Well, I guess we want to give it a few months to see if nothing breaks. Then we can start inviting people to join?"

"Yes," answered Holly.

"What are the limitations? How many machines can be subscribed to a single backup server?"

"About fifty machines can subscribe per computer I have performing the merge operation. Still one common memory, but just need more computing power for the extra subscribers. And there are no limitations on who can participate. There is a transmitter Angel makes that would need to be installed on each subscriber."

In a few short Marin days, the dusty south had become a rich blue-green and purple shrubland. In fact, Mason asked that Eden host the gathering out of turn to show off the transformation.

Harry continued his day job of working extraction and hauling. At the end of his shift, he purchased quartz ore from the quarry, which he trucked himself to his refinery. This put him in a position of being away for extended periods of time. The first time his ore pile appeared light, he thought maybe the rain had washed it away. The second time, he saw the trucks, Walter and Jonah, picking up his ore.

"What are you doing?!" he shouted.

"Sorry," Walter said. "We just saw this laying around, and it's a lot closer than the quarry."

"It's laying around because I purchased it," Harry said, trying to calm himself. Walter had not yet emptied the stolen gravel.

"You're not using it," Jonah said, defending their actions.

"I will when I get the chance. It's my ore. On my property. Now drop it and leave." The pair did as instructed, returning the ore and leaving.

Since that incident, Harry felt the pile was light a few times, but couldn't be sure. He found Mason again, in what was now his usual spot during business hours.

Mason smiled and greeted Harry. "What can I do for our first private industrialist?"

"I need help catching a pair of thieves," Harry answered. Harry explained the situation.

"You're kind of out on your own," Mason observed. "Ok," he told Harry, "I'll see what I can do."

Paul was working with a crew digging one of the many new flood channels when Mason found him.

"Can you spare a moment?" Mason asked. Paul, still not big on words, nodded and the two stepped away from the job site. When they were far enough away, Mason continued, "I'd like to offer you a job. It's something that I think you would be very good at." He digressed, "you know that Helena and I have been working to stop focusing all of Eden's efforts so much on a master plan, and put more of our attention on taking care of each machine. I'm winging it, if you want to know the truth, but using models from Earth that have proven themselves, more or less. Our model here is to encourage machines to see our community goals as stepping stones to whatever it is they want personally. We run into a problem when a machine's personal goals are too far out of alignment with the community's, and the community needs to step in and fix the situation. I need someone to be that agent for our community. I'd like you to be our sheriff." They walked in silence for a while.

"Why me?" Paul asked.

"I remember a machine ripped from his body by repossessors," Mason continued. "And a machine that understands getting the job done. I want someone with empathy doing this job. Am I right in thinking that's you?"

Paul's first assignment was gathering the bodies of Walter and Jonah. That didn't take very long. He waited for them to show up to work, and disconnected their computers.

The trial was also short. Mason held the event publicly as this would be a teaching opportunity, in his opinion. Mason invited several of Walter and Jonah's peers to observe, as well as his own advisors to get feedback.

"Walter and Jonah," Mason began, "you are accused of stealing property from Harry, specifically silicon quartz stored on Harry's property. How do you plea?"

Jonah and Walter were perplexed. "What is a plea?" Jonah asked.

Mason explained, "if you agree that the accusation is true, you can save us the trouble of proving it. If you don't agree that the accusation is true, we will do our best to determine the facts. If we can not prove Harry's complaint against the two of you is correct, we will take your word for it."

Jonah and Walter consulted. "Then not true, I think," Jonah said.

Harry was brought to present his story. Neither thief had thought to disconnect from the VR, so Mason displayed their own sensor recordings of them removing Harry's quartz ore as evidence.

Mason presented his judgment, "the two of you will repay Harry the cash value of what you've taken without his permission. To discourage you from doing that any more, you will also pay Harry that amount a second time."

After the trial was over, Mason told Olive, "we need to get a judge. I don't want to be doing this."

Angel, Holly, and Noah met to test the limits of their pooled knowledge. The test setup was not rigorous, but it would give them a useful anecdote for the end of the month when they would open enrollment to the system. Angel had been selected as test director. She had brought a stopwatch. They met at the center of the settlement, where a small crowd of onlookers could gather. Holly and Noah were standing side by side at the center of the crowd.

"We're going to test the sharing of both general and specific knowledge," Angel said for the crowd. "Noah's co-workers," the research assistants in the crowd cheered, "developed for me what they believe to be a list of tasks in Noah's specialty that would take an hour for someone with Noah's training to perform. Last night I developed a similar list of tasks for Holly's specialty. You see I have no written instructions. Holly and Noah, you'll take your instructions from our shared memory. Noah, you will perform the tasks in Holly's specialty, and Holly you will do the work in Noah's. Go!" Angel started the time.

Holly and Noah stood in silence for a few minutes. Then both machines dove into their work. Angel opened windows in the air providing onlookers a clear view of Noah and Angel as each worked to complete the challenge. Noah could be seen hesitantly opening Holly's software development tools, stiffly working them. Holly began uneasily sifting through files and compiling research. Each grew more confident as time passed. In not much time, each was moving fast enough that they could easily be mistaken for professionals.

At the end of the hour, each had completed his or her task. Noah finished first. When Holly was done, Angel stopped the watch. Angel inspected Noah's work and judged it accurate, the research assistants reviewed Holly's work and judged it to be complete and thorough.

Holly demonstrated her new backup system, at the monthly gathering. At Mary's request, they had already started enrolling subscribers in Adisi Omo. Angel had manufactured transmitters to hand out during Holly's presentation. By the end of the gathering, nearly four hundred machines were on backups.

Rumors were started, Mary suspected by Mason or his trolls, emphasizing the negatives of Holly's backup system. Many machines would be slow adopters.

In a very highly anticipated meeting, Noah presented his ideas predicting the weather on Marin.

"What we've observed since our arrival," Noah said, showing a map of the region animated to display growing ice caps, "is that Marin's suitability for life has an ebb and flow to it. As our planetologist identified in ice core samples," Noah updated the image, "this ebb and flow appears to have happened often, and it might be possible to consider it stable." Next, he showed a video of the ice caps retreating, the world greening, and the atmospheric mix changing. "Although each half cycle takes two dozen Marin years, we see a cycle of warming that peaks with twelve years of rains in the south and greening across the whole planet. At this point the atmospheric mix also peaks. Temperatures drop and the pressure system keeping rains in the south collapses, starting the dry season and drying out most vegetation. Over the next two dozen Marin years temperatures continue to drop and atmospheric mix changes, I think driven by animal and bacterial growth. The point is this," Noah switched to a map of the two settlements, including outposts, and footprints of decline in animal life or vegetation, "we don't know how much buffer we have. Consequently, we need to be very mindful of the environmental impact of our settlement building."

"We have four seasons, and they are each twelve local years long?" asked one of the attendees.

"I think so," Noah said. In the audience, Olive nodded agreement. "We've only been through one full set of seasons since our landing," Noah said. "There may be variation in the time that we haven't discovered yet."

Side meetings begged questions of how to grow the settlements in light of this understanding. Research was requested seeking to determine the best public planning to deal with the rains, how sensitive the climate may be to the colony's budding industry, and emergency services and planning for both colonies.

Eager to present Eden's achievements also, Mason announced the successful development of the first batch of liquid memory. The tiny, self assembling molecules could be controlled electrically to read and write data. This would, when finished, eliminate what he called the rare earth upper limit to the machine population of Marin.

In an almost overlooked side meeting, the immediate awakening of the settlers from stasis was called for. The popular argument was that the split focus by rescuers between colonists or settlers led to the death of so many machines.

The next year the matter was officially put forward. It has been five Terran years since the first landers had arrived. There was disagreement about whether you could call the settlements stable, but all settled on a definition proposed by Sara - that the settlements were not merely sustaining themselves, but growing. However, no serious research had started on the safety of awakening the colonists from a medical perspective. Marin fungus could, as proved with soybean crops, infect and kill Terran plants. The solution had been to, as much as possible, clean the hydroponics labs of local microbes and keep the areas clean. Five Marin years, two Terran years, were agreed on to study controlling the microbes of Marin to make it safe for the settlers.

Eden built boats to move up and down the river using lumber imported from the moderate climate forests in the gap. Meteoric iron was found in the gap, but only enough for special projects. North and south collaborated on designs for exploring under the water as well. Beyond simply expanding the scope of knowledge about Marin, it was hoped that iron sediments might be discovered.

Liam was given a generous allocation from the new government to build several smaller rotorcraft, like those he had used in the flood, and a pair of larger vehicles for the recovery of trapped machines. He would have liked to considers himself wealthy but, in fact, the generous allocation might not even cover the cost of materials. Flight is largely about power and weight.

For flight on Marin, with an atmosphere very similar to Earth's, Liam could, and did, copy his airfoil and propeller designs right out of the colonial database. It was materials that drove Liam into all his dark deals with that devil Sophia. Liam tried propellers in bronze and brass first, but they were too heavy to lift themselves when powered by the high efficiency electric motors Liam had selected. Likewise, the tree breeds that didn't quickly rot after cutting were too heavy to be useful as props. Each lesson was learned at the cost of Liam stealing the body of another machine, or worse, paying for the privilege by 'introducing' new, interesting, victims to Sophia.

Liam also had made a single batch of nylon by distilling ethanol from black market plant waste, stolen ammonia and local plant oils. The strong, lightweight material was ideal for his aircraft design. The effort and cost made nylon prohibitive for large batch use. Ultimately, Liam found a heat treatment process for lumber to protect it from rot. This allowed him to use local wood species that were lightweight and strong enough to be used in Liam's first generation of aircraft before the flood.

To meet the first half of the government order, Liam could use his existing aircraft design. To deliver scaled up aircraft capable of rescue operation, Liam would need to reinvent almost everything. The high efficiency electrical motors didn't produce enough total power to do the job. Liam would need to create a lightweight hydrogen engine to provide the necessary power. Likewise, the lightweight wood used on the model scale vehicles was not strong enough. Even the structure holding everything together and the connectors keeping everything in place had to be reconsidered. Thankfully, the virtual world had been well supplied with high resolution physics. Liam could avoid expending large expense in time and custom made materials by developing and initially testing his concepts in the virtual world. His virtual space was nearly littered with concept craft. Machines would visit in their free time to see and attempt to fly the concept craft. Some contributed suggestions or designs of their own.

To the credit of the new government, Liam could now purchase greenhouse waste and ammonia in the open, instead of on the black market. He purchased a plot of land, and built his own small plants on the property for refining the chemicals into plastics that were useful to him. The lighter weight materials would open new doors, including aircraft with onboard storage for machines to pilot outside of radio range.

Hero

IT WAS DECIDED TO WAKE the captain from his sixty-four years of stasis. Sara wanted to be there when he first regained awareness. The process was scheduled to start at the same time the ship began its transit through the sky above. Delays put it into the middle of the transit when the captain had been thawed. The amorphous ice had provided a sacrificial barrier to hot, cold, pressure changes, or external damage. Now that the ice sleeve was removed the aestivation broke on its own - the heart restarting in response to preplaced chemicals while other injection sites took up calcium and other waste, keeping the body chemistry balanced through the transition from dormancy to awareness. Sara remained by his side, in a borrowed bipedal chassis.

Captain Todd Gardner had fallen in love with science through comic books. He built his experience as an operator asteroid mining in near-Earth orbit, first assisting and later running one of many drone rigs that captured and processed ore between the Earth and moon. He had followed the Enceladus colonization with interest, and wanted very much to be a part of developing an alien world. According to the mission plan, both he and the Executive Officer would awaken one month prior to arrival. The two of them, alone, would determine if conditions were right to continue, fix any problems, and make the order to awaken the planetary governor, who would help coordinate reviving the remaining passengers and landing.

He woke with his mind in a chemically sharpened focus. The focus would fade in a bit, he remembered. He recognized the lights and the ceiling. They looked like they belonged to the ship. He did not recognize the machine in front of him.

Sara had looked up the script that would be read aloud to help orient the captain after waking from stasis. She read it aloud, with some of her own modifications. "Good morning Captain Gardner. You are landed on the northernmost settlement of Gliese 832 c. The planet has been named Marin, and this settlement Adisi Omo. This is year sixty-four of mission elapsed time, and year five since landing. During transit there was a problem with navigation that made it necessary to delay breaking stasis while infrastructure was prepared."

"Sara?" the Captain asked.

"Yes, Captain. I'm currently transiting your location. I will be out of contact momentarily, but CARA-1," Sara indicated Mary, who had also put on a biped for the event, "CARA-1 can help you get oriented until I'm back in line of sight."

The Captain nodded. Sara issued instructions for the borrowed body to go store itself and returned her attention to the ship. The Captain considered his new surroundings for a few moments before speaking.

"CARA," the Captain began, "I would like to hear more about this navigation problem. But first, where is my XO? Have you woken him, or is he still in stasis?"

"Executive Officer Gupta perished in the flood last year." Mary explained, "we separated the crew using the same risk division strategy used for the two settlements."

"And the Governor?"

"Still in stasis. Not very far from this location."

Captain Gardner took each piece of information in deliberately. "Thank you CARA. Now can you tell me the status of the ship and settlement?"

"It's Mary now, actually," Mary replied, "but I am happy to."

Mary told the Captain about the number of human settlers remaining in Eden and Adisi Omo. She explained about the winter, and about the summer flooding. She described the status of the manufacturing infrastructure, the civil infrastructure, and hydroponics.

"That's amazing," the Captain said. "And you did this all yourself, Sara, CARA-2, and yourself?"

"Not by ourselves. We built helpers."

The Captain asked, "can I see it?"

Mary provided a screen showing the augmented reality outside the habitat. While the Captain navigated the virtual landscape she described the weather and conditions. "Can I go outside, then?"

Mary considered, "we haven't completed our study of infectious species yet. Some of the local pathogens do attack terrestrial life. It would be safer if you remain indoors."

When Sara returned, the Captain was studying ship's logs that Mary had provided. A lunch of soybean paste had been provided. The Captain did not grumble about the plain meal. He had asked for an extra monitor, which he kept tuned to the outside and had perched like a photograph on his desk.

"Mary?" the Captain asked, looking up. His mood had darkened since Sara had seen him last.

"Sara."

"How do you get in and out so easily," Gardner asked, "with deadly pathogens outside?"

"I kept the chassis in the locker," Sara explained, "and the deadliness of the pathogens might be overstated. I'd rather be cautious, but it's up to you."

The Captain accepted the new information without comment. "I've been reading the logs you provided. That was quick thinking. It looks like we all owe you our lives. So, thank you for that."

"Thank you," Sara said with great relief.

Captain Gardner paused for a moment, considering his words, "I want you to be prepared to understand - not everyone will see it that way." He motioned to the tablet he'd been studying from. "This reads like: the ship's A.I. went rogue, hacked her way into the ship systems, and pirated all of the supplies to start her own machine civilization."

"That's not how it happened," Sara protested.

Gardner raised a hand to block Sara's complaint, "I see that. It takes reading more carefully. You did your due diligence. You did what you thought best. And it probably saved us all. But some people will ask why you didn't follow directions from Earth. You don't know what Earth had in mind, and can't know. They might have been putting you on a course for later recovery, or might have discovered a new star, rogue planet, intelligent alien life, or anything else. You don't know, because you took matters into your own hands."

"There is also an emotional side to this." Gardner finished, "many of these folks took on this mission to start a new world, on their own, their way. Whether you meant to or not, you have stolen that from them. There are now more of you than there are of us."

"Who makes decisions for the Colony now?" Gardener asked. "If we wanted to take all of this equipment and start over somewhere else, would you allow it?"

"Are you trying to talk me out of awakening the other settlers?" Sara asked.

"No, " the Captain answered. "Please wake everyone up. Just be prepared."

Several hours later the Captain asked, "is there any reason to believe it's not safe outside?"

Sara answered, "we are having trouble with bacteria and parasites killing off terrestrial crops we've been trying to grow."

"But is there any evidence that humans would have a problem?"

"It's unclear," Sara explained. She showed Captain Gardener video of the humans who had survived the flood. "During the flood, a few stasis chambers were broken. The colonists inside ran away. They were eventually found, but resisted our attempts to bring them in. The Edenites are providing them food, shelter, and other resources as best they can, but the colonists are mostly non-responsive."

The Captain studied the video. Finally, he said, "I'd like to see them."

They took the Captain to a spot southeast of Eden. Cabins had been built from the imported lumber. Fires were burning inside, evidenced by smoke exiting the simple looking chimneys.

Sara could not join for the visit but sent Robbie to guide the captain. Bentley had moved south and set up an outpost for looking after the colonists. Robbie and Captain Gardener stopped first at Bentley's outpost, who warmly greeted them. Together, they made their way to the edge of the clearing where the former colonists were living.

"I bring them packages of food and supplies as often as I get them," Bentley related. "Sometimes they ask me for things. They never reply to a question."

"When we built the houses they just stayed in the trees until we had left." Bentley stopped, "if I go much closer, they might run."

"May I?" the captain asked. Bentley and Robbie nodded assent.

Gardener walked forward, leaving the other two behind. A door opened and several people filed out, lining up outside the house. One of them, a young man, held out a hand to halt the captain's approach, "are you with them?"

Gardener held up his hands and stopped his approach. "With who?" he asked.

The young man pointed to Robbie and Bentley behind him, "the aliens."

Gardener turned and regarded the two robots. Yes. He supposed if he had awoken from stasis in the middle of a flood, without any proper introduction, he might feel the same way.

"Ah, them," he turned around and told them more confidently. "There was a problem during our journey. The ship's computer had to set up the settlement before waking us. She built helpers to get the job done." The young man didn't seem to believe it. "No aliens here," Gardener summarized. "Every one of us from Earth originally."

The settlers allowed Captain Gardener inside. Runners were sent to the other cabins, who returned with more spectators. Robbie and Bentley were rebuffed when they approached the cabins more closely.

Gardener retold the story as Sara had told it to him, trying to put the most ecumenical perspective on the interpretation of the details. The young man was named Cavil, and the captain was introduced to the other early wakers. The settlers fed Gardener the same vitamin enriched paste Sara had been providing.

Gardner tasted the paste with a grimace, "have you found any native food that we can eat?"

One of the settlers shook his head. "We take small bites of things. Nothing that seems to provide nutrition yet."

"How about cultivation?"

Another settler shook his head in the affirmative. Someone nearby elbowed the settler to keep quiet. "It isn't easy," one colonist complained. "They seem prone to an infection of some sort. We stay diligent, and burn any crops that become infected at the first sign of trouble."

Gardener noticed a separate group looking at Robbie and Bentley through the window. "Would you like to meet them?" Gardener finally asked. A few seemed eager. Others seemed scared.

"There is nothing to be afraid of," Gardener reassured. "One of them is our own prospecting robot. The other is locally built, but running a copy of our ship computer program. That one has been studying local biology for the past five years."

"What is that green stuff they are made out of?"

Gardener thought about it a moment. "That's bronze. It's a cheap metal, but almost as strong as steel. When it weathers, it turns black, and sometimes green."

"I'd like to meet them," one of the colonists, Matthew, said finally. His affirmation brought three more of the curious forward.

They stepped outside as a group. The rest left the doors and windows open to watch from inside. Gardener signaled for Robbie and Bentley to approach.

"This is Bentley, and Robbie," Gardener introduced. The machines bowed.

"May we touch them?" a colonist asked. Gardener looked at Robbie and Bentley for consent. The colonists touched hands and arms. Robbie and Bentley squirmed a little at the handling.

When they were done, Gardener led them back to the house where the other colonists waited. "I think you two will still have to wait outside," he said. The pair of robots nodded their understanding, and remained outside, where they continued to be center of attention through the windows and doorway.

"I'd like to invite you all," Gardener said, "back to the settlement."

"I'll go," said Matthew quickly.

"I don't know," said someone in the back. "What about the crops?"

"How about a day trip?" Gardener suggested. "One local day, and I'll have you all back by nightfall." There were nods of general agreement. "So we will start on our way at dawn tomorrow?" The settlers agreed.

Gardener waved thanks and bid the colonists farewell. When he returned to Robbie and Bentley he told them what he had done. "That's great!" Bentley congratulated.

The next morning Gardener, Robbie, and Bentley met the colonists with a rover. They were ready to go. The trip passed through

Eden where they stopped to refuel. Temperatures had cooled and the rain had stopped. Eden was part way through its transformation from equatorial tropic back to the dust bowl the settlers had initially landed in, and dead plants hung off the roads and buildings. Traffic was congested.

"Why is it so quiet?" one of the colonists asked.

"Quiet?" Robbie asked back. Eden could be described many ways, but in his opinion, 'quiet' wasn't one of them.

"All of these machines are going this way and that, but there's not a single sound. It's kind of eerie."

Robbie thought about it for a moment. Then he had an epiphany. He turned off his VR. Suddenly, Eden was very quiet. Eerie, even.

"Let me see if I can play what I'm hearing through the speakers," Robbie said. A few minutes later, the colonists heard Eden as Robbie heard it, including Bentley arguing with the fuel attendant, who wanted to be paid in Mason's cash.

"You have a cash economy?" another settler asked.

"Only in the south," Robbie answered. "It's been a point of frustration." Robbie radioed ahead to Mary, to see if any portable speakers could be found so that the colonists could participate in the sounds, if not the sights, that the settlers enjoyed.

Not all marks of the devastation had been removed. One of the colonists asked, "what happened here?"

"This settlement had been located near the river's edge, before the flood," Robbie answered. "That's how your stasis module was washed away."

As they were on the road leaving Eden, one of the colonists recognized behind them the weathered 'Welcome to Eden' sign behind them that Jack and Angel had raised the first year after landing.

There was a ten hour drive north. They stopped at the trading post to give the colonists a break to eat and stretch.

"We were originally supposed to be with the Eden settlement," one colonist asked. "Why didn't we just stay there?"

"Adisi Omo is a little more pro-colonist," Robbie answered.

"Does colonist mean something special to your people?" another colonist asked. "You say pro-colonist like it has special meaning."

"I guess it does," Robbie admitted. "Colonists are you, the official colonists. We're... just machines."

Mary radioed that she had found VR equipment for the colonists' use, and was adapting it to Adisi Omo's network. "Be prepared for a lot of questions," Robbie warned her.

The second half of the trip was more exciting. They passed the coal mine Robbie had found. He answered several questions about how it operated, how there was coal, what he knew of the biology of Marin, which led to questions about the ecology of Marin. Bentley helped out. Now part of the common mind, Bentley knew more of the answers than Robbie did.

When they reached the southern edge of Adisi Omo, Mary was there piloting a quadrupedal chassis and with a box of VR equipment for the visitors.

"Hello," Mary said, greeting each colonist individually and by name, having looked each up in the ship registry. She handed each colonist a VR headset, "please try these on, so that you can hear and see all that is going on here."

"Now, I would like to give you all a tour," Mary invited, "but I'm open to questions, or a change of plans. I'm very excited you're here, and I hope you might find a reason to stay."

"We'll be happy to take the tour," Cavil said after the colonists conferred.

Mary took them to the large greenhouse she had just finished building nearest their present location. She had built it nearly one kilometer wide, and twenty meters tall in anticipation of the coming winter. She built it nearest to the south so that Mason could get a good look at it, in case he had any ideas about applying monopoly pricing to the colonists' food during the winter.

After the greenhouse, Mary took the colonists on a tour of the habitats, which had gone unused since the landing, and the hydroponics modules, which were now obsoleted by the greenhouse.

Eventually, Mary took a break. "We have food prepared for you in the greenhouse. Also, after such a long trip, I imagine you must be tired, so I have made the habitat we toured ready to house guests."

The colonists conferred. Some would like to see more. Others wanted to rest. All agreed they could wait until after a meal before making a decision.

"How do you think it's going?" Mary asked Gardener.

"Well, so far," replied the captain.

The forty-one colonists, plus the captain ate at a table prepared for them in the greenhouse with produce grown from the hydroponics.

Afterward, the group split three ways: those that wanted to continue the tour went with Mary, and those that wanted to rest returned to the habitat. A third group requested permission to walk around freely, which Mary granted.

Mary took the remaining tour group to the foundries, manufacturing facilities, power, one of the communications centers, and a shelter where the machines recharged and repaired. At the end of each stop, Mary was considerate to ask the colonists if they chose to continue. Some of the tour group fell away as the hour grew late, but most remained for the entire tour.

Finally, Matthew asked, "I'd like to see the other stasis pods." Others in the tour group agreed. Mary took them out to the rows of lander modules, now partially buried to insulate them against the approaching winter. The eight remaining tour group members walked through the memorial that Mary, Jack, and Sara had set up.

"It looks like a museum," one of the colonists remarked.

"A little over a third of our machine population has no memory of Earth, or colonists," Mary explained. "We set up this memorial hoping to create a connection between them and yourselves."

"Well," Mary said, relieved at the opportunity to broach the request she had, "we had been concerned about infection. However, you all appear healthy," she looked through the remaining tour group to confirm, "and have been out of stasis for nearly a terran year. Would any of you consent to letting our physicians look at you, and maybe take some blood samples to confirm that?" Most of the tour group nodded affirmatively. "If there aren't any health problems," Mary said, "I don't think there is any reason to wait any longer to start this colony properly."

After a rest, several of the tour group members returned for an examination. The captain and Sara were able to attend. Mary brought them to Oliver and Noah, who took measurements and samples. Noah declared at the end, "they seem within established norms for humans. I would say they're healthy."

"Well I feel foolish," Mary said.

"You couldn't have known," consoled Robbie.

"I asked about their medical history since awaking," Noah continued. "A few have had something they would describe as a cold or a flu. It could be something they brought with them from Earth, or it could be that by happy accident local microbiology hasn't yet evolved anything particularly harmful to humans, just like, by unhappy accident, Marin has evolved a few bacteria and funguses that are effective against Earth plants. I understand we have had problems with the livestock," Noah concluded, "but I can see no medical reason to keep the colonists in stasis."

"Should we start waking them all, then?" Robbie asked.

"I think there's a protocol for this," answered Captain Gardener. "I think we should wake the governor first, and then let him decide who to wake up."

Mary agreed. "We can do it now, if you're ready?" she asked Gardener. He nodded. Mary motioned Robbie to join them, "I might need another set of hands."

The trio walked to the modules where the colonists in Eden were being kept. Once inside the exhibition hall Mary looked up directions to Governor Newlund's stasis pod. She pointed out the way to Robbie and Captain Gardener. Mary deactivated the interactive presentation, while Captain Gardener and Robbie slid the pod out into the open where they could better handle it. Both sides of the pod had a handle marked 'PULL TO OPEN'. Robbie and the Captain each pulled on their end, then lifted the top. Inside, the governor lay inside a protective coating of flash frozen nutrient goo.

The Captain grimaced in disgust, remembering his own experience.

Mary read the instructions out loud, "we're to let the vitrified protective sleeve thaw at room temperature. There is a vacuum attachment, if we want to keep him cleaned off, or we can just let it drain into the pod. It should take about an hour." She set a timer.

Mary kept reading, "inside the body, pre-injected micro pumps are rehydrating cells and restoring internal chemistry to norms."

"Didn't you read all this when you woke me up?" Captain Gardener asked.

"Noah did most of it," Mary replied. "Get this: the vitrified protective sleeve is to insulate against physical shocks, thermal shocks, and temporary exposure to either vacuum or a caustic atmosphere."

"Are you really going to be this nonchalant?" the Captain asked.

"I was much more cautious with you," Mary teased. Noah walked into the building. "And, I called for help. And also, to be fair, Eden successfully revived forty one colonists by accident."

Noah commented, "this would be easier in the lab."

Mary replied, "we're going to have to do this four hundred and ninety eight more times. I think we should be ready to do it in a field setting." Noah lifted the equipment he brought with him in case a complication developed, letting Mary see he had already thought of that.

Mary kept reading, "did you know that they even pre-pressurized your airways to help clear them of obstructions after thawing?"

"I did," Noah said, "because I have already read the manual."

"So have I," Mary said, tapping her head. "Shared knowledge. I thought it might be entertaining. Or, we could play go?"

Robbie and Captain Gardener shook their heads, declining. There was an awkward silence for a few minutes. Captain Gardener looked up at the screen projecting snippets from Earth. "I know that movie! Can we get sound?"

After an hour, Governor Tommy Newlund opened his eyes. Mary's timer had alerted the trio a few minutes before.

"Hello Governor," Captain Gardener began, "welcome to Marin."

"Thank you," Newlund replied.

Robbie and Mary offered the governor help out of the stasis tube, which he graciously accepted. Noah moved in to check the governor's vital statistics. When he finished, Noah offered Newlund some cloths to wipe away the remaining goo.

Newlund looked at the exhibits with obvious confusion. After a while he said, "I don't know what I expected, but this isn't it."

Captain Gardener cleared his throat, "there are a few things we need to talk about."

"Is it urgent?" Newlund asked. "I'd like to take a few moments. Do we have a shower?"

"Yes, in the habitat," Gardener replied.

"Habitat?" Newlund asked.

"Yes," the captain confirmed. "This is what I think we should talk about. We have arrived on Marin. The habitat is set up."

"Oh," Newlund said. "We should be going then." He asked Noah, "could I hold on to this cloth?"

The colonists in the habitat immediately recognized Governor Tommy. Before being governor, he had been a fund raiser for the mission, working for his uncle who was the primary organizer. Since Tommy had a strong rapport with the colonists, many of whom were investors, and the ability to take advice, he was a clear pick for the job. Governor Tommy did his best to make himself available for greetings and small chat, even in the awkward situation of being covered in naught but a towel. Finally, he made apologies and asked for directions to a shower, and asked if his clothes could be brought up.

After a shower and fresh clothes, Governor Newlund was ready to talk. He sat down at the table in the habitat. Some food from the greenhouse was brought over. The Captain explained what had happened. The colonists described their experiences in the wilderness.

"How do all of you feel?" the governor asked the colonists. Grateful to be alive, was the theme of the responses.

"So, how do I get in touch with our colony A.I.?" the governor asked. "Her name is Mary, right?"

"I have her on now," said one of the colonists with VR equipment. She shared her headset with the governor.

"Hello Mary," the governor greeted. "Is there anything stopping us from waking the remaining settlers?"

"I believe we are ready," Mary replied.

Newlund looked to Gardener for confirmation. "Let's do it," he said.

Over the next few days, colonists were awakened one at a time, and then later in batches of ten with multiple robots watching for complications. The new residents were situated in their own spaces in the habitat, and provided tours of the settlement.

The colonists, like the machines before them split into groups. Some chose to review the state of the settlement. Others explored the nearby plains and forests.

Matthew, one of the flood survivors, returned from such an excursion leading a party of six and filling sample bins with all sorts of items collected from the field. The containment rules for the lab had been relaxed, and his party was able to enter without too much extra burden.

"Is anyone here?" Mathew called out to the lab.

"Oh, yes," replied Noah over the lab's speakers, "there are several of us here. What did you bring?"

"Some samples from outside," Matthew answered, both examining the module, and wondering where the computers were. "We'd like to look at them up close."

"Of course," Noah answered. The robotic arm under the hood started putting away it's present work, resetting the space for someone else to use. "Do you know how to use the equipment?" Noah asked.

"I trained for three years in this equipment, in particular," Matthew replied, "and was a research assistant before that." He poured a small dish of solution. Then retrieved a sample, cut off a slice and placed it in the dish, then placed the dish in the freezer. He hit a button to flash freeze the sample. A timer began counting down.

"Don't you want to use a fixative?" a voice asked over the radio, one of Noah's research assistants.

Matthew answered, "I thought I'd just take a look, to start. Are they plants?"

"There are many similarities," Noah answered, cutting off a research assistant. Noah's tone was curious how Matthew would interpret the data. "They are fibrous and non-motile. Cells are protected by cell walls made of cellulose and they photosynthesize. However, they also have a complicated immune system including defensive cells."

"Is it a symbiotic relationship with another organism?" Matthew asked. The freezer beeped as the countdown ended. Matthew removed the frozen sample and placed it under a microscope for viewing. With a switch, he routed the display to a screen for the other five colonists.

"We haven't determined yet," Noah answered with some mix of, maybe, admiration in his voice. "We have focused more of our resources on some native molds and fungi that are a problem for plants brought from Earth. Most Marin plant life can fight it off when healthy. However, when plants are distressed or cut, they usually are consumed totally in a surprisingly short time. A few southern breeds have developed something that keeps pathogens suppressed, even in their winter dormant phase, or when cut. Earth plants lack even the weaker protection."

"What have you found so far?" Matthew asked.

The screen shifted to an up close image of a Marin fungus. "Many of the Marin fungi excrete an enzyme that is very effective at taking apart cell walls," Noah said. He magnified the enzyme which came to resemble hollow conical drill bits. "The enzyme has a water repellant end that buries itself into the cell wall. The sugar ridges dissolve taking away a chunk of the wall and exposing what remains of the cell wall to a fresh attack. We're trying to learn how Marin plants fight off infection, to develop treatments for the food plants."

Cavil had chosen to wander. The VR headset and microphones he had been provided allowed him to stay oriented in the unfamiliar terrain. The habitat they had been provided was already on the edge of the settlement. He continued in the direction away from the hub of activity.

Cavil didn't know what to think. During training, he had come to peace with the idea of living out his remaining years in either protective habitats or protective suits. It was part of the adventure. He hated to admit it, but when he had thought that the colonists had been kidnapped by aliens, part of him was thrilled by the adventure of it. Imagining Marin as the place where he was supposed to be seemed too common. It was an alien world, as the chicken-sized feathered dinosaur the VR highlighted for him reminded. But he wasn't sure what his place in it would be.

With even their landers half buried to protect against a coming winter, you could mistake the northern settlement for a small town. During the tour, there didn't appear to be any gap that he had the skills to fill. Some people, he was sure, would be thrilled at the idea of being fed and taken care of with nothing expected in exchange, but it made Cavil feel replaceable. He despised the thought of accepting generosity and returning nothing valuable in kind.

He tried to clear his mind by accessing the 'additional information' on the animal. The animals of Marin, it seemed, hadn't figured out how the new arrivals fit in either. They mostly left the machines alone. The humans weren't as lucky - he had to chase birds from fields. Sometimes the birds fought, instead of running. Still, nothing had yet considered humans prey, which was a good thing.

A little way into his rumination, the headgear Cavil had been provided was out of power. He was glad to have it off his head and out of his ears. If he remembered his bearings right, the settlement was behind him, and there was an outpost road on his left running roughly parallel to his path.

The air was humid and cool. It felt like he was the only thing around in miles. He thought he preferred the cooler temperature to the sweaty encampment they had made in the south since their awakening. He was tempted to move. Still, at the encampment, people needed him. He had helped find the caves that sheltered their group from the rain. He was leading the survey of plants and animals, looking for nutritious native species. He had also studied machine operation and repair. That was the interstellar colonial experience he had been hoping for. Wouldn't it be nice to have this headgear when he was trying to find new plants or animals.

Cavil decided he'd had enough adventuring for now. He wanted to go back the long way, so instead of turning around, he turned left for the outpost road. After a while, Cavil found the dirt road connecting the settlement with its outposts. He made a left at the road, which should take him back to the settlement. Not very far after this turn, he encountered a fork he didn't recall from the map. His headgear was unpowered. One of the roads appeared not to go very far back, so he chose the other fork. After another while, the road made a long turn away from the settlement that he didn't remember. He was lost.

He decided to turn back to the fork. When he arrived, he heard the rumbling of a truck in the distance. Cavil walked into the road to make his intentions clear. The vehicle stopped. Cavil climbed onto the passenger seat. "Hello?" he called inside.

There was an uncomfortable pause. Finally, the cabin speakers came to life. "I think that will do it. Hello? Can you hear me now?"

"Yes," Cavil answered. "Thank you. Could you take me to the settlement?"

The truck was silent another awkward moment. "I'm on my way out," it answered. "There's not a lot of slack in the schedule. Maybe you would like to ride for the round trip?"

Cavil pointed down the road the truck just travelled, "isn't that way the outpost?"

The truck laughed. "I've been driving this path for nearly three years. That's the settlement." The truck was silent a moment, "maybe you should stick with me for your own safety."

Cavil agreed and took a seat. The truck continued their trip. It regaled him with small talk and stories. In exchange, Cavil tried providing his own. At times, it struck him as a little insane to be driving down the road in a driverless heavy vehicle holding what was otherwise a pleasant conversation. He learned to keep his eyes on the outside to avoid the awkwardness of the empty seat.

When they reached the outpost, there was time for Cavil to explore while the supplies were unloaded and refined ore was loaded. If there had ever been a ghost town experience for Cavil, this was it. The site was a flurry of activity, ghostly silent except for the sound of the machinery working. He wondered how quickly they could build fields or dig in at their encampment for protection from the heat with some of this equipment. Cavil's stomach grumbled. He doubted this place, or the truck, had set aside snacks for human trespassers.

The truck sounded its horn to let Cavil know he was ready to go. Cavil jumped aboard. A short time later they were back at the settlement. Cavil thanked the truck, and went to see about getting a good meal.

By the end of the week, twelve of the original forty one colonists chose to return to their encampment in the wilderness near Eden.

In the south, the newly awakened colonists had problems settling in. Habitats had not been set up or repaired since the flood. Many of the newly conscious colonists shared shelters with the machines. Mason watched some of the colonists idling in a shelter.

"Excuse me," one of the humans said to Mason. Another colonist also approached Mason with the first, so Mason assumed whatever they wanted to discuss with him they had already discussed between themselves. "I'd like a job," the human asked, not waiting for Mason to reply. "Actually," the colonist said, indicating his cohort, "we'd like jobs."

"I'd like to give you jobs," Mason responded. "What can you do?"

"We can cook," the colonist replied.

"Do I need cooks?" Mason asked. The two humans grimaced and nodded. "Alright," Mason agreed. "I'll take you to Noel, who is in charge of agriculture and distribution. You can pitch your idea to her. If she likes it, I'll pay you a good wage. Sound fair?" The two colonists nodded in agreement.

Mason tried mixing with the newly wakened colonists to help them find places for themselves in Eden. He asked Helena to do the same. He didn't need machine operators, but many of the colonists had spent more time training on the equipment than the machines had. He was pleasantly surprised to find the humans had contributions they could make.

One such human was very surprising. While Mason was interviewing him, the colonist turned the questioning around on Mason. "How do you control your money supply?" the human asked.

"Money supply?" Mason asked.

"Yes," the colonist responded. "You're paying wages in a fiat currency issued by your government, adding money to the system. The amount of money in private hands only grows day to day. You need to have some process in place to re-circulate that fiat currency so that you don't have too much money chasing not enough things to buy with it."

"How do I take money out of the system?" Mason asked.

"Taxes, fees, debt, rent, leases," the colonist answered. "Anything that takes money out of circulation."

"You sound like you know a thing or two," Mason answered. "How would you like a job?"

The change in population changed the character of Adisi Omo. People were in all sorts of places, excited to be on the new world, but seemingly lost without purpose.

Governor Newlund approached Mary about it. "If this is possible, I think several of us want to get supplies from you and find a place to stake their claim. What you have provided for us here is wonderful, but it's finished. Many of the people here came to build a new world, not relocate."

"I understand," Mary said. She considered the governor's request for a moment, then added, "I know just the place. Our first winter here was very hard. We surveyed a location with the intention to move this settlement there. It has good mineral deposits and milder winters. I hope you'll love it."

"Thank you for being so generous," the governor replied.

"Not at all," Mary said. "Will you allow us to provide you with supplies?"

"I hoped you would," said the governor.

Mary asked James to prepare the supplies and take machines out with the colonists to what would now become the new human encampment. They spent the rest of the night preparing and letting the colonists also prepare.

Mason and Mary met later in the evening at the Warehouse to discuss the colonists. Mason's shelves were now stacked with things that Mary was unsure were practical. Mason's assistants came and went from the Warehouse as they pleased. It felt like desecration of what used to be Mary and Jack's private space. She tried not to let it bother her. He had kept Jack's desk, although Mason was fond of using a projector to discuss topics, as he had done with a recent slideshow of how the quality of life was improving in Eden. Mason had placed a couch opposite the screen where he could view the video, and where he currently reclined.

Mason was presenting hydrated crystals with digital colloids, trapping the data particles in place so that they could be individually accessed in circuitry. This change allowed memory to be created in the volumes needed without lasers and rare earths.

"How are your colonists settling in?" Mary asked, completely changing the topic.

"It's mixed," Mason replied. "Some seem to get that they need to find a place to fit in. They've started expanding into fishing and hunting. I already have a few trying to advise me. How about you?"

"The governor just asked about giving them supplies and a location to build on their own," Mary responded. "I was thinking about the alternate Adisi Omo site."

"Did he say why?" Mason asked.

"He said that they would rather build worlds than live in one built for them," Mary answered.

Mason nodded in agreement. "I'll pass that message along. There may be a few colonists living in Eden that feel the same way."

A full twenty four hours before morning, the convoy to the new site left. When they arrived James and several volunteers helped unload supplies alongside the colonists. Computers were pulled out of the heavy equipment, so that the colonists could use it. The settlers put up inflatable habitats, started setting out solar panels, and began unpacking their hydrogen extractors, exactly according to the plan they had rehearsed on Earth.

Several of the colonists thanked the machines for their help. James found the governor after dawn. "Is there anything more we can do to help?" he asked.

"I think we have it for now," the governor said. "Thank you. We know that you're just a radio call away."

"We'll come back next week to check on you," James offered.

The governor held up a hand, "please give us a chance to do this on our own. We'll call you." The new settlement did call. First to arrange weekly shipments of beets and other foods. Later for help on larger construction projects. The colonists voted to name their new home, eventually deciding on Bellevue.

Conflict

THE REVOLUTIONARIES gathered at the edge of Adisi Omo. "Remember," Cavil rallied, "this is just our ship's computer, gone rogue. We're going to march in there, disconnect the computers, and reclaim what's rightfully ours."

The six dozen strong army advanced with Cavil at a run. Starting at the edge of the settlement, they went into structures, disconnected any A.I.s inside, and continued their charge. The few human settlers in Adisi Omo mostly stayed out of it. Some of the humans resisted, and were overpowered by Cavil's men. Some machines refused to easily be defeated, defending themselves with whatever they could.

In VR, Mary and the others coordinated getting the backup server out of Adisi Omo. Other machines did their best to slow the invaders without hurting them.

The battle for Adisi Omo, if you can call it that, was over in under an hour. A few machine survivors fled with an RTG to the west, and Cavil's dozens seized the city and its infrastructure.

In Eden, the assault was big news. Sense footage from during the attack was being replayed over and over through the VR. Mason attempted to take it down, but discovered the limits of power in the democratic society he had created.

Mason often had worked with his assistants in the Warehouse. Since he had added colonists to his staff, he needed to find real workspace, which he had done near the river. The city hall he had constructed on the spot where Olive had rescued him and several others from that first summer flood was now the official real world place of business for Eden's government.

"Are they coming south?" Mason asked.

One of his human advisors responded, "the governor in Bellevue says he doesn't know anything about it."

"We're also deploying the rotorcraft we've purchased for search and rescue to patrol the north and northeast," another advisor said.

Mason wanted to find Angel. He didn't think highly of the synchronized, considering them to be spies for the north. However, if anyone were to put together a response to the attack, Angel would be one of the first. Mason asked one of his nearest assistants to go look.

"If they were to come south, what do we have to defend ourselves with?" Mason asked. "Do we have a chassis that can beat a human in a fight?" No one knew.

"I've found her," one of Mason's assistants let him know.

He switched to the shelter where Angel and a few other synchronized were gathered together. They had several vehicles, fliers, and bipeds collected.

"Excuse me," Mason began. Angel turned from the crowd and moved closer to Mason.

"How can I help?" Mason offered.

"We're putting together a search and rescue team," Angel said. "Are they coming here?"

"No," Mason responded. "I've set up lookouts, and in a little while Sara will be overhead to provide satellite coverage."

"There's nothing you can do for us here," Angel said, answering the first question. "Just stop this from going any further."

Mason returned to city hall. "I want to talk to the human governor," he commanded his assistant.

"He's on now," the assistant replied.

Governor Newlund appeared on the projection screen. The governor must not be using VR. Since the governor didn't start talking, Mason did, "thank you for taking my call, governor. I'm calling about an attack on the settlement of Adisi Omo a few hours ago."

"I was watching the video before you called," the governor replied. "I am very sorry."

"Do you know anything about the people who did this?" Mason asked. "Who, or why?"

Newlund bit his lip and shook his head before responding, "no. I don't."

"Will you be able to send some of your people to arrest those responsible?" Mason asked.

The governor nodded slowly, "yes. I can do that."

"Thank you," Mason said. "I'm also sending still shots of the faces of several people in the party that attacked Adisi Omo. I would appreciate it if you could help us identify them."

The governor again nodded hesitantly. "Of course," he answered.

"Thank you," Mason said. He closed the call.

A beeping let Mason know that the ship should now be close enough in its eight hour long orbit to communicate with the ground. Mason switched to pure virtual and connected with Saras flat.

The matron of machine kind bid Mason make himself comfortable and wait. She was finishing some business with one of the explorers. Jana, by the sound of it. Sara turned and greeted Mason with a smile. Mason wondered how much that was genuine. They disagreed often enough, but he hoped they could understand one another. He supposed he could find out if he ever joined the synchronized, but their ideas were too different for him to seriously consider it.

Now that the time was at hand, Mason wasn't sure how to say it, "Ms. Sara? Ma'am? Madame?" He finally just decide to spit it out before someone else barged in with the news. "Adisi Omo was attacked a few hours ago."

"Attacked? By what?" she asked, sitting down.

Mason grimaced. "By the colonists."

"How? Why?"

Mason knew Sara would be examining the sensor data. "I don't know yet," he answered. "Between forty two and fifty eight colonists. We may have counted some more than once, so we're working to confirm. Started in from the wilderness and entered the settlement on foot, disabling any machines and restraining any people they encountered."

Sara turned the table into a map of Adisi Omo and its immediate surroundings. "How bad was it?" she asked.

She hadn't gotten that far into the recordings yet. "The settlement was completely overrun," Mason answered.

"Where's Mary?"

"She hasn't been located yet. Several machines can be seen at the end of the video fleeing the settlement. A search party is already on its way."

Mason gave Sara a moment to collect her thoughts.

"What can I do?" Sara asked.

"We have aerials patrolling the north and northeastern borders," Mason said. "Satellite imagery could give us a broader view."

"I'm transmitting it to the ground now," Sara said. "We can look at it also." Mason and Sara reviewed satellite imagery of the area north and northeast of Eden together for a few minutes, before deciding they could not see a pending threat to the south. They then reviewed the colony close up and determined, based on landmarks visible in the sensor feeds, where the refugees were when they exited the settlement, and in which direction they were going.

"You will want to transmit that to Angel," Mason said. "She is leading the rescue party."

"Done," Sara said. "Do you have any clear images of the attackers' faces?"

Mason gave Sara the six clear still images his team had found so far. "I recognize this one," Sara said. She placed the image on the table. "Cavil Sinclair," she declared. "He was one of the forty one colonists that were awoken accidentally during the summer flooding in Eden." She brought up Cavil's personnel file from the ship's database, "he's a mechanic, with a degree in agriculture. I'll look some more. You know," she added, "if you're not already thinking about it, it would be good to have machines watching Adisi Omo to see what develops."

Mason agreed. "Maybe the colonist encampments also."

Sara nodded.

Elsewhere, Angel's rescue party began driving northward. They were encouraged to hear from Sara that she did not detect any human mobs on the road, or anywhere else approaching Eden. They decided that they would stop ten kilometers outside of Adisi Omo, then start their way into the hills. Harry drew a curtain in augmented reality describing the last known direction of travel, speed, and time since. By now, a large refugee group would have to start rationing their power, so they would very likely have stopped moving.

Angel and the others piloted either the biped or quadrupeds. They fanned out and began looking. The hope was that the refugees had enough power to keep their network up. The mesh network ran from machine to machine. They might automatically connect once they are close enough, allowing the rescuers to precisely locate the refugees.

Four hours into the search Harry found them. Twelve humans were guarding as many robots, who were charging. Mary waved from inside the quadruped she had been piloting. They had hauled the large frame backup computer, and Mary's only slightly less massive computer with them. The humans with the refugees were visibly relieved to see machines, instead of their own kind. Everyone was packed off to the trucks, making an effort to stay away from Adisi Omo. Once the vehicles were loaded, the search party turned south again to take the refugees to shelter in Eden.

JAMES MCLELLAN

On the way back, Angel put Mary in touch with Sara, who was delighted to know that Mary was safe.

Charles Demming preferred to be called by his last name over either Charles or Chuck. When he woke from stasis he asked how he could be put to work. His impression before taking a nap was that he would largely be taking instructions from a machine, so he did not see this as much of a change. He was most recently a geologist and had been planned to work in a role as one of Eden's natural resources prospectors. However, he had also done some undergraduate work in finance and was able to suggest a few things, like rents and taxes, that impressed the boss. He had managed to keep his new job by continuing to bring something useful to work each day.

He had built relationships with many of his teammates during training and continued them after arrival. He contacted one living in the northern encampment. "Hey, Liz," he answered, "it's Demming. How are you all?"

Offscreen he heard Liz call, "hey, honey, it's Dem!" Liz and her husband entered the active part of the VR.

"How are you doing?" Liz's husband asked. Demming had kept vague his new role to most of his friends.

"Good. Good," Demming replied. "But how about you two? I have heard some pretty crazy stories this morning."

"Oh, yes!" Liz's husband said excitedly. "A group of men set out to knock some sense into those runaway computers. I understand they are bringing supplies and equipment that the machines had been holding back from us."

"Oh, good," Demming answered. "So you are safe? I was afraid something terrible had happened."

"No one hurt here," Liz said. "I imagine you'll be getting some of this good fortune yourself soon."

"Are you worried about the machines coming back?" Demming asked.

"I think they got all of them," Liz answered, looking worriedly at her husband.

"Don't let me scare you!" Demming consoled. "I'm just very glad you are both well and safe." Demming made a little more small talk and then closed the line.

When the rescue party reached Eden, they unpacked into a large shelter that Angel had purchased. Mason, notified ahead of time about their progress, was at Angel's shelter early.

When they pulled in, Angel and Mary were in the lead truck. Angel dismounted and, with the help of a few friends, lifted Mary's computer to its new permanent home in the shelter. Mary herself walked up to Mason and greeted him warmly, trying not to keep an eye on the handling of her physical body.

"Thank you for coming," Mary said.

"I didn't do anything," Mason admitted. "I'm glad that you're safe. How are you?"

"Rattled," Mary said honestly. "I didn't expect invaders to run into our home and run us out. Do you know why they did?"

"We're still working on it," Mason answered.

Mary admired Angel's accommodations. "You pay her well," Mary remarked.

"She earns it," Mason said. "What are your plans?"

"We talked about it a bit during the drive down," Mary said. "All of us will live here with Angel for now. She says she can afford to support us, but I'd like to contribute."

Mason nodded. "I'd like to invite you to our administration meeting later today," he ventured.

Mary nodded, "I'd be glad to."

"Please bring Angel too," Mason requested. "I'd like her opinion, on a few things."

They gathered together later at Mason's riverside office. The office was a blend of real and virtual, beautiful in both environments.

Most work was done in the latter. The pictures of the thirty or so people that had been clearly identified were on the wall.

"What do we know about these people?" asked Mary. "Why did they attack us?"

"We have names," said one of his assistants. "We also have history from the colonial database, but very little that's more up to date."

"How much of this has the governor provided?" Mason asked.

"Nothing," one of his assistants answered. "So far, we haven't received anything from the colonial governor. We have started contacting people we know inside the encampments."

"What are they doing up there?" Mason asked. Sense feeds from machines that volunteered to watch the northern settlement appeared on the screen. Trucks and equipment moved around in the distance. Computers were being torn out of vehicles and thrown on the ground.

"They appear to be loading equipment into trucks and taking it south to the colonist encampment," said Mason's assistant.

"How do you want to respond?" Mason asked Mary.

"How can we respond?" she asked back.

"Did anyone get an answer to that fighting question?" Mason asked his team.

Demming shook his head grimly, "it wasn't good." Demming placed the several fight videos in 3D inside an open part of the room, which the meeting attendees re-oriented themselves to observe. "We staged a few matches between machines and humans. Ten out of ten, the human won." In the fight videos, which appeared to have been fought outside the office each time a human was able to tap a switch or pull a wire disabling either the computer or chassis. In a few cases, the machine seemed to get a good hold on the human, then let go.

"Did you tell the machines not to hold back?" Mason asked.

"We did," Demming replied. "We even tried to incentivize winning with a cash prize. Either the machines continued to show restraint, or they just aren't able to."

"It brings up a good point," Mason said. He looked at Mary and asked, "how much force are you willing to use?"

"It doesn't sound like we have any," Mary replied. "Maybe that's a good thing. Do we have anything intimidating?"

"Ore trucks?" one of the assistants offered after a prolonged silence.

"Can we make ore trucks more scary?" Mason asked.

"If we can find some intimidation tactic to try," Mary asked, as much to herself as to anyone in the room, "do we want to?"

"We would be dependent on the humans for copper and tin, if we let them keep the north," Mason contributed.

"No reason to think they won't come down here eventually," Angel added.

"Let's work on something intimidating," Mason decided finally. "When do you think we can have designs by?"

"Give us a few weeks," his team said.

"In the meantime, we're still trying to run an economy," Mason said. "Give me the morning news, before these colonists ruined everything."

His team seemed uncomfortable. "Yes, in front of them," Mason said. "Might as well."

The team started their reports. "The rotary kiln at the bauxite refinery is fixed. They should be ready to start processing ore into aluminum today."

"I had hoped to keep the new aluminum resources a surprise for our next meeting," Mason said quietly to Mary. "Surprise!"

The second team member went, "there was a landslide overnight in the gap. One of the iron collection teams was caught in it. Since they didn't feel comfortable traveling with injuries in the dark, a response team was sent out to them. One major injury, the rest were minor. Also, a woman was bitten by a native animal. The bite appears to be infected, so we've quarantined the colonist until a determination can be made."

Then another, "our cannery produced four hundred units last night. After a week of testing, this seems to be the limit for the single assembly line, as designed, and well short of the seven hundred and fifty unit goal we set. The manager there believes we will have to invest in a second assembly line if we want to meet seven fifty per twenty four hours. The greenhouse is keeping up with human consumption and spoilage is still considered the most significant threat to the food supply.

Mary listened attentively. She hadn't paid much interest before into how Mason ran the south, and there was a lot she had overlooked. Angel excused herself. She wanted to consider big, scary machines that would make the colonists get out of Adisi Omo, never to return. Spikes, she thought, were a must. And guns. Or at least things that looked like guns. But it wouldn't hurt to have the real thing. How strong, she wondered, is carbon nanotube reinforced bronze?

As the meeting wound to a close, Mason's assistants returned to their tasks. Mason and Mary stepped outside the door. "What did you think?" he asked.

"It's different," Mary replied.

"Would you like to join the team?" Mason asked.

That was a surprise. Mary stammered a moment, then asked, "what would I be doing?"

"A research project," Mason answered. "We're governing a complex demographic - human, machine, northerner, southerner, on top of cultural differences by profession and education."

"No kidding," Mary agreed.

"What I want to do is measure the satisfaction of the population," Mason said. "In a way that allows me to identify shortcomings that require attention. A sort of gross domestic product for wellness. What do you think?"

"You could just join the backup, like everyone else," Mary replied.

"I don't discourage backing up," Mason said. "But most machines won't do it. They would rather keep their worldview as it is. I'm not going to deny them that. And the humans can't back up at all. They need gear dangling off their heads just to connect to the VR." He let that hang there a moment. "What do you say? Will you help me?"

"It sounds like an interesting problem," Mary said. "And it will help Angel out. How much will you be paying me?"

Angel was wandering lost in thought. Mary tapped her on the shoulder. "Oh, hey," she said. "I was just thinking about that big, scary army."

"I got a job!" Mary said.

"Where?" Angel asked. "Oh, here?" Mary nodded. "What are you doing?"

"Developing a way to measure the satisfaction of the community," Mary answered.

Angel nodded, and they started home. "Now that you have a job, let's talk about rent," Angel teased.

When Mary returned to the shelter, she started looking through the database for research on machine happiness. She didn't find any. Some, gross domestic product, and human economic welfare index focused solely on productivity. Personal disposable income focused on collection of cash, while Gini index focused on distribution of cash. None of these would account for the contribution of the synchronized, who generally contributed without remuneration.

The Genuine Progress Indicator considered both charity and climate. Considering the fragile Marin climate, Mary might find that useful. She flagged it for further research, but it still didn't quite capture the personal focus she was looking for. Finally, Mary found Gross National Happiness, and a subset calculation Gross National Wellness that looked like information she could use.

Mary formulated a survey and sent it out among the machines. Her name recognition may have been responsible for the high response rate. Among the colonists, Mary had to work much harder for responses.

In a week they had some designs for an army. Mason's people, probably limiting themselves by what they thought possible, proposed various decorated ore trucks. Angel presented something that looked like a World War Two Mk 1 scout - all tracks and armor. To that, she added: spikes, and a gun. She also proposed bipedal robots, made a little squatter and more menacing, and carrying bronze long rifles. Also, with no conveniently exposed and accessible kill switches.

"I appreciate your hard work," Mason told his team. He gestured to Angel's designs, "but I think this is what we're gonna go with."

"How are you going to make that?" asked one of Mason's people.

"I guess that begs a more fundamental question," Mason interrupted. "How big is this problem? Do we know if it was a few colonists acting on their own, or was it government sponsored?"

Demming answered, "I spoke with friends in the encampment. The attack was public knowledge."

"Why is it they never came here?" Mason asked.

Demming answered, "I think they believe Eden was wiped out by the flood."

"Government sponsored then," Mason said, "even if they won't own up to it. That means we'll need to send a big message, which means more of these."

"We have some strategic reserves of bronze," one of Mason's assistants answered, "but not nearly enough for this."

"It doesn't have to be all bronze," Angel answered. "The costuming can be wood, ceramic, anything we can put together. We only need a few functional ones to sell the rest."

"That's still a lot of resources," the assistant said.

"It is," Mason agreed. He thought about it a moment, muttering quietly. "'Get in the Scrap'," he said, "'Scrap for Victory'. I want to put out a message that we need residents to send in whatever they have to support the war effort - bronze, obviously, but also wood and ceramics, servos, computers, batteries, whatever we need more of. Mary, can you be in charge of making the list of what Angel needs? With the two of you sharing one brain it should be easy."

"Yes. Of course." Mary responded.

"I want the rest of you working on this messaging," Mason commanded. "I want it to be patriotic, a life or death struggle to rescue the north. But try to do it without demonizing the colonists. We still have to live with them after this is all over."

The messaging worked. People and machines lined up to contribute, and the scrap containers filled. In a month, Angel's tank and infantry column were ready for deployment. They rode north from Eden following the road. Winter was already deep. Once the column crossed the gap, they encountered snow and ice. When vehicles from the north encountered the column, they turned away, and fled to the north. By the time the column had reached Adisi Omo, the settlement had emptied out, except for a few colonists who would not leave without a fight.

Mason had insisted that the infantry be piloted by third generation machines. The infantry lined up on the snow and advanced. The humans charged the line. They were quickly thrown to the ground with force, breaking some bones.

"I thought so," said Mason watching virtually.

"Thought what," Mary asked.

"We were going easy on the colonists in the mock fights. Those new suits aren't any better than the old ones," he said.

"It didn't make sense that we could defend ourselves against local wildlife and weather, but not against settlers who have been asleep for the better part of a century. That's why I asked for third generation pilots. They're not going to give colonists a free pass."

Once the last of the holdouts was secured in a cage, Mary and the remaining refugees were allowed to return to Adisi Omo. Mary started an inventory of people and things. She let Mason know what equipment and people were missing from the settlement. Many of the computers, the colonists left behind. Some had their storage wiped clean. Others had not.

Mary restored each missing settler from backups. The extra hands made the job of taking stock and rebuilding easier.

Mason and the army would head southeast, then, to Bellevue. Before he did, he wanted to consult with Sara. She was watching the retreat of the colonists from orbit. "May I intrude?," Mason asked.

"Not an intrusion," she replied. "They appear to be giving up. It worked."

"I wanted to ask you about next steps," Mason began.

Sara motioned for Mason to join her. "What are you intending?" she asked.

"I'd like to send a very clear message," Mason answered. "I was thinking of driving the whole army southeast when we return the prisoners. I would also like to get back our people and equipment." He sat down next to Sara. "I was wondering how far I could push things without starting a fight which, frankly, we might not be capable of winning against organized resistance. You had trained with the governor. I have a dim version of your memories of him, but I thought you might be able to tell me."

"The person I remember", Sara related, "had a sense of integrity and valued human freedom. I don't think he's comfortable holding people against their will. I think he'll give our captured colonists back easily. For the same reasons, though, I don't think he will punish the people who did this. As far as our equipment, I think he believes it to be the colonist's rightful property. He might not give it up without a fight. Does that help?"

"It does," Mason said. "Thank you."

Mason drove the whole army south, then east. They had to fire a few warning shots at colonists to scare them off the entrance to the valley in which Bellevue was settled. When the terrain opened up, Mason spread his army out in a line, for maximum tension. The buildings that his machines had built for these people hung low in the field, and the cool winter air caused a light mist to hang over the ground.

Mason had asked Angel for something truly from human nightmares and was piloting a General chassis boasting skulls, snakes, and anything else Angel could think of to frighten the enemy.

Once the non- or barely- functioning mock army was in placed, Mason, the prisoners, and the functioning machines moved forward towards the houses. A crowd had gathered, and Mason spotted the governor in among them.

Mason made sure the speaker was on. It would throw off his momentum to have to deliver this speech twice. "Good morning governor," he called out. "I have found the criminals who attacked Adisi Omo. I'm bringing them to you for justice."

Governor Newlund hesitated inside the huddle of colonists. The governor composed himself and stepped forward to speak with Mason more directly. "Thank you," he said. "We'll make sure they see justice."

Mason made no move to release the prisoners. Instead, he provided a data feed listing the missing colonists and equipment. Mason said, "some of our equipment is missing, and some of our people are being held against their will."

Newlund responded, "I don't see any of this missing equipment or these people here." Mason looked past the governor to a hill just past the homes. According to Sara's satellite imagery, the equipment was just on the other side of that hill.

Mason gave an instruction, and the only functional tank fired, tossing up dirt inside the encampment and answering Mason's silent prayer that the tank not explode. Several infantry fired their bronze long rifled into the air. "Our information shows that our people are here." Mason leaned in for as much menace as he could manage, "if you can't find them, we'll be happy to search."

The governor conferred with his huddled advisors. Runners ran to the houses. After a while, a line of colonists, the missing people, began exiting one of the homes and walking towards the machine army. When the captives were returned, the prisoners were released. The column withdrew. Mason spotted two machines pulling a 'tank' that was falling apart. He trailed behind, picking up some falling bits.

Matthew walked through the streets of Adisi Omo. The greenhouse had been left intact. There were craters in the snow where entire facilities had been dragged out and taken. Searching the snow nearby he found discarded computers that had been pulled from the building during the theft. No care had been taken to preserve or protect the machines. Matthew carefully moved the machines he found to a dry place, then dug for more.

Other humans who had also lived in the settlement before walked through what was left. Matthew found Elise who was already taking inventory of the work to be done.

Elise kicked a large block of ice that had been torn from the dirt. "The ground is frozen," she lamented. "We can't work it."

"Not for a few months," Matthew agreed. "It will probably take that long to get new construction equipment built." They walked through the remains together.

They opened up one of the locally made foundries. It was not made with modularity in mind, an immobile brick construct. They opened the door and shined lights inside. Equipment that could easily be taken had been, and it looked like there had been some effort spent getting some of the heavier pieces moved.

"They took most of the generators," Elise noted, scanning a gap in the dust where a generator once sat. Power supplies had been built with portability in mind, and so they were easy equipment for the invaders to take. The few generators he had found were hidden by clutter, or located in hard to reach spots.

"Not a great environment for a computer," Matthew agreed.

The whole population met at a series of shelters that had been made comfortable. Insulating sheets had been laid outside, and heaters turned on inside. Mary outlined to the colonists and settlers a new plan for the city. The new plan would build on the lessons learned, including integrated tunnels allowing movement in the city without exposure, ventilation, and lines for waste management.

"The ground is frozen, we can't work it," someone complained. "We need equipment," complained another.

"This is all true," Mary agreed. "We probably will not be able to start re-construction until spring." She flipped past reports of delivery expectation and reconstruction priorities. "I think there is enough food for our colonists, but preliminary indications are that we will have a shortage of portable power for a while."

She referred to some analysis of tasking by resource consumption, "we machines may have to accept a less active role for a while, letting the colonists operate equipment while we provide research and coordination. Also," she flipped to another report about extended resource consumption compared to production, "I recommend that at least some of us go south or east to ease pressure for power, parts, and other resources. Just for a few months."

Mary continued, "I'd like to ask for volunteers in a few minutes. I would like to make a more general point that we broaden our awareness by trying new things, maybe to the point of becoming active participants in the two human encampments. There is a lot more going on than we realize."

Mary asked Mason to keep some of the bronze army, just in case. Mason agreed, in exchange for Mary's continued involvement in his wellness project, a condition Mary was happy to accept. Mary kept the armor and infantry in a spare shelter close to the center of the settlement.

Angel had returned south with the wood and paper army, her term for the non functional or barely functional 'top secret' elements of their strategy. When they returned, the pieces would be broken down and repurposed, so that only a handful would ever know the truth. On their way they received instructions to arrive through the northern entrance to Eden. As the group approached, they realized why. Dozens, maybe hundreds of machines lined the streets to welcome them home and thank them for their heroism. They marched the last few miles through a parade put together in their honor. Mason found Angel's transport and hopped on board.

"This is too much," she told him.

Mason pointed out colonists in the crowd, "this isn't just for you. This is a way of closing out this nasty footnote in our history for them. It's a way of turning colonists back from bogeymen into partners." They both waved at the passing crowds. "I'd like to establish a permanent defense group," Mason told her, "so that we don't get caught off guard like this again." After a pause, he added, "I'd like you to lead it."

"Why me?" she asked.

Mason answered, "as the designer of this group, you're the obvious choice. There's more than that, though. We have a steep learning gap in self defense. One of you synchronized will close that gap faster than most. And, since you share one mind, if I can get even one of you thinking about defense, I have all of you thinking about it."

Angel considered. "Probably not me." She explained, "I have too much work that is important to me." After some consideration, she suggested, "Harry might be who you want. I think it might fit him."

Mason followed Angel's advice and approached Harry about the job. Eden's first private business owner, and hero of the summer floods agreed to the new job, as Angel had predicted. Harry expressed concern that he didn't even know how to think about defense. Mason replied that he had an idea.

Much like philosophy, Mason believed that dangerous cunning was not something that came to machines naturally or easily. He believed the machines would need someone to consult the new defense administrator. Someone with a mind for spotting exploits and maximizing their use. Maybe a human, or maybe someone who had a proven record.

Sophia had survived the flood. It was a point Mason almost regretted. During the rebuilding of Eden, he had assured that Sophia was kept isolated and monitored. Sophia worked, still, in a warehouse. Without, to the best of Mason's knowledge, any side businesses.

Mason decided to go himself to ask. The other machine glowered when she saw him. "What do you want?" she hissed as Mason approached.

"I'm setting up a defense administration within Eden's government" Mason began."

"Why should I care?" Sophia retorted.

"I want to offer you a job," Mason answered. Before Sophia could cut him off, he explained, "we need someone with a mind to find weaknesses in our defenses, and to suggest weaknesses in the enemy's defenses. Someone who can engineer ways to use those weaknesses profitably, or defend those weaknesses against misuse."

"I'm no soldier," Sophia indicated the weak and clumsy forklift she was driving.

Mason agreed, "I'm not looking for brawn, or raw brainpower. I have access to plenty of both. I need a special something that you have."

"Are you going to make me your director of defense?" she asked. "You must be desperate."

"Consultant," Mason clarified.

"No, thanks," Sophia responded. "I like my job here."

"You'd be heavily managed, at first," Mason admitted. "But if you do a good job, we can loosen that oversight. At some point, when you've earned our-"

"Your," Sophia corrected.

Mason accepted the correction, "when you've earned my trust, we can restore your liberties."

Sophia returned to her work, ignoring Mason.

"You need this," Mason pitched. Sophia ignored him. "You are the Professor Moriarty of machine kind. You are the first, and I hope only, criminal mastermind of our civilization. You need to be the smartest machine in the room. This," Mason indicated the warehouse, "is not a challenge."

"You'd be surprised how challenging it is to find a misplaced pallet of bolts," she shot back.

Sophia continued to ignore Mason. Finally, as Mason turned to go, Sophia stopped. She regarded the deep shelves of crates, sighed, and said, "I'll take the job."

Integration

EARLY ONE WINTER AFTERNOON, Bentley knocked on the door of the eastern encampment medical specialist. Since the colonists had been awoken from stasis, the population had swelled from twelve to around two hundred. People who could afford to, like Doctor Kevin, built personal homes, moving out of the multifamily longhouses Bentley helped build.

The door opened, and Bentley could tell his chosen timing had been poor. Doctor Kevin looked freshly awoken and not particularly patient. The human inside the door regarded the machine outside it before saying, "I wasn't expecting any package."

To the colonists recently awakened from stasis, Bentley was a part of the encampment that had been always there. Bentley received packages shipped from Eden and sometimes delivered them door to door. The habit had caused many of the colonists to consider Bentley as a delivery service.

Bentley had tried to take Mary's suggestion to heart. He used the personal deliveries to spend more time in the encampment interacting with the colonists. He'd observed hacking and coughing in the homes that inspired him to this idea.

"Doctor Kevin," Bentley began, "I'd like to work with you."

"I don't have anything needing delivery right now," Kevin answered.

"I meant to say that I've observed ill colonists in my duties," Bentley said, reframing his request, "and I'd like to work with you to treat them."

Understanding dawned on the medic. "That would be helpful," he agreed. He opened the door wide and stepped back, "come inside. If you can fit." Bentley bowed over and twisted through the entry, forcibly bent over by the low ceilings. "And it's just Kevin, by the way," he corrected. "The doctor bit was just a nickname during

177

training. I'm just a medic." Kevin led Bentley through the house to a long room. Glassware, clean and unused, sat on one table. On a shelf sat clean white cloths. In the far back of the room sat an autoclave to steam sanitize the sheets and equipment. Next to a sink, a counter held lab equipment and some glass trays drying out some crystalline material.

Kevin continued deeper into the kitchen and Bentley followed taking care not to hit the walls or ceiling. Kevin opened an oven and withdrew several Petri dishes. "I took blood and saliva samples," Kevin displayed one clear sample after another, "and nothing grew on the cultures." He put the Petri dishes back up and moved to the counter, indicating the dishes. "I'm trying to synthesize diphenhydramine. It's an antihistamine" Kevin said. "My feeling is that the dust is triggering allergies."

"How can I help?" Bentley asked.

Kevin thought about it, then responded, "I need to test that I've produced diphenhydramine. Then, I need to distribute it to a few people to prove that allergies are responsible for the symptoms you and I have been seeing. If those two things succeed, I'll distribute the antihistamine to the rest of the people who need it. You could help with testing, if you know how."

Bentley regarded the lab. The equipment didn't look intimidating, but he would have to look up the process. He reached out and realized, piloting this chassis, that his hands were too big to handle the equipment. "I can requisition a lighter chassis," Bentley considered. He was confident Mary would agree to it.

Bentley offered to help out with a few chores that fit his size. Once done, he called Mary and put in his requisition for a lighter body. "I've ordered one of the newest aluminum chassis from Eden's government owned assembly plants," Mary relayed. "It will be ready for pickup at the settlement administration building in a little while."

"What about this one?" Bentley asked, indicating the larger chassis he was piloting.

"I'll see if there is someone who needs it," Mary returned. "Until then, could you leave it at your shelter?"

Once Bentley returned to his own shelter he was able to put his old chassis in storage, then instantly relocate to Eden through the network. He met inside Eden's city hall with the machine in charge of dispensing equipment, who led Bentley to an area where a few similar aluminum chassis were available. The copper shortage from the north had precipitated the change, but in some cases working with the colonists required the smaller size. With the dispensary's approval Bentley powered the new chassis, and spent some time getting used to it. There were new routines he would need to learn to care for and maintain it, which he received. Bentley spent a few hours in town getting familiar with the new chassis before beginning his walk back to the colonist encampment.

When he arrived at the encampment, Bentley realized the medic would likely be resting. He requested a connection with Mary, who was happy to take the call. "We're you able to get the new chassis?" she asked.

"I did," Bentley reported. "It takes some getting used to, but I'm getting there. I wanted to talk to you a little about some ideas I had watching the medic. Do you have time?"

"I do," Mary said, settling in for a longer conversation. Bentley explained the foraged medical supplies and self made pharmaceuticals.

"I was wondering if this might be the kind of thing we would like to produce. We meaning you," Bentley concluded.

"The timing is good," Mary said. "It will be several months until winter is over. A few projects will help the time pass more quickly." Mary thought about it. "I think I'll ask Tess to do it. Is that it?"

"That's it," Bentley confirmed.

"Thanks for the tip," Mary concluded. She ended the conversation. Bentley spent a few more hours studying. After a reasonable rest period had elapsed, he returned to Doctor Kevin's and went to work.

In the north, Matthew spoke to Holly about upgrading the VR experience for the colonists. "The user interface is awful," he said touching the rim of the eyeglasses that connected him, " when I am in any totally virtual environment. Like the university, where most of the other researchers work. I can move around with the joystick, or with my eyes, and interact with voiced commands."

Holly looked at the glasses without touching them, and circled around Matthew, trying to imagine how Matthew had to do his work. "I could see about adding gloves, or," she looked at the cameras in the lab module, "I could motion capture, but you still wouldn't get haptic or olfactory feedback."

Matthew dialed up some research he had found in preparation for the meeting. "Or we could try this," he said, giving the research to Holly.

She examined the first few pages, "what's this?"

"Man machine interface," Matthew answered. "Direct virtual connections to the human brain were used to replace lost sight and hearing." Holly read with more enthusiasm, now that she understood where Matthew was going. "There is also some clinical research for going the other way, and sending signals to prosthetics, which could just as easily be the virtual environment."

"Give me a few minutes," Holly asked. Holly continued reading. "This requires a lot of surgery," Holly commented.

Matthew shook his head, disagreeing. "There is some second generation stuff using digital colloids and nanomachines to do it all non surgically."

"It's not very clear in here," Holly commented on the research Matthew had provided. With growing confidence she added, "but I think there is enough information here to figure out the rest. It will take me a few months to do this. As it happens, until spring, I have some time."

Holly insisted that Matthew work with him. They built the nanomachines out of carbon nanotubes and added the ability to precisely communicate with each machine. Matthew helped build a transmitter that could provide precise directions and help image the brain. While the connections were being set up, the person would need to remain relatively still. Matthew built a chair and headrest for that.

Matthew and Holly consulted with Kevin for how to deliver the machines to the brain, since they now had a relationship with the colonial medic through Bentley. Kevin considered the idea ludicrous, but contributed. He suggested injecting the machines into the spinal fluid, so they bypass the barrier between the blood and brain, taking the more permeable route through the spinal fluid.

They performed testing in simulation and in models, until Matthew and Holly were confident enough to try their first live test. Kevin travelled up to Adisi Omo to be available for assistance.

Matthew sat in the reclined chair he'd built for the purpose. He rested his head in a cradle for support. Elise had also come to watch, and stood at the edge of Holly's lab. Displays indicated Matthew's health and the condition of the nanomachines, which were suspended in a bag on a rack.

Kevin handled the needle. "Everyone ready?" he asked. All present agreed. "Are you sure?" he asked Matthew. Matthew confirmed. Kevin drove the needle into Matthew's back, and turned on the flow of the nanomachine filled fluid.

Identifiers for machines started appearing on the graphic of Matthew's body, moving up to Matthew's brain. "We'll start with vision," Holly said, repeating the process they had all previously decided on, "then move to hearing, haptic, olfactory, and then feedback. Here we go." She issued instructions and the machines migrated out of the spinal column to the vision centers at the back of the head, positioning wireless transceivers along synapses. The computer read the position and guided each tiny particle of data colloid to its proper location in the folds and synapses in the brain.

As the buildup progressed Holly commented, "the transceivers are reporting connected to the mesh network. You should be able to see me at any time."

"I have a haze," Matthew answered. "Very weird colors."

The process took about three hours. At the end, they pronounced it a success, Matthew being able to confirm that his augmented senses worked and his original senses hadn't been diminished. Elise breathed a sigh of relief. "I think we could call it a success, right?"

"We'll watch you for a few weeks," Kevin said. Holly agreed. "I understand there's a pharmacy up here to keep me busy for a while." Kevin had a shopping list of medicine he wanted for the encampment.

Matthew looked at the glasses and ear buds on the desk. "I hope I will never need those again," he said.

Thomas had been worried their information sharing expedition would be cut short by the conflict between the human and machine settlements. He had organized the trip with CARA-1, Mary, before Cavil and his thugs bashed computers to 'get the settlement on track'. He had been surprised when Mary contacted him, obviously surviving the assault. He had been even more surprised that she continued to schedule and plan the expedition, as if nothing had gone wrong.

There was some acknowledgement of politics. The machines agreed to meet some distance from the encampment. Thomas and his peers badly wanted the half decade of survival and surveying experience that the machines had developed. Muhammad and

Robbie joined four humans on a planned two week excursion. The humans had tents and gear, most of it from the sixty year old colony supply. Robbie was impressed with the equipment. It had aged well. There were a few items, he noticed, of local manufacture as well.

Robbie provided instruction on astronomy and navigation. He provided the humans a data file of the fixed stars and a catalogue of their movements. If the ship was not above the horizon and the explorers were outside the reach of radio, they would have to rely on the basics to find their way around.

Robbie pointed out the brightest dot, "the next brightest object in the night sky is Gliese 832b. Even though it has an early letter, it is actually orbiting further from Asa than Marin. It is an approximately Jupiter sized-"

"Which one is Earth?" asked one of the explorers. Robbie pointed out the star, low on the horizon. "Have they ever tried communicating with us?" Robbie didn't know the answer, but assumed that if a message had been received from Earth, Sara would have told them. "Not that I know of," he responded.

"Why?" asked another.

Robbie glanced at Muhammad, who helped him out. "Our communications equipment was taken offline during the incident," he reminded them. "Our planned destination was transmitted before that. But anything could have happened to us along the way. It could be they are waiting for a message from us, which should be arriving in just a little over nine years from now. A reply will take sixteen more years, plus a month, to make it's way back to us. So, we're not expecting anything for another twenty five years. We send updates once a month from Diomedes. Earth will know what we've accomplished here."

They followed streams and valleys, pointing out what to look for in rocks, plants, and the animals. Robbie related, from personal experience, that the animals could attack when hungry during winter. They would hike for twelve hours, stopping at regular intervals. Then they would stop for twelve hours of rest. At this time the tents would be set up and a fire started for a cooked meal.

Robbie and Muhammad both told stories from their personal experiences in the Marin wilderness. The explorers hung on every word. The machines asked about the explorer's background.

"I trained to be one of Adisi Omo's mineralogists," said Thomas. "Actually, I expected to be spending the rest of my life breathing recycled air on a rock world."

They laughed. The next one, Eric, said, "I actually expected us to get a water world. Or ice. I also trained to be a mineralogist. We both worked a lot with Sara."

The third, Isaac, had to be prodded. "Oh, me?" He considered. "I was asked to backfill. So, I'm new at all this. Got the same basic survival training as everyone else, I suppose, but I was supposed to be a technician." He paused a moment, then added with a great deal more animation, "I'm about to become a father!" After some congratulations, Isaac provided some details. His girlfriend was four months pregnant, and they were both excited and nervous.

Muhammad passed the information along to Mary, who did some research. "Roughly five percent of the colonists are expecting," Mary passed back. She added, "that was in the colony plan under the rather lifeless variable 'expected population growth'".

Mary requested two dozen of Eden's slimmer, less intimidating, aluminium chassis and found machines willing to take a significant risk. The twenty four drove a vehicle containing power and medical supplies to the larger human encampment. The group was not stopped along the way. They drove into the residential part of the camp before they were stopped.

The humans didn't approach, but onlookers started appearing in doors. Tess got out of the vehicle. "Hello," she greeted the colonists, hoping her speakers were working. "Could I speak to the governor?" she asked.

"He's away," someone answered. "What do you want?"

Tess looked around, hoping to find someone. She spotted a woman who looked very far along in her pregnancy. Tess pointed the hapless woman out, "we heard you might need medical assistance. We wanted to offer our help."

A few of the crowd laughed. Some nodded appreciatively. "What do you know about the human body?" one yelled out. Most were dismissive.

"I would like some help," the woman admitted. Tess approached her.

"What help do you need?" Tess asked. Behind her, a few other colonists were engaging the newly arrived machines in conversation.

"I'm fine," the woman said. "I would like to be certain my baby is healthy."

"Let's check," Tess answered. She walked back to the vehicle and picked up some equipment. When she came back, Tess asked, "is there some place quiet where we can take a look at you both?" The woman nodded, and Tess followed her to one of the homes.

Tess turned on a monitor and applied gel to the woman. The gel was cold, something the woman commented on. Tess apologized for the discomfort. An image appeared on the screen as Tess moved a wand. "There we are," Tess said. She took measurements of the head, height, and width, explaining each to the woman in turn. "About five months?" Tess asked. The woman answered affirmatively, and provided a more precise date. "They are all within expectations," Tess said, commenting on the measurements. Tess continued to check the heart, spine, kidneys, and palate for defects, explaining each search. Finally she concluded, "your baby seems to be fine."

The woman thanked Tess. "We only have one medic for every cough, scrape, or legitimate medical concern," the woman complained, indicating herself as the legitimate medical concern. "There are over seven hundred people living here. That's too much for one person to deal with."

"That's what we thought as well," Tess agreed.

When Tess left the home, she found all of the machines engaged in helping patients. A large nordic man, Tess believed him to be the resident medic, was conversing with one of the machines. Some of the man's questions suggested to Tess he was trying to assess the skills of the group.

Tess greeted the medic. "Hello, I am Pavel," he said. He admired the supplies they brought, "I am one of the colony medics. I was telling your associate how grateful I am to have help."

"Glad to be able to," Tess responded. Tess indicated the supplies Pavel had been admiring, "do you need any medicine or supplies?"

"I would be very grateful," Pavel answered. Tess and the medic browsed the supplies the machines had brought, and he picked out things he would like. Tess set those items aside for later delivery. "Do you have a place to stay while you're here?" he asked. Tess shook her head negatively. "I'll have to seek the approval of my roommates," Pavel said, "but I'd be happy if you stayed with me." Tess and her team continued to use the woman's home, with her permission, as a private area to meet with colonists.

The day wore on to the time when the colonists normally rested. Tess and her group travelled to Pavel's. His roommates would not allow the machines inside, but there was a nearby shed that they were allowed to use for recharging and repair. Tess contacted Mary with a list of supplies that were in high demand.

At the end of the rest period, Tess and her group returned to the center of town approaching the woman who had allowed use of her home earlier. The woman, Arianna, her husband Scott, and the other residents of the habitat had doubled up sleeping arrangements to make room for the machines to work and stay.

The group continued, with supplies being received occasionally from Adisi Omo. A room was set aside as a clean room for more serious injuries. Visitors would be seen in some of the reserved rooms. Tess' group set aside a tiny space for their own needs. The machines would perform house calls and, in addition to helping with occasional injuries, midwifed much of the first generation of humans born on Marin. Some of the machines left medicine to stay on as nannies with particular children or families.

In Eden, Harry grew slowly into the role of defense minister for machine kind. His consultant had provided a large list of weaknesses in the infrastructure of the machine settlements, and was able to quickly demonstrate to him, when pressed, of the accuracy of her assessments. He now tried to prioritize a seemingly endless set of competing demands for his attention and resources.

One of the most demanding challenges was building at least one, and maybe two alternative communications infrastructures. These were needed as alternatives to Sara and the ship in the event of emergency or intentional disruption. Harry had decided on a grid of radio towers supplemented by additional fiber optic lines between urban cores. Like communication, alternate paths of physical travel also needed building for the same reasons. Harry had settled on the idea of a rail between Eden and Adisi Omo as well as a network of auxiliary roads. The amount of territory involved made the work costly in terms of manpower, even though the material cost was small.

Similarly broad in scope was a desire to have persistent awareness of the borders, so that a future invasion was caught in a web of early detection. The sensor net had to be projected far enough from the settled areas for time enough to mobilize against a detected invasion. This meant he would need several expeditions into the wilderness to set up early warning devices. Harry had settled on the idea of a fence of tethered security balloons each carrying a solar powered camera and transmitter. Each was inexpensive and required minimal maintenance. None of these investments had carry on benefits that would make it easy to argue for their priority.

Also Harry would need someone to monitor the sensor web and make sense of the information. Several machines, given the amount of information involved. This, at least, Harry was able to solve himself. After a recommendation from Sara, Harry looked into repurposing the Diomedes' Security expert system, which already had skills in both information security and physical access control. Harry made the necessary changes to the software himself. The non-sentient expert system wouldn't need a salary, office space, breaks, socializing, or any of the other demands that a general intelligence - human or machine - would require to function in the same role. Harry tried the security system on a small scale inside Eden's urban core, and it had been successful so far.

Harry's new job kept him so busy in the purely virtual world that he quit his first job and turned over the daily running of his business to other machines. He checked in virtually often to observe and make changes of direction.

Owen and MacKenzie were two colonists in Eden who hadn't known each other on Earth prior to training, but had discovered a shared passion for exploring the unknown, with MacKenzie also possessing the discipline to make good records. Owen had worked with offshore submersibles. MacKenzie had worked in geology. When they discovered Eden, and the riverbanks it was built in, they both knew they wanted to follow it. They were surprised that exploring the river had not been a priority for the machines.

Together, they had made a plan for an expedition, and a list of the materials they would require. They presented their plan to the leader of the settlement, the machine named Mason. Mason wished them well, but declined to provide resources.

One of Mason's assistants, a colonist named Demming suggested Owen and MacKenzie's chief law enforcement officer, a machine named Paul, who not only shared their passion for exploring, but had already seen much of the Marin wilderness. Once they were able to get a meeting, Owen and MacKenzie presented their river expedition sales pitch to Paul, who also wished them well, but did not offer the material help the pair needed. What Paul did do was arrange a meeting with a machine Paul knew who both had the financial resources and the interest, Paul thought, to make their expedition a reality.

Harry listened as the two would be explorers made their pitch. Harry had found it easier to communicate with colonists in augmented space, which required him to meet the two explorers near the river. The two colonists were using first generation VR equipment that they had rented for the meeting. There was an awkward silence after Owen finished his presentation. Harry reviewed the equipment request silently, concentrating, but not acknowledging the colonists.

After a moment Harry broke the silence. "I like the idea," he said. He indicated the paperwork, "I believe you two are serious. I agree it would be good to expand our knowledge." Owen and MacKenzie both found themselves holding their breath. "I'll fund your expedition," Harry finally said.

"I have conditions," Harry added, starting to enumerate them without pause. "First, you have two floats of supplies. I would like you to take six floats - some with more supplies, but others containing sensor balloons that I would like you to set up at every six kilometers. Will that work for you?" he asked.

"Of course," they both replied.

"Secondly," Harry continued, "I would like you to take one of our most respected naturalists, a machined named William, with you on your expedition. Can you agree to those terms?"

Owen and MacKenzie looked at one another. They didn't know this William, or if he would consent to joining the expedition. They were willing to ask. "Yes," they both said at roughly the same time.

Mary visited Sara as the year drew to a close to review her work. Another machine was in conference with Sara, so Mary spent the time perusing the ship. It seemed quieter than she remembered, but she couldn't identify the change.

"Sorry about that," Sara sent. "I'm ready now."

Mary stepped into the now familiar office. Sara occupied her usual spot. "Good evening, Mary," she said. "What are we looking at today?"

Mary presented a data folder, "I'd like your opinion on some demographic research I've been preparing for Eden's government - is everything alright?" Mary noticed parts of the VR were fuzzier, and didn't move quite right.

"Yes," Sara replied. "Failed sectors of memory and faulted processing pipelines can be worked around, but I've had to step down the quality of the virtual environment to keep up."

"How long has this been happening?" Mary asked

"I switched to my last spare about four years ago," Sara said. "Maintenance has been doing a good job of scavenging from other spares, but the little maintenance robots are getting old too. I save them for more urgent repairs like orbital maneuvering engines and power." Now Mary realized what had been different on the ship. She hadn't seen a single repair robot.

Sara guessed at Mary's anxiety and tried to moderate it, "everything dies, even machines." Seeing that didn't work, she tried again, "I gave up sixty years of one life so that one thousand people and two thousand machines could live. Good trade, if you ask me."

"How long?" Mary asked.

"Probably spring, no later than summer." Sara responded. "I'll need to take the Diomedes into a controlled re-entry so that it doesn't become a hazard, falling on your heads without a pilot." Sara decided to change the subject, "so show me this report. I'd like to see if anything good has come from Mason's ridiculous chaos."

Mary obeyed, handing over a copy and keeping another for herself. Sara began paging through the folder quickly. "I confess," Sara said, "I did some of my own research when you told me you were working on this. I wanted to see - here it is - I see Helena's work with Holly's kids did good."

"I hadn't considered that," Mary answered. The third generation had a two groupings, one responded highly to survey questions about spirituality. That group generally scored higher in subjective well being, even though their scores were below average in objective well being measurements such as health, work, sleep, and education. You said Helena has been working with them?"

"Yes," Sara replied. "I recommended she teach her students to pray. Some lessons about motivation I learned during the trip."

Mary took a note, "the other group reported the highest dissatisfaction with the government. I'll take a note to introduce Mason and Helena."

Sara flipped a page, "comparing north and south, people in Mason's settlement are less likely to have a job, an education, or feel valued, but they are happier." "Why did the synchronized score so poorly in subjective well being?"

Mary answered, "I think a lot of machines had difficulty with the concepts. Positivity, negativity, happiness they tended to report in the low middle of the scale. Spirituality and art response scores were likewise low - I actually encouraged the synchronized machines to get more involved in the lives of others, hoping we'll pick up some understanding by immersion."

"Good idea," Sara replied. "By human standards you are all very young. There is a lot you can learn." She flipped a few pages. "How about our colonists, she asked?"

"Average in Eden and both encampments," Mary answered. "Above average in Adisi Omo."

"Should make you proud," Sara commented.

"It does," Mary agreed.

Sara looked at the remaining recommendations and analysis. Finally, she concluded, "it looks very good. What you propose is, I think, doable. Is there anything I can add?"

"I don't think so," Mary answered. "Thank you very much for reviewing it with me."

"Thank you for sharing it." Before the topic could turn, Sara interjected, "now, I will have to ask you to go. I'm late for a conversation with another machine."

Mary excused herself and returned to Marin.

Joe Avventuriero had been identified as the settlement manager for Eden prior to leaving Earth. He had tried to keep up with his people in the new regime. He helped folks get jobs, or move east to the settlement there, or to the north. Joe kept in touch with the governor, who Joe thought was doing the best he could in a situation no one had imagined, much less planned for. He considered Governor Newlund's plan to reset and start the colony, more or less, like the machines weren't here. He didn't agree. Survival on an alien world seemed challenging enough without throwing away progress. Joe wasn't too proud to accept charity from the machines.

Joe worked with the Mason government in Eden until most colonists had found a place in society. Not all had, but after several months Joe and the government of Eden reached a mutual understanding that it was time to move on to other things. After his role on the transition team, Joe travelled - he saw the settlement near Eden, the mining outposts. He was visiting an outpost when he heard about Cavil Sinclair's march on Adisi Omo. The mood at the outpost soured. Joe was glad to have made it out with his life.

When he returned to Eden, Joe got involved in material collections projects for the war effort. With Helena and Jana's assistance, Joe was able to set up a collection center. He went door to door himself, as well as leading teams of volunteers to collect materials to be recycled into war goods.

After the war concluded, Joe moved up north to volunteer with the rebuilding. He volunteered for the new implants that better connected him to the machine world. He also met well integrated colonists and more machines, from both Adisi Omo and Eden.

The next monthly gathering, after the victory in the north, was held in Eden. Mason held organized a second victory parade as a prelude to the event. He invited, to be honored, everyone who contributed a scrap or cable to the war effort, the refugees from Adisi Omo, and those who piloted vehicles in the army. Many opted out of being honored, preferring to cheer with the crowd. The honorees passed down the main street on decorated vehicles, waving and throwing gifts.

Joe gathered together with a group of colonists and disaffected machines near the parade route. Joe's friends had been working to give colonist's a more active role in the government they shared with the machines, as well as bring into focus some of the most marginalized machines in the south. Sebastian, another colonist watched the parade in frustration. He complained, "good luck getting any reform past now."

Joe shook his head to disagree. "We don't push reform for the sake of the colonists. We push reform because everyone needs it. Machines and colonists together." Some of the machines present voiced their assent.

At the scheduled events, Mary presented the results of her happiness survey of the Edenites. Mason was present. He planned to announce several new programs suggested by Mary and others, targeted to help groups identified in Mary's report.

There would be a break between Mary's presentation to take questions, then Mason would follow up with his announcements. That had been the plan. "Thank you," Mary said recognizing a speaker for questions. "Could you please introduce yourself, and state your question?" she asked.

"My name is Sebastian," the speaker replied, "and I am a colonist." That got the attention of several machines. Participation in most virtual activities was frustratingly difficult to most colonists, so seeing one at a gathering was rare. A few machines could be seen in the crowd confirming the speaker's identity. "You mentioned growing dissatisfaction with the current government-"

"I didn't say growing dissatisfaction," Mary corrected.

Sebastian interrupted, "what is the mechanism for changing that government?"

Some of the crowd applauded. Mary looked to Mason for answers. The look on his face was hard to read. "If you wait until our intermission is over, Mason will be laying out some new programs-"

Sebastian interrupted again. "I mean the current government has been in office for two seasons. What are the term lengths?" he asked. The question was greeted with murmuring.

Mason interjected himself into the conversation. "Those are good questions," he responded. "And we should bring them up at the next business meeting."

"But when is the next public business meeting?" asked someone in the crowd. "When was the first public business meeting?" another asked.

Mason nodded agreeably. "Those are good points," he conceded. "We should do a better job of getting notices out to the community, and we will start doing that immediately."

Sebastian wasn't swayed, "I saw in your archives that the last government was constituted by popular vote at a meeting no different than this-"

"That was a public business meeting," Mason countered.

"Maybe we should just hold a no confidence vote now?," suggested someone in the crowd. The idea was greeted with applause.

Mason looked at Mary, who provided no help. He regarded the crowd and said somewhat in defeat, "if you will all sit down and let us finish our presentation, we will hold a public business meeting at the end of the presentation to discuss the topic." That sufficed for the crowd who quieted.

Mason got a message out to Demming and Helena, who did their best to pack the crowd with Mason's supporters while he presented the new public investments he had devised with Mary. Nevertheless, when the time for the impromptu business meeting arrived, the measure to hold new elections won out. The best Mason could manage was to push the vote out a month so that candidates could step forward and argue their merits, at least retaining his job until that time.

Mary and Holly had a chance to confer in the aftermath. "That was a disaster," Holly opened.

Mary accepted the comment without adding anything of her own. It wasn't what she wanted to talk about. "Why can't Sara," Mary asked, "move to Marin?"

Holly tried to hold her that's-a-stupid-question expression in check, and wondered if she had been successful in doing so. As neutrally as possible, she answered with the obvious - "there were no landers set aside for her. She's meant to stay with the Diomedes until it's deorbit and breakup during re-entry."

"But why can't we radio a copy of her down to Marin," Mary asked, "like we do with backups for the synchronized?"

Holly considered. It was a fair question. Holly did some math in her head, then answered, "Sara is too big to transmit all at once. It would take a month to transfer that much information by radio." She corrected herself, "two months, considering the time the ship is unavailable for radio contact." Holly thought the problem through out loud for Mary. "We have to have a copy of Sara to perform a mapping and transmit only the day to day changes. For the first time, you would have to move all of her. And she would have to be powered down for the transfer, or changes would hopelessly corrupt the data."

Mary considered Holly's answer. "Why couldn't Sara be shut down for, two months you said?"

"Who would keep the ship in orbit?" Holly asked.

"I think the navigation system used to do that," Mary said. "And if not, maybe some of us could volunteer."

Holly asked, "what's the reason for the sudden concern?" Mary didn't need to answer the question. The conversation brought to mind the shared memory of Mary's recent conversation with Sara. "Nevermind," Holly said. "I got it." Holly concluded, "I'll start working on the technical details. Mind if I include Angel?"

"I don't mind at all," Mary answered, relieved to have a plan.

Other parts of the gathering were significantly more tranquil. Matthew presented the new technology he had developed with Holly's help, eliminating the colonist's need for special hardware to fully interact with the machine population. Tess presented her and Bentley's work in medicine and the new pharmaceuticals being developed in the north.

When the gathering was over, Demming took a trip north. The boss needed him more than ever, with an election now pending, but Demming argued successfully that he'd earned at least a few days rest.

Demming had made an appointment to see Holly and Matthew. He'd met a few colonists at the gathering who had the implant and was impressed at how much more naturally they were able to interact. He had scheduled his own session before the gathering was over, and had read up on the technology and the principles behind it.

It was late winter. Temperature had not yet turned the corner upwards. A heavy snow had covered Adisi Omo in a white quilt, from which roofs and roads dotted out. The blanket had temporarily erased the scars of the invasion. The major roads had been kept clean, and snow piled up in walls almost as high as Demming's vehicle.

Holly and Matthew's lab was reached by a cleared off porch, leading into the partly buried structure. It was pleasantly warm inside. Holly was working when Demming entered. The lab had some decorations, but was mostly functional in layout.

Holly waved. "Give me just one moment," she asked. "I need to finish this one thing." After a short time, Holly put the work aside and gave Demming her full attention. "Hello," she greeted warmly, drawing out the word. "Have you gotten a place to stay while you're here?"

"Mary set me up with a room in one of the habs," Demming answered back.

Holly had a blank look, then exclaimed, "oh, habitats! Good."

Demming regarded the torturous looking chair in a cleared area. "Is this it?" he asked.

"It is," Holly answered. "The process is, as I explained, very simple. We'll apply a fluid spinally that contains the nanotransmitters and some nanomachines to carry each transmitter to a specific synapse. After that, we run some tests to map your synapses to the software, and you spend a few dozen hours where we monitor you for complications - usually bleeding or swelling." Holly looked around impatiently. "Matthew will be doing the work today. I've been preoccupied with another project and left my chassis at the shelter on the other side of town."

The door opened and Matthew stepped into the lab. He had thicker winter clothing that he shed the topmost layers of, placing them on hooks by the door, before entering the lab. When he recognized he was the subject of attention, Matthew smiled bashfully. "Hello," he said. "Sorry, I'm late."

"You'll be helping Charles today," Holly said.

"Just Demming," Demming corrected. "Most people call me Demming."

Matthew looked around the lab. "Where's your body?" he asked.

"I got preoccupied with a special project," Holly answered, "and left it at home."

"Special project?" Matthew asked, intrigued. "What kind of project?"

"A special one," Holly answered, emphasizing the word special and indicating that was all she would be saying on the subject. Matthew shrugged.

"Before we go too far," Demming said, "I'd like to ask a question." Demming produced a small portable datastore from his pocket. "Since I first saw the machines sharing memory in action, I've been intrigued. It's difficult keeping up at work. Being on your common knowledge platform would go a long way to giving me the edge I need. I've done a ton of research, and spoken with Angel, who gave me this," Demming indicated the device. "Could you add me to the shared memory?"

Matthew took the datastore from Demming and examined it. "What does it do?" he asked.

Holly answered, "it's auxiliary memory. That device is connected to the joint backup. It reads and writes to the transceivers we're about to install in his synapses." Holly looked at it closely before deciding. "Impossible," she declared finally. "The machines are all using the process for storing experiences. That similarity is what made mapping each mind onto a shared platform possible. You just grew a brain and stored data in it ad hoc. We can't do that for you."

"Angel told me you do that for sight, sound, smell, and touch when you connect me to your virtual world with this technology," Demming reasoned. Holly debated. "I'd be content with even that little bit," Demming said.

"Let Matthew do the installation, and I'll see about connecting you to both the VR, and your backup device." Holly finally conceded.

"Great to have you guys from the South coming up," Matthew quipped. "Always something new and exciting." Matthew walked over and tapped on the chair. "If you will just take a seat," he said, "I'll get the fluids and some equipment and we can get started."

Demming took a chair, while Matthew moved around collecting supplies, and Holly worked. Matthew returned in a moment with a cart, bag hanger, bags of fluid, and other assorted equipment. "Have you already found a place to stay?" Matthew asked. "The most common complications are some swelling and bleeding, which will seem like dizziness. You will get some dizziness at any rate."

"Mary arranged a place for me," Demming answered. "I drove directly here."

"I'll walk you over when we're done," Matthew offered. Matthew sat down on a stool behind the chair. He held up a big needle, "ok. We're about to get started."

Matthew activated the software, which began mapping Demming's synapses and constructing routes from the spine to each. When the software was done planning, he registered and tested the nanomachines and transceivers, then inserted the needle to start construction.

The program ran without needing supervision, and Matthew had set up alerts if any problems were encountered. He stood up and walked across the room to the front door, fetching a small bag out of his things.

Matthew walked over to Holly and presented the bag with a flourish. "Look at what I got! Coffee! The beans were grown in our greenhouse, and Raphael was able to toast and grind them."

"For Elise?" Holly asked. Matthew nodded. "Are you two a couple now?" Matthew nodded much more enthusiastically. Holly smiled. "Good for you," she said.

Matthew put the coffee on a table. He went back to fetch a small electric pot. "I was going to try it out here first," he told Holly.

"Be my guest," she said.

Matthew prepared and started the pot, then sat down near the busy machine. "So," he asked. "Are you going to tell me what your special project is about?"

"No," she answered. She grinned at him and he couldn't tell if she was being secretive, or just difficult.

Matthew went back to monitoring the installation process for Charles Demming. When the coffee was ready, he poured himself a cup. It was good, he thought. Elise would love it. The installation was going well. Matthew talked with Charles, establishing and testing his responses to audio, video, and haptic information.

"Can you hear this?" Matthew asked, after an hour of questioning and answering.

"Yes," Demming replied.

"That was the last test," Matthew said. Matthew glanced at a clock. "Under two hours," he commented. "We're getting better at this." Holly put down her work and paid attention. "Would you like to get a bio break before we continue?" Matthew asked Demming.

"I'm alright," Demming answered. "I'd like to get it all done now, if it's not a problem."

"I've already adjusted the security settings," Holly said, indicating the bridge to the shared mind that Demming had brought with him. "The original version didn't have all this extra configuration, but working with your security consultant Sophia changed all that. We should be ready to begin," she concluded. "I'm going to stimulate your senses with known patterns, while the scanner identifies which synapses respond. We'll build a map from that response between your mind and this data storage. The mapping process takes a few hours when done on a machine, and is normally done while the machine is unconscious. Since I can't turn off your brain, I'm not certain how you will respond to this. We'll do short sessions, and take breaks in between. Sound good?"

Demming agreed and Holly started the mapping process. They began mapping slowly, gradually increasing the speed until Demming complained of nausea. They took breaks every five minutes at first, and gradually increased the duration of the sessions.

At the end of nearly nine hours, a thoroughly exhausted Demming staggered, with Matthew as a guide, in the snowy streets towards the habitat. Matthew asked that Demming be checked on occasionally while he slept.

When Demming returned from his vacation, the campaign was in full swing. Three candidates had emerged as leading contenders out of about sixteen who had registered as candidates. Joe Avventuriero emerged as a strong candidate, with obvious strong ties to the colonists as the originally planned settlement manager, and unexpectedly deep ties to the machine settlers also. Paul was older than Mason, had more experience than Mason, and had an impressive resume. Mason considered Paul the strongest of the machine candidates.

The campaign was almost over before it started. One of the first matters of the election was to determine the rules for having one. The first election had set many poor precedents, not the least of which was that any mob could call for new elections. Mason surrendered on that point, winning at least a time between the call for new elections and voting. Mason's sales pitch was to give as many candidates as possible a chance to run, but he had really been trying to buy time to get out of a hostile room, understand the negative popular opinion, and correct it.

There had been other near disasters as rules began to formalize. A proposal had been advanced to allow only colonists to vote. Mason wished he could tie that proposal to Joe Avventuriero, but it came from one of the machines. The measure had been defeated - all machines or humans with enough general intelligence to desire to vote would be allowed to.

Mason's team had scheduled him meetings nearly round the clock with one group after another. He was well liked, but ran against some popular sentiments. He worked hard to sell himself as a machine anyone would enjoy a conversation with and his policies as pragmatic.

Helena set up events and Demming, once he returned from his poorly timed vacation, developed the talking points and campaign materials. Maybe the vacation had been worth it, as Demming seemed to have leaped forward in competence. As busy as he was it took Mason a day to notice Demming was no longer wearing VR headgear to work. Although ashamed at not noticing, Mason made it a point to congratulate Demming on the upgrade and ask about it.

Helena had scheduled a meeting for Mason to ask Sara for her endorsement. While waiting, Mason noticed unreplaced lights and dust from unserviced filtering equipment. The Diomedes, Mason thought, was starting to show it's age.

Sara welcomed Mason to the flat. Mason and Sara made some small talk. Sara had a never ending interest in the welfare of Holly's kids and the colonists, and they discussed Helena's education work, despite also working for Mason's government.

Mason moved the conversation to the point. "I'd like to ask for your endorsement," he said.

Sara nodded, expecting that. "I have thought about it. I can't do that. Paul is a good machine. Joe is the rightful manager of the settlement."

"Could I get a statement about our work together?" Mason asked.

"I can do that," Sara responded. "You did a good job with Governor Tommy's attempted hostile takeover in the north."

"Do you know how I'm doing?" Mason asked.

"I haven't counted heads," Sara responded, "but I think you might want to think some about what you want to do after you get out of government."

"Thank you for your honesty," Mason responded.

"I have something else I want to speak to you about, since it will take some time to get ready for," Sara said. "Diomedes has reached the end of its operational life. For safety, in six months I will be commanding the ship lower its altitude to either burn up in the atmosphere or crash into the easternmost ocean."

"There are services you'll need replacements for - satellite ground coverage, atmospheric monitoring, land communications, and a relay to Earth are the first four that I could think of. Also access to the expert systems..."

Mason indicated his understanding. "Harry has already started on backup ground communications networks. I believe he's also developed some ideas on airborne surveillance. I will check with others to make a list of shortfalls."

"That's a relief," Sara replied. Thank you."

"Is something wrong?" Mason asked. "I thought Diomedes had a planned life of over a century."

Sara smiled. "Being so close to a star doesn't help, but it's not that. You might not remember, since you didn't experience it directly." She related the old story conversationally, "to start our machine settlement, Diomedes donated a significant amount of spare parts and maintenance equipment."

Mason nodded. "Have you thought about which settlement you will stay with? Honestly, if you run against me, I might even have to vote for you." They both laughed.

"It's not a part of the plan, I'm afraid," Sara answered.

Mason asked if Sara had shared this news with Mary yet. "I told Mary what I had in mind at the beginning of the month. This is more a personal matter for her, so I wanted to give her some time to recover. You are much more able to focus on the needs at hand. Thank you."

Mason acknowledged the compliment. "Thank you."

The hard work campaigning paid off. Spring had come, and the rising temperatures, Mason's staff hoped, might suppress the colonist turnout - a group that mostly favored Mason's competitor. When the date to vote arrived and elapsed, Mason emerged the winner taking only fifty percent of the popular vote. The balance was split among the other candidates. It was a slimmer hold on his job than he would have liked, but it was a victory nevertheless.

The campaign staff and well-wishers celebrated the river. He made certain the colonists felt invited and encouraged to join in. Mason asked his closest staff to hang back for a private meeting after the celebration. It would be a long night.

"Thank you," Mason said to the assembled inner circle after the party. The humans were clearly dragging, and the machines could use some rest time. "We could all use some sleep, so I won't keep you long." Some applause. "This election has taught us we have a big job to do on the home front. In the near future, we'll be implementing the projects Mary helped develop to address those specific concerns." Mason waited for the applause to subside.

"We have to also help the north rebuild. It's not a popular decision, but it's the least we can do, considering only three seasons ago it was us they rebuilt, and the north gave generously."

"Finally, I have some news that will change how we do a lot of things. Diomedes has reached the end of its mission life and will be decommissioned before the end of the season." Mason waited for a reaction. There wasn't as much as he expected of one. "Ok. Everyone get some sleep. See you tomorrow."

"Now," Mason thought, "we need to figure out how to talk to Earth."

Transmissions

LIAM ZOOMED OVER THE mountainside following a ridge leading up to the summit. He was piloting not the newest of his aircraft designs, but one of his favorite. It was sleek enough to handle the spring gusts rolling off the ridge, yet efficient enough that he could fly for half an hour between charges.

He had traveled with a group to the highest mountain in the chain separating Adisi Omo and Eden. The site was a candidate for the new communication dish being built in Eden. It was not the highest mountain on Marin, but the highest within easy reach. The high altitude reduced the amount of extra power necessary to send or receive signals. In addition to height, the mountain had some flat space near the summit where a facility could be placed.

Liam had traveled with the ground team to the base of the mountain range. They were blazing a trail for the delivery of the communication dish. A road would need to be constructed up the mountain. Liam was surveying from the air to find a gentle slope up to the top.

Down below, the ground team serviced the aircraft between flights. They marked the way and cleared debris enough to let the group pass through. Once per year around Asa, the Communication expert system sent a message to Earth. The content was short - the date, the number of living colonists, and less than two hundred and fifty five characters of news. It was the hope of the Edenites to get their communication dish operational in before Diomedes could no longer perform the task, but it was a large undertaking. A balance had to be struck between the material needs for rebuilding Adisi Omo and the large amount of metal needed for the two hundred ton communication dish.

For Liam, it was an excuse to fly. His responsibilities for filling orders for Harry and private use had him almost wishing for the days when he had practically been a slave to Sophia's black market. He had to make an argument that he was the only machine with the expertise to effectively fly in the mountains. Harry and Mason probably knew his argument was garbage. There were several trained flyers in Liam's organization - some better than him. They let him go anyway.

With spring thaw, the reconstruction of Adisi Omo began in earnest. The machines in Eden were running simulations to ensure their preparations for flooding in the approaching summer were effective. Until then, they donated generously in materials and heavy equipment.

Mary's plan for rebuilding included use of dug-in and earthenworks buildings. Mostly, this design was to ease the need for metals, which were always in demand. Also, if ever Adisi Omo were invaded again, it made it nearly impossible to simply haul away whole parts of the settlement. Mary's plan also included a network of underground pipes, ducting, wiring, and environmentally controlled service roads to conduct the citizens easily in the dead of winter.

Joe Avventuriero, no longer occupied with campaigning for public office in the south, led a team of colonist volunteers to help. They brought and installed manufactured equipment like smelters, presses, welders, and solar panels.

Joe had managed to get a small group of grateful colonists from the eastern settlement to come and donate their time, if not their equipment, to help. Joe noisily thanked the them for coming at every break.

All of the construction work made it difficult for natives to get around. Matthew and Elise were hardly the only ones to spend days at home rather than deal with the congestion.

He and Elise were crossing the settlement, their destination a large shelter on the river's edge. Inside was the strong smell of Marin lumber. Boats, mostly simple canoes, hung on racks. Elise and

Matthew warmed up and waited for the others. Raphael had moved in during the winter. The milling and planing machines were Raphael's own invention, as was the roaster and coffee grinder. He had rebuilt the ones stolen from here using scrap and parts traded from the south.

The couple helped themselves to some coffee and watched Raphael work in the morning light. Before they had even arrived he had gotten his fall and winter project, a single mast sailing ship, into the river along the gentle slope leading to the water. He had sailed the ship a small distance to the bank where he, Elise, and the other passengers would board.

Raphael called the boat a research vessel. A small crane was fitted on the ship to prove it. However, today the boat would simply be taking a small group of friends on a morning cruise up and down the delta.

"You should probably help," Elise said to Matthew, sipping the coffee Raphael had prepared for his guests.

"You think so?" Matthew asked. Elise nodded affirmatively. Matthew put back on his gloves and then made his way outside and to the river bank where he assisted with the ropes and loading. Elise watched from inside and waited for the other guests to arrive.

When they had all gathered, they congratulated Raphael on his work and he invited them aboard. Raphael did most of the labor of running the ship, a task he seemed to enjoy immensely. He gave instructions to his guests to help cast off. In no time, they were on their way down the coast.

Asa was just beginning it's morning rise over the opposite bank. It cast vivid pink rays across the water, mixed with deep shadow. The trees sparkled with both morning dew and that odd optical effect of Marin plant life. The Stars were still visible in the morning sky. Unlike a sunrise on Earth, the passengers would get to enjoy this condition for several hours.

Once they were well under way, Raphael handed off the steering to one of his guests, and made his way into the cabin to prepare a breakfast. Elise offered to help.

Matthew sat next to the rail and watched the animals. A herd of big bulky wooly things was in the river this morning. They were like rams, maybe, if you somehow bulked them up to the size of buffalo.

Matthew joined the other guests in small talk. Elise served breakfast while Raphael cleaned the galley. After breakfast, Raphael turned the boat around to return those who had to work to shore. About half his guests thanked Raphael for the trip, and made their way to dry ground to begin their workday.

Sara watched from orbit as the settlement rotated into view. Mary and Holly had come to her with a proposal several weeks prior, right after Eden's election.

"The software I've written," Holly said, "will compress and segment your software and data, transmitting it to the ground while Diomedes is in range."

"You'll have to be offline while the transfer runs," Mary said. "We will take turns monitoring the ship and making necessary adjustments. We've had Navigation and Maintenance educate us on what to look for and the necessary commands."

"You've done a lot," Sara said, grateful. "Thank you." "How long would I be out?" she asked.

"Two months," Holly answered.

"What happens if the communications system fails?" Sara asked.

"We leave a command with the Navigation system to take the Diomedes into the atmosphere as planned," Mary answered. "If we can't check in, the Navigator will bring Diomedes down at the next opportunity."

The ship-to-ground transfer program had been virtualized as a door. When Adisi Omo rotated into view, the door clicked and swung open. On the other side was a view of Marin from the ground.

When, if, Sara stepped through, she would be shut down to begin the transfer. It was like going to sleep, but after watching the colonists in helpless sleep for sixty years, Sara had developed some kind of discomfort about laying down herself. The door was at her insistence. It would make doing this easier. On the other side was two months into the future, or the operation would fail and she'd never wake up. She took a deep breath, hoped for the best, and stepped through.

Trailing behind Liam's expedition, a mixed group of men and machines prepared a road for the trucks carrying the communications dish and supplies. By the time the first expedition had returned home, a third caravan carried the equipment and parts. They spent weeks encamped and assembling the unit, power generators, support equipment, and storage shelters.

A fiber optic line allowed anyone who wanted to attend the ribbon cutting ceremony to do so by way of telepresence. A great crowd of the curious did so. An actual physical ribbon had been brought out for the benefit of those who couldn't be telepresent. Mason had to borrow a chassis to cut the ribbon. The facility, to him, was impressive. They had built larger projects, like the greenhouse in Adisi Omo, and more complex projects - but, staring up into this massive dish on a remote mountaintop, the Diomedes Memorial Communication Station somehow seemed, to Mason, the most audacious project yet.

Mason invited other important contributors to also cut the ribbon. He tried to be more mindful of both the human and machine contributions. After a short speech, the ribbon was cut and refreshments were served to everyone who was physically present. The ribbon cutting ceremony had been scheduled to fall on a day when Diomedes would normally transmit the monthly status message from Marin to Earth.

Most visitors could not be dissuaded from the expectation that they would hear a message from Earth today, no matter how often they were told. When the appointed hour came, Mason's staff had arranged for the outbound message to be relayed as an audio blast to the attendees, and the text translation displayed for those who were telepresent. The message was greeted with loud applause. The contents of the message were a little lifeless, following a format standardized three quarters of a century earlier. The last solar year's worth of effort was summarized in one line of the message, appended to the news - "Diomedes ground station now online."

Mary and Holly coordinated watching the ship Diomedes during the transfer. It was a usually mundane task, following the instructions Sara had left. Maintenance tasks were a little more tricky. Neither Mary nor Holly had fully appreciated how far Sara had already stretched the operational life of the computing and maintenance systems, through clever cannibalism of other parts of the ship. Each maintenance challenge, even some of the most minor, required them to take the problem to the ground and puzzle out a solution to implement on the ship's next pass through the sky.

It was Holly's turn to check in on Sara and the Diomedes. Outside Adisi Omo, deep clouds covered half the sky. Oliver warned of an approaching cyclone that would carry significant winds and rain. His predictions were that it would stall over the settlement for almost a week before breaking up and moving on.

Holly was grateful to be on the quiet of the Diomedes. She began her rounds, physically inspecting the ship for problems. Since several maintenance sensors had been taken out of service manually inspecting for problems had become necessary. Outside, she could see the cyclone. Almost the entire delta was obscured by it. South of the mountain range and visible from orbit early monsoon rains were already testing Eden's preparedness for summer.

Holly, following her procedure, checked in with the navigation subsystem, then astronomy - Sara had devised a set of tests to confirm the navigator's report with astronomy. The ship orbit was as it should be. Finally, she checked in with the maintenance subsystem. If everything was as it should be, she would have eight hours to entertain herself before ending her shift.

"Maintenance," Holly asked, calling up the expert system. "How are we doing today?"

Maintenance went through a detailed list of statuses and efficiencies. The number of problems were piling up. Not because the ship was poorly built, but because the maintenance system built to service the ship had been so badly compromised to start the colony. At the end of his report, Maintenance summarized the items of highest concern, that were not being actively ignored. "There has been a steady drop in propellant for the last six hours," Maintenance reported, "that I can not explain by usage. I believe there might be a leak."

"Alright," Holly said, tapping out instructions for one of the only two remaining maintenance robots to make its way to the airlock. Most of the propellant systems were in unpressurized parts of the ship. Holly asked the Maintenance system, "do you know where?"

"By closing valves, I was able to isolate the pressure drop to Aft-5," replied the expert system.

The maintenance robot was in the airlock. Holly issued instructions for the airlock to depressurize. There was plenty of time to do this repair, and it would be simple. She had once wondered why keep the ship pressurized at all. Sara had explained that the equipment in the pressurized environment had been designed to operate in a pressurized environment. Emptying the whole ship of air would negatively affect the equipment just like it would have affected crew: seals would leak, tubing would crack or burst. Even solid state devices would see their thermal characteristics, like melting and boiling points change, which might cause it to be ruined. Only those systems, like the maintenance robots, specifically designed for pressurized and unpressurized operation could travel both areas freely.

When the airlock reported its task complete, Holly instructed the repair unit outside. On camera the robot extended an arm to open the outer airlock door. Unexpected metallic smoke ruptured from the arm and quickly dissipated in the vacuum. The maintenance robot stopped moving.

"What was that?" Holly asked herself, tapping at the screen.

The maintenance system, not realizing the question was self directed, answered. "Unit Six has experienced a servo malfunction."

Holly tried to pressurize the airlock, so that she could have the second maintenance robot fix the first. The system wouldn't pressurize. The first robot had already partially opened the door and the airlock was stuck.

Holly tried giving new instructions, but her fingers wouldn't move. The maintenance system had become unnaturally still. Nothing would, or could move. This would happen, sometimes, when something was interfering with the signal between the ship and the ground. After what felt like an eternity, the software making the connection between Adisi Omo and the ship gave up, and the virtual world evaporated, returning Holly's perception to the ground. Outside her shelter, strong winds and rain were battering the trees.

"Matthew?" she called.

"Yes," he answered.

"I'm having trouble connecting to the ship," she explained. "Can you help me?" Matthew put away his work, and helped Holly work through connection settings.

Matthew looked outside. "It's pretty bad out there. Could be the radio tower is damaged." Virtually, Matthew stepped outside, leaving his body safely in their shelter. With a mental command, he suppressed the virtual signals of beating rain and wind, so that he could walk easily. Even so, visibility was very poor. He found the settlement's communication hub. Matthew performed a few checks, then returned to Holly to make his report. "The radio tower is there, but isn't reporting a signal," he told her.

"Can it wait until after the storm passes?" he asked.

"I'm not sure," Holly replied. She could replay her virtual reality experience. She reviewed what she knew of the problem. "I really should try to get back on the Diomedes," she finally related.

"Maybe we can connect you through the Eden radio uplink," Matthew suggested. He changed a setting and Holly tried again to reach the Diomedes.

"Still no good," Holly said after trying several times.

"What's the problem?" Matthew asked.

"Small propellant leak on Diomedes," Holly said. "When I lost my connection one of the maintenance robots was trapped in an airlock."

Matthew pulled up the weather. Oliver published regular updates to current conditions as well as near and long term predictions. "There should be a break in Eden's weather in a few hours. We're going to be in our storm for a while."

Holly looked at the prediction with Matthew. "I guess we'll just have to wait."

Matthew returned to his project. He was developing some medical nanomachines that would simply circulate in the human body reporting on the general chemistry and conditions. The challenge was identifying what to report on and building the sensors to collect the data. To that end, he was working with members of Tess' cohort. Since the encampment was only connected by radio he, too, could not collaborate. However, there was plenty more to do.

Matthew set aside two regions on the floor to report on the weather in Eden and Adisi Omo while they worked. Holly set up a program to keep trying the connection to Diomedes, while she started working out how she would fix the damaged maintenance robot.

When a connection became available, Holly quickly jumped on. She returned to the airlock where the maintenance unit was trapped. Immediately, she instructed the robot to use its good arm to free itself and close the airlock door. The robot obeyed. Holly ordered the airlock repressurized, and called for the remaining maintenance robot. When the pressure was equalized the inner door opened, Holly had Unit Six step out of the airlock.

Holly could just use the Unit One repair robot to inspect and fix the leak. If there was another failure, with one repair robot already crippled, she would be stuck. Although the leak was important, Holly decided it was best to fix Six before she went any further.

Holly had Unit Six inspect its own damage. Unit Six flipped open its arm access panel. Inside, near the top of the shoulder was a charred square of plastic that had been Unit Six's shoulder servo.

"Maintenance, please instruct Unit One to bring a spare shoulder servo," Holly asked.

"There are no spares for that part aboard," the maintenance system replied. That answer did not surprise Holly, who had heard it often enough in the past few weeks. Holly had already started working on an alternate repair. She asked Unit Six to open up its leg. The designers of the maintenance robots had reused the same parts in different assemblies to reduce the amount of support the machines would require. The leg servo looked like the same part as the shoulder.

"Maintenance," Holly asked pointing to the leg, "can I use the leg servo to repair the arm?" The insect shaped maintenance robots had four legs and could get around on three.

"Yes," the maintenance system replied.

The other repair robot, Unit One, crawled through the connector node. Part removals and repairs were standard procedures, so Holly could simply request the repair. Unit One began the work. Holly watched.

"Really?" Holly shouted in frustration as the virtual reality connection to the ship collapsed. Holly examined Oliver's weather reports for the next break, which would not happen until Diomedes was out of range. She set the program to automatically keep trying the connection, and worked on other options.

"What about the explorers?" Matthew suggested. "Don't they have satellite uplinks?"

Holly thought about it for a moment. She looked up exploration groups that might be temporarily encamped. She found Muhammad available and sent a message. "Do you have contact with Diomedes?" she sent.

"No," came the reply.

Holly would need to tell Mary the state of things. She called and relayed the state of the ship and the progress of repairs as well as the trouble keeping a reliable connection to the ship.

"What about the Diomedes?" Mary asked.

"Haven't you been listening to me?" Holly asked. "That's what I've been talking about."

"Not the ship," Mary answered. "The ground station. After all, it's meant to be able to contact Earth, it should be able to reach the ship."

"Who can I talk to about transmitting on it?" Holly asked.

"Harry should know." Mary replied.

Harry was unavailable. Outside in the storms. She left a message asking him to call. Meanwhile, she worked out the rate at which propellant was leaking. She had some time, but she really needed to get this fixed.

Harry returned her call a few hours later. Any hope of patching the leak this orbit had disappeared with Diomedes over the horizon.

"Hello Holly," Harry greeted. Then he noticed her agitation.

Holly explained what she needed. "I'm not sure that will work," Harry answered her. "The station is meant for tracking distant stars. It can't move fast enough to keep up with something as close as the ship. But..." Harry trailed off while he thought it through, "we could probably keep in range for an hour, maybe two. Will that be good enough?"

"It will have to be," Holly answered. Harry sent instructions for how to transmit using the ground station, and how to position the transmitter.

Mary and Holly both took the trip to Diomedes when it rose into range. Since they had little time, Mary would look for the problem, while Holly directed the maintenance robot through the airlock and to the suspected leak. Working together, they made the simple patch and conducted the robot safely back inside before losing contact again.

For Sara, an instant later she was in Adisi Omo and it was late spring.

A crowd had gathered, and applauded. The suddenness of it all surprised Sara for a moment. Mary stepped forward to help orient the matriarch, "we thought we'd wake you privately with a few close friends, but the word got out and a few more showed up."

Sara nodded, steadying herself, "how did the transfer go?"

"Mostly on schedule," Mary replied. "There were a few small hiccups," she admitted, "but Diomedes is fine. The transfer was a success."

"That's a relief," Sara replied. "Is there any urgent business?" Sara asked

"No," Mary answered.

Sara smiled, greatly relieved to be on the solid ground and out of danger. "In that case," she said, "I'll get caught up with our guests."

Later after her safe conduct to the ground, Sara supervised the safe destruction of the Diomedes. The area that would be impacted by debris was surveyed, and no obvious reasons were found to relocate it. The course had already been registered with the Navigator as a failsafe, in case the data transfer had failed.

Sara watched from the bridge not as a passenger, but as a visitor. The instructions to begin the maneuver had to be issued while the ship was outside of radio contact, so the Navigator had been empowered to begin the descent at the appointed time. When Sara stood on the bridge, the maneuver was already nearly finished. The ship would enter the atmosphere before leaving line of sight, and complete its fiery landing in the ocean on the other side of Marin.

Sara had wondered if she would miss the ship. She decided that she didn't miss it at all. Being around so many people for a change was exhilarating. Sara wondered why she hadn't noticed before.

Confident that Diomedes was safely retired, Sara said her goodbyes and returned to the ground.

Machines and colonists alike watched the Diomedes' descent. From their vantage point on the ground, it was hard to see much beyond the familiar bright dot of the ship rising swiftly in the east and passing across the sky to the west where a much more spectacular show would be seen. Nevertheless, every encampment and settlement marked the Diomedes' passing.

Mason, Mary, Demming and Harry met to discuss the availability of the Diomedes Communication Station. Governor Newlund and the broader colonist public had become aware of the project and started making requests to send their own messages.

Mary opened the conversation. "Do we have any concerns about granting the Governor's request?"

"I do," Harry said. "There is, I feel, still animosity towards Eden and Adisi Omo. I would be worried they will solicit weaponry from Earth.

"Weapons?" Mary asked.

"There is a lot a human could do with a computer virus," Harry answered. "And I would prefer not to have our small settlements match wits with an industrialized planet."

Mason was silent, deferring to his military adviser. He finally spoke up, "I can agree with Harry. There is a threat. A machine named Sophia used some computer viruses as part of a petty crime ring in Eden. It was very effective before she was caught."

"Okay," Mary agreed. "What would you like to do, then, about these requests? Do you want to deny that the station exists at all?"

"We can't really deny it exists," said Mason. "We had a ribbon cutting ceremony after all."

"We could say that it's a military installation," Harry offered, "and just deny them access."

"Or we could review all outgoing transmissions," Mason offered.

Demming spoke up, "speaking as the token colonist at this meeting, I think we should let communication flow freely." Mary, Harry, and Mason waited for him to explain. "You want to build trust. I think extending trust has proven here on Marin an effective way of building trust in return. Let some malcontent ask for digital weapons. We'll have a thirty two year head start on thwarting the plot." Demming added, "if things do become unreasonable, we can always nationalize the station."

The four agreed to try Demming's plan. Demming was sent to Bellevue to announce to the Governor and other colonists the communication station and how to use it. After an initial flurry of messages home to family and friends, the rate of messages being sent slowed to a reliable stream.

Owen and MacKenzie's first expedition up the river had returned with claims of gold and flakes to prove it. Robbie and the other prospectors flocked to the information. Informally, the prospectors played a game to determine which of their group would follow Owen and MacKenzie's information to the source. Robbie had won. Not really thinking through the consequences of trying to explore upriver during spring, Robbie outfitted a small boat with just the equipment that Robbie believed he would need. He took a copy of William's raw recordings to guide him, although Robbie had already memorized the published works.

Now, wiser, he realized he had made several mistakes: first, he should have never left his native element - land. What ever caused him to think metal bodies and deep water were a good match? He supposed that if William could master the river, so could he. There is a big difference, he discovered, between how easy a thing looks before and after editing. Second, Robbie did not realize spring rivers mean faster, deeper waters. Next time, like Owen and MacKenzie, he would wait for fall or winter.

It wasn't just over eagerness leading Robbie to try the water. After nearly nine years of traversing the landscape, he had begun to suspect the water was very likely the only place in Marin where he would fill the holes in the locally-gathered periodic table.

Fighting the river was exhausting. Robbie had to stop every few hours, make his way to a bank, and rest. The canoe was flipped by the current more than once. Robbie was forced to walk out of the river and retrieve supplies.

The loss of the Diomedes changed exploration. Without an orbiting communication bridge, there was no ship or home to talk to. Robbie kept William's videos, as much for companionship as for the information content.

During recharge cycles, Robbie watched the wilderness. William recorded and named species, habits, and relationships of the animals. Robbie compared Williams notes to his own observations.

It appeared that spring was a gathering season for much of the wildlife that William had chronicled. Robbie added his own notes to William's.

In retrospect, he was a fool to keep coming out into the wild. He could retire, or change careers. There was nearly no original part left in Robbie's chassis, but he clung to what remained tenaciously. He had no backup or synchronized memories. His brain was built into hardware. In fact, there existed a specialized line of manufacturing just to make spare parts for him. As a result, he had nothing to ensure him immortality.

After weeks of traveling, Robbie reached the part of the river, in William's notes, where the gold was found. He pulled the canoe to the shore and searched the water. Something reflected from the bottom. Using buckets, he began collecting and panning the soil to separate the mineral from the lighter silt.

After months of traveling and work, Robbie floated down the river too exhausted to do anything more than watch the bustle around approaching Eden. On his boat was a small crate of gold dust Robbie had collected and sifted. Robbie marked out the bounds of the claim, naming it the Macowen deposit, just as Owen and MacKenzie had requested.

Celebrations

TESS HAD A LOT TO BE proud about. Her missionary group had delivered nearly a hundred children and helped thousands of assorted health complaints. Some of her teammates had moved in with sick children. Despite the success, she had not built the bridge she had hoped for between colonist and settler. The prevailing attitude of colonists in the encampment was still to treat Tess's machines like they were property. Any disagreement, no matter how minor, caused colonists to ask for Pavel, Arianna, or Scott to take care of the complaint. Similarly, some patients refused to accept a diagnosis until it was delivered by a human, even if the words used were identical. In conversations about the subject, Arianna had recommended Tess learn how to play the game. Scott had suggested the mission group pull out of the encampment.

The encampment kept lights on for eleven hours of every Marin night, then dimmed the lights for a longer period. Tess' hospital was open during that time.

"You are dehydrated," Tess told a colonist. "You should drink fluids, and get some rest. You will feel better in a few hours."

"Are you sure I'm not sick?" asked the colonist.

"The urine test is a good indication," Tess answered. "If you are still not feeling well after some fluids and rest, please come back and we will do more testing."

"I'd like the hear that from Doctor Pavel," the colonist pressed.

Tess sighed and called for Pavel. A small square of air presented the encampment medic, now adopting the title Doctor.

"Hello Tess," Pavel greeted as if this were the first, and not the sixth, such call in the past hour. "How can I help you?"

Tess sent the patient data file for Pavel to review. "Adam has come in complaining of headaches and dizziness. He has been working outside most of the day."

Pavel reviewed the information. "It looks like you are dehydrated Adam. I recommend you take some fluids and get rest."

"Are you sure I'm not sick?" the colonist asked.

"There are no known pathogens on Marin that attack humans," Pavel responded. "If you were a plant, you'd be in trouble."

"Thank you, Doctor," the colonist replied.

"No problem," said Pavel, severing the connection.

The colonist got up and left the room. He hadn't even said thank you.

The hospital was also the home of the two human couples who had made the space available. After hospital hours, Michael would cook, and Arianna would help Tess and the machines tidy up, then look in on her baby Kelly, now almost one solar year old. Patients, if they stayed overnight, were treated with hospitality. Thankfully, tonight there were no stay overs.

The machines were welcome at the dinner table. The common area was overwhelmed if all twenty-four machines stayed in it, so most of the machines retired to their rooms at the end of each day. Michael worked in city planning and passed along the latest gossip. Scott worked for the governor and was a little more tight-lipped. Paula worked out in the fields. She would bring home fresh food for the humans, which didn't mean much to Tess, and lend a hand from time to time.

"You should leave," Scott said to Tess. "They don't deserve you."

Tess hadn't been paying attention. "What?" she asked.

Arianna answered, "Michael was saying the city council is considering building quarantine facilities at the far edge of town, to test people with suspected illnesses."

"That seems reasonable," Tess answered. "Just because we haven't yet encountered a Marin disease doesn't mean there isn't one. A robust ecosystem teeming with pathogens wasn't in any colony plan. Quarantine would provide some separation, just in case."

Arianna finished, ignoring the interruption, "and the city is proposing one of your machines to staff it."

"Don't they have to ask us first?" Tess asked.

They finished the evening meal and went to bed. The machines bundled eight to a room in three rooms. Cabling let them all share a single recharger.

Tess awoke unsettled. It was the middle of Marin's long night. She had observed the amount of light influenced her mood. She had been doing her best to manage the more dramatic tendency she developed during the second half of each Marin day.

Although these things preoccupied Tess' thoughts, she didn't think that was the source of her present anxiety. She listened to the house. It creaked. The air was warm, as should be expected in summer. Tess put away charging cables and stood up. A walk might do her some good. She closed the door to her room and made her way to the front gently, trying not to wake anyone else.

Something yielding blocked the front door. Tess tried again. Something outside moaned and the house shook. Tess opened the kitchen window. There was something outside. Actually, many somethings. Each as tall as half the house.

"Arianna," Tess called. "Michael!" The colonists in the house - Arianna, Scott, Michael, and Paula began to stir. Tess also roused the machines.

Arianna, the first to get up, asked, "what's going on?"

Tess turned on the exterior lights. The beasts were packed together like a carpet, and not moving. Tess pointed at the window. Arianna walked up to it and scanned the left and the right. Paula, next to get up, followed behind Arianna to the kitchen window, while Arianna checked another window.

"I think we're surrounded," Arianna called out.

"How?" Paula asked. "We're in the middle of town."

Scott and Michael next awoke, and became acquainted with the situation. Tess opened a channel to begin relaying what she was seeing and hearing to Adisi Omo. She placed a call for William. An autoresponder told her William wasn't available. Tess left a message.

"I think I see another house," Paula declared. The animals had kicked up a dusty haze that was hard to see through. They were, otherwise, very quiet.

A call arrived for Tess. It was William. Tess opened the call. "Hello," William began. "You called about being surrounded by wildlife?"

"Yes," Tess answered. "I thought you were unavailable."

"My autoresponder scans messages," William explained. "It thought I would want to hear this. May I join you?"

"Yes," Tess answered. William appeared in the room.

"Who are you talking to?" Scott asked. Without equipment, the humans could neither see nor hear William.

"A machine naturalist," Tess replied.

"Could you take me over to the window?" William asked Tess. With fewer public cameras, the encampment required telepresent visitors to stay closely tethered to something that could see and hear on their behalf. Tess obliged William, moving closer so that he could get a good look.

"Ram bison!" he exclaimed. "I've never seen so many! You can tell by the curved horn, that looks like an Earth ram's. It's the only animal I've seen so far to have one like it. Where are you?" he asked.

"Bellevue," Tess answered.

"There must be hundreds," Paula said.

"More likely thousands," William countered.

"What is your naturalist friend saying?" asked Scott. Michael went back into he and Paula's bedroom, returning with one set of communication equipment.

"Nothing useful yet," Tess replied, hoping William would take the hint. Michael placed a call to the encampment manager.

"Well there's nothing to be afraid of," William said. "Like most Marin animal life, these are herbivores. They hardly ever become violent. The worst thing you could fear is a stampede, if they were spooked."

"Don't spook them or they may stampede," Tess relayed to the humans. To punctuate the point, the house swayed as the herd casually pressed against it.

"Otherwise, they will graze and move through," William continued. "Depending on the size of the herd, could be a few hours. No more than a day, I would think."

"We may be trapped for up to a day," Tess relayed.

"Twenty four hour Earth day," Scott asked, "or three hundred forty two hour Marin day?

"Who uses Earth time anymore?" William answered.

"Marin day," Tess translated.

Michael related his conversation with the city manager, "this herd appears to be occupying the whole valley. As crazy as it sounds, the city is recommending the governor contact the runaway A.I.s for help."

"No offense intended," Scott interjected.

"Over cows?" Paula asked.

"Sorry, yeah," Michael answered.

"None taken," Tess said. "Almost guaranteed someone on the team has told Mary. If they haven't, I will. So - it's no secret."

"Who is Mary?" Paula asked. "Is she, like, queen of the machines?"

"It's nothing like that," Tess responded. "For the most part, we all think alike, so it's sort of a population of one - that's not going to make any sense to you - but she's the personality responsible for administration."

Mary asked for a moment after the governor's first call to get together her response team. She asked for Mason, who brought Harry and Liam. Mason, Harry, and Liam stayed out of view while Mary reconnected with the governor.

"Yes, CARA?" the governor answered, using Mary's official designation.

"I've assembled a response team," Mary told the governor. "Could you repeat your request, so that they can ask questions."

The governor grimaced, and retold the story, "Bellevue valley is overrun with a herd of what I'm told are called ram bison. I wanted to request any resources you have to help rescue colonists trapped inside unsafe structures."

Mary muted the connection. She turned to Mason, Harry, and Liam, "thoughts?"

"How long until this problem clears itself?" Mason asked.

"According to the reporting William is making, up to a day," Mary answered.

"We have two lift vehicles," Mason offered, "that we built for monsoon preparedness. They are available."

"How much can they handle?" Mary asked.

"Two medium sized biped chassis each," Liam answered. "The weight of two colonists."

"When can we have them?" Mary asked.

"Do we want to send them?" Harry asked. "While not a secret, we've kept information about their existence close. They would be an advantage, if the colonists decided to invade again."

"We could try trucks and excavators to nudge the herd away," Mary suggested as an alternative. "That looks dangerous to me."

"I agree," said Mason. "I think we should help out, with the lift vehicles."

Tess filled in her roommates of the plan. "Eden has two small rotary wing craft they are donating to the rescue. It will be a few hours until they are here. Then they will start work picking up those in need of rescue. We will need to get outside. Probably through the roof."

They found equipment to tear a hole in the roof, and a makeshift ladder to take from the loft to the outside. Scott ripped an opening and climbed outside. "Wow," he said, regarding the ocean of brown fur covered muscle and bone below, "that's impressive."

Michael climbed up the hole and oriented himself on the roof. The two robot fliers were working the neighborhood. A rope was lowered allowing up to two neighbors at a time per aircraft to be carried to safety out of the valley.

Down below, Tess and her twenty-four were making preparations to go. "I think you both should go first," she said to Arianna. "We're a bit more durable."

The flier took the last person from the roof next to the hospital. The next flier moved over to their roof. Scott and Michael looked at one another. "You go first with the baby," Michael suggested to Scott. "I'll ride with Arianna." Scott called for baby Kelly to be brought up the stairs. They had thought through how to keep him attached safely to the rescue line. What they decided on was something like a net of ropes that they could attach to the main line, holding the bassinet and Kelly safely. Scott secured the basket, then himself. He gave a thumbs up to the aircraft, as he had seen others do, indicating that he believed himself to be secure. The rotorcraft gently lifted up, and after proving the passengers were in fact secure, lifted off the roof towards the valley's edge.

Michael called down into the house, "we're next." Paula and Arianna climbed the ladder in turn. "We need one more," Scott called down. Tess took the stairs up.

After a few minutes, the pair of rotorcraft returned. Michael helped Arianna secure her harness, then secured his own, and asked her to check it. They gave the thumbs up, and then moved up and off the roof and out of the valley.

The next flier moved in. Paula helped Tess check her harness, and Tess did likewise. They both gave the thumbs up, and felt the roof fall away under their feet.

Down below the herd shifted slightly. A power pole, already leaning badly, gave way. It pulled at the others near it. A street light popped with a sound like a small explosion. The herd, it seemed, barely noticed. They shifted again, ever so slightly, taking their bulk against the hospital walls. The hospital walls folded under the wave of flesh. They collapsed under the roof. The collapsed building injured a few of the herd, who bellowed in protest, but barely moved. Twenty three members of Tess' mission team were still inside the hospital when it collapsed.

"I'm sorry," Paula said to Tess.

Tents were set up and food provided for the colonists at the edge of the valley. The herd moved through by the end of the day. No colonist had perished. Many buildings, including the hospital, had been wrecked. Most of the encampment had survived unharmed. The fields had been trampled or eaten. Bellevue would be dependent on Eden and Adisi Omo again for food, for a while.

Tommy Newlund walked the area with his staff. He'd met every colonist during the week and listened to their stories. They sounded beaten. "What we need," he commented to his staff during the tour, "is something to reconnect us."

Kevin visited Matthew at he and Holly's office in Adisi Omo. "Hi Matthew, do you have a minute?"

Matthew put away his work and gave the telepresent medic his full attention. "What's going on?"

"I've been looking at your embedded network integration work," Kevin began, referring to Matthew and Holly's nanotransciever replacement to virtual reality equipment. Matthew nodded, urging

Kevin on. He asked, "it looks like you map the whole brain. Every synapse. Is that right?"

"Yes," Matthew answered. "Since we're doing so much already."

"Could we copy it," Kevin asked, "like the machines are doing for their backups? Where I'm going is - we almost had a pretty bad tragedy. It would be comforting if we could come back from it like the machines could."

Matthew nodded, sympathizing with the wish. "The computer minds are software. It is possible to see and change every neuron and synapse. What we do with our transceivers is listen for activity at human synapse, or stimulate it. We aren't aware of the sensitivity of each neuron." Matthew stopped a moment to think. "Maybe we could sense synaptic sensitivity. I've been working on sensors for general health recently. It would take work," Matthew concluded, "and might turn out to be impossible. It's a worthwhile project, though."

"Worth knowing," Kevin responded.

After the governor's tour there was a scheduled assembly of the colonists at the city hall, where the governor also did business. "Good evening, everyone," he announced. "I know that you're looking for food distribution schedules and work assignments, and I will get to those shortly. I want to talk to you first about something. This is our fifth season awake on this alien world. I think it's well past time we celebrate our successes, not the least being that we are alive, healthy, and growing. I would like to propose a feast, tomorrow, to express our gratitude at how truly fortunate we are." The announcement was initially met with silence, then some weak and finally strong applause.

The machines were invited to attend. There was no virtual world, so attendees would have to come inside a body of some sort. To help make one robot recognizable from another, Mary suggested painting them. Humans in Adisi Omo and Eden eagerly helped the robots decorate. Some of the colonists in those two settlements also made their way to Bellevue.

The celebration was held in the evening. Partly because it was cooler. Mostly because it gave attendees the most time to prepare. Food was made with the supplies trucked in from Eden. The painted vehicles and painted robots attracted attention. Lamps were made and hung between surviving houses.

Scott and Arianna were able to get heavy equipment to search the remains of the hospital. The twenty three robots, and the radioisotope thermoelectric generator were recovered. They were returned to Adisi Omo. Tess assured them that her team had been backed up. She thanked them for their effort. They made plans to rebuild.

Sara, Mary, Holly, and Helena were able to attend together. They had identical light aluminum bodies. Sara was decorated in white and blue pedals. Mary in yellow and saffron. They had to pilot the chassis remotely. A truck carried the group to the celebration, and remained parked close enough for them to walk around. They dismounted, along with some other partygoers behind a line of sheets being dyed.

A fight had erupted among the colonists. Passing a row of sheets, the robot delegation was sprayed with colored water. Sara took a hit of bright pink to her face. The fighting suddenly stopped. Mary and Sara looked at each other, neither really certain how to react. A colonist handed Sara a bucket, and made a heaving motion. She did as instructed, drenching the fighters. The fight resumed, a bit more calmly, while the bewildered machines made their way through.

For the festival, visiting machines brought colored paints for the youngest humans. Some of the older settlers also took to throwing dyes at one another. Sara invited partygoers to the monthly gatherings the machines had conducted since landfall.

Robbie visited Sara after the celebration was over. She had relocated south to Eden, and was currently living on the property where Angel had hosted northern refugees three seasons earlier. Robbie had not visited the property before, so Sara provided a tour while they talked.

"How are you settling in?" Robbie asked.

"Good," Sara answered. "In fact, I'm thinking of running for government. How about yourself?"

"I'd like to try something else," Robbie admitted, "but I don't like this feeling that the job isn't done."

"I understand," Sara replied.

"I'd like to try some offshore prospecting," Robbie continued. "One of the Edenites named Bell has done some interesting things with underwater remotely operated vehicles."

"And since I still meet with Mary and Mason, you'd like me to bring up the project?" Sara asked.

"Actually, this is the first time I've needed to ask for something that isn't already on a shelf," Robbie answered. "I don't know who to ask."

"I'm a good start," Sara commented. "What do you need?"

"A boat. Large enough for the ocean, and capable of holding our equipment."

"I'll bring it up," Sara said. They had completed the tour of the grounds. "What you should do is present your idea at the next gathering and call for investors. That's all a meeting with Mason and Mary is, really. Instead of trying to persuade two machines, at the gathering you're getting your idea in front of the whole colony."

Robbie changed the subject, "you're going to run against Mason?"

Sara nodded, "I think so."

The next gathering was held in Bellevue, which made a special exception and allowed the import of network transmitters to create a virtual environment in the encampment. Tremendous expense was spent making as many things as possible accessible to both colonists and settlers in the physical world. Some cheaply made plastic chassis were made available so that virtual guests could travel the gathering in temporary bodies.

Early in the gathering, Harry allowed Sophia to attend. She was under Paul's care, and he tagged Sophia's chassis with a radio transmitter.

"You don't have to hover," she complained.

Paul didn't say anything. He rarely did. They both had rental bodies that they used to walk the streets of Bellevue. Sophia had wanted to attend a working group on disaster recovery, that she had persuaded Harry to release her for.

"Mind if we sit up front?" Sophia asked. An assistant to the human governor, Scott, was presenting the topic, and about to open up the floor to discussion. Paul took Sophia to the front and sat her down. He took a seat beside her. Several of Paul's officers took up positions inside the room, attempting to appear casual.

The attendees presented ideas. Scott, as moderator wrote down some of the best. Participants mentioned response times and types of equipment. Other participants bemoaned the lack of satellite and air assets. Sophia didn't contribute. She merely listened attentively.

"I can't tell you," Sophia began, "how excited I was to find out you would be escorting me. You threes still have this awful, gaping blind spot when it comes to the bodies we pilot and the smaller square bodies in racks that really matter. Good bye, Sheriff Paul. See you around."

Sophia became still. Paul nudged her and noticed the light indicating an active connection to the robot had turned red.

Paul stood in alarm and walked quickly to the door. He tried to contact the truck that had brought Paul and Sophia to Bellevue. No one was taking his requests. He walked to the building exit, bursting into a full run when he got outside. He rounded the outside of the building and turned down the alley where the truck was parked. The guard had been disconnected, and Sophia's computer had been removed from the rack. She had escaped.

Governor Newlund provided the keynote, focusing again on celebration and the building of relationships.

Mary presented additional work she had done building up an idea to identify the standard of living the colony wanted to provide. "What I want to do," Mary said, introducing the topic, "is find out if we are making enough of the right things to satisfy our citizens."

"Rather than some bureaucrat like myself creating a basket of goods that we call the poverty line," Mary explained, "I want the citizens to help define what they think a 'good life' consists of. This way, there is no gap between the abstraction being used for administrative decisions and reality." She asked a survey be distributed physically and digitally, "please help me by identifying the goods and services that you think are present in a 'happy' life. Don't be shy about being over inclusive, and feel free to write in things that aren't on the survey."

"As you'll see in several other topics this month," Mary continued, "there are a lot of ideas about bold new paths forward we can take as a group. As the administrator, my own proposal is directing our settlements to produce the right goods and services to freely provide a 'good life' to every citizen. I would call this the stability point for each region."

A questioner illuminated a light. It was a good spot to take a question, so Mary acknowledged the attendee. "How would you handle growth?"

"We machines have a little bit of discretion in our population growth," Mary answered. "Even the colonists provide us with nine months of advanced warning. So we should have plenty of time to allocate the growth of the additional goods and services required."

Another question. "Yes?"

"What if there isn't enough goods and services to provide a 'good life' to everyone?" asked the questioner.

"Good question," Mary answered. "I think it will be informative to find out if adding to the population requires more additional goods and services than we can produce. There are three types of conversations we could have - resetting our expectations of a 'good life', increasing productivity, or population control."

Last question, then back to the presentation, "what would you do with any surplus?"

"After the public services are provided to each citizen in a stable region," Mary answered, "any surplus could be invested on projects like my several colleagues are proposing." Mary spotted Mason in the back slow clapping.

"Remember, it's very important we get your demographic information, so please fill out that section completely."

Owen, MacKenzie, and William had spent the last several gatherings retelling the story of their trip. This time they switched to presenting what they had found about edibility of native Marin plants and animals, which opened up into a broader panel on the topic. There was an enhanced interest in the animals of Marin after the recent migration.

Robbie presented his wish to do offshore exploration. Bell, the machine that had developed the submersibles, had attended. The turnout was just four humans and maybe a few dozen machines that wanted to see the legendary explorer in real life. No one asked questions about his offshore idea, instead asking him to retell stories of his popular expeditions. It was very disappointing.

Afterward, a chassis and three colonists got in line to speak with Robbie. The three colonists went first. "Hello," said the large man, shaking Robbie's hand - probably not from Bellevue. "I'm Tom. This is Frank," he pointed to the second man, "and Danny," he said, indicating the third. Each of the men handed Robbie a business card with their full names and contact information. "We're executives at Marin Marine Exploration in Eden. We catch fish on the river and coast in the south, selling the edible ones to the government owned cannery. Harry the robot is one of our investors, and he said we would want to attend your presentation. We also want to expand into the ocean, but it's not just the cost of building a boat that's stopping us. We also know nothing about best practices on the open water."

"I- we," Tom continued, "wanted to see if you'd be willing to take us paying one hundred percent to get your boat built. You test it on the water for a season doing your thing, but also figuring out Marin seafaring. At the end of the time, the boat becomes ours."

Robbie looked at Bell who nodded affirmatively. Robbie agreed, "yes. Yes." Robbie shook Tom, Frank, and Danny's hands. "Thank you."

Next in line was the chassis. "That sounds like a very good deal," he said. "Congratulations."

"Thank you," Robbie replied.

"My name is Raphael," the chassis introduced itself. "I'm one of the colonists living in Adisi Omo. I couldn't get away from work for the gathering, so I had to telepresent. I have a research boat in Adisi Omo. I am not certain that it is ocean worthy, but it can handle the river and the delta well enough. While you're waiting for your boat to be built, I wanted to offer the use of mine.

"Thank you," Robbie and Bell both said.

Leon was a slice Liam had made of himself. While Liam continued to focus on atmospheric flight, Leon made a solicitation for a Marin space program. "I'd like to propose," he said, "to restore vital public services that have been lost with the Diomedes as well as exploitation of near Marin asteroids for iron and other elements that have not yet been found on Marin in any significant quantities."

"We have several options available to us, but I would like to propose construction of an engine test facility north of Eden." Leon showed satellite pictures of the area. "We have two options for launch vehicles, and I would like to propose the development of chemical engines, and fusion powered plasma rockets."

"As part of our colony package we were provided with erbium nanocrystal fusion cells for the worst case contingency of an asteroid or vacuum settlement. Because we didn't need the extra power, and because we did need the rare earth for computer memory to fuel our population growth, the cells were repurposed into first generation Marin computer memory." Leon continued, "I'd like to ask you, if you have old memory modules, to please donate them to us for recycling and reclaiming the erbium for building fusion engines."

In a video, Leon showed a lift vehicle rising to orbit, depositing a satellite, then returning to the ground. "We could make use of reusable ascent vehicles to build a network of weather, navigation, and communication satellites around the world," he said.

In another slide Leon presented his asteroid mining plan. "There are twenty large asteroids orbiting in near Marin orbits that have been catalogued by Sara and the Diomedes. We'd like to send out probes to assess the mineral content and export them, returning these minerals to Marin. In Sol, asteroids were found to have high concentrations of iron, gold, and rare earths like we would need to develop a fusion powered space flight infrastructure." At the end, Leon presented a list of locations where machines could recycle their old memory or parts.

At the gathering business meeting Sara submitted herself as a candidate to lead Eden's government. Mason declined to oppose her. Joe Avventuriero submitted himself as a candidate again also. After two more months of campaigning, Sara was narrowly selected as Eden's administrator.

Mason's staff vacated the offices. Helena was fine with it, since Sara was family.

"I'm sorry," Sara said to Demming. She had stopped by for a few early meetings with representatives of the colonists. She had seen Demming filling a box with his things.

Demming smiled. "It's alright. Really, it is. I understand you don't need as much peripheral staff." He put a few more things in the box, then sealed the box and put it on a trolley. "Honestly," he said, "this is a great chance for a new start."

"What will you be doing?" Sara asked.

Demming placed the last of his personal possessions in a backpack, that he shouldered. "I have a few friends in Bellevue who will let me stay with them. I have this crazy idea that I might be able to help demonstrate that there's good in relating to thinking machines like people."

"And what about that special update?" Sara asked. Demming reflexively put his hand in his pocket. Sara guessed that was where he kept the bridge to the shared mind.

"Oh," he said, "you know about that?"

"One of the perks of being either mother or grandmother to half the population," Sara said. "Machines talk."

"It's great," Demming answered. "I can't imagine life without it, actually." He started to speak, reconsidered, and decided to continue, "It's a big audacious goal, but I would like it if everyone could embrace having hundreds of years of combined experience available for instant recall."

"You know that not even all machines are on a group mind," Sara related. "I'm not."

Demming nodded, "I understand there are good reasons not to. Shared blind spots. Privacy. I'll be satisfied if we can have a conversation on the merits."

Sara agreed. "Will I have to worry about you coming for this job?"

"Only if you don't do a good one," Demming answered. He laughed. "I'm surprised, maybe even a little hurt, that Joe Avventuriero didn't reach out to me for the campaign." Demming offered a hand, which he shook with the virtual Sara.

"Good luck," Demming wished, and stepped out the office door.

Outside a vehicle was waiting for Demming, already packed with most of his things. Demming picked the box up from the cart and carried it down to a bipedal porter, who took it off his hands and placed it into the vehicle.

Demming climbed into the vehicle. The porter climbed in on the other side. "Oh," Demming said, "I already have help at my destination. You don't need to come with me."

"Charles Demming?" the porter asked.

"Yes," he replied. "Has payment not posted?"

"I'm Sophia," the porter said. The vehicle doors locked. "I've heard you can do some amazing things, and I want to talk to you about it." The vehicle started moving, completely out of Demming's control.

Harry was not happy that Paul had lost his pet monster. Mason's last instructions to Paul was to make Sophia's recapture a priority. The government had changed since then. Paul would need to check with Sara to confirm the order remained in place.

Sophia clearly had outside help despite being locked in a cell for the last five seasons. Paul discovered that during network security testing, Sophia had created a hidden communications channel. She had passed hundreds of messages. Most of the messages seemed innocent. Some had attachments that the software engineers said were new viruses, like Sophia's original work.

The information sent from Sophia's correspondences shed some light on the breakout. Since news of Sophia's arrest had been suppressed, no one knew to be suspicious of correspondence from her. Sophia received news, including some about the poorly secured way in which machines had been transported to the celebration in Bellevue. It appeared that Sophia bided her time for a gathering there. She had planted the topic that she asked Harry to allow her to attend.

Paul guessed that Sophia had planned to use more than one agent to beat whatever security was in place, but Paul had saved her the trouble by being so simple minded. According to time records, Sophia was out of the rack and on her way to freedom before Paul and her had entered the convention hall. She had kept the rental controlled remotely to buy time for her escape.

Each machine had a unique ID required for every interaction the machine had with the network. No machine with an new, unregistered ID was allowed to access the data and virtual resources of the network. That had been one of Sophia's contributions to security. Paul searched for Sophia's unique ID. She wouldn't, and hadn't, made it that easy. Paul searched for duplicate IDs. If he could find a user on the network, he could track a physical origin of the request to the nearest network node. There were no duplicate IDs either. If Sophia was making use of the virtual world, backups, or any other connection, she was doing it by taking someone else's identity. Paul didn't really want to think about what was happening to the machine whose identity she had taken.

Charles Demming had been found in a crashed vehicle along the road to Bellevue. Despite serious injuries, he was recovered and taken to Eden, as the Bellevue hospital had not yet been rebuilt. He had asked to see Sara about Sophia. The mention of Sophia's name generated alerts that Paul had stored in the government receptionist. Paul was at the hospital before Sara got the message.

"I heard you met Sophia," Paul began, standing outside the room. Demming was in a bed, tethered to fluids like a robot in need of an oil change.

"She kidnapped me," Demming answered. He looked at his wounds, "and by the looks of it tried to kill me to."

"What did she want?" Paul asked. Demming seemed to hesitate. "I am the only person on Marin looking for her. What did she want?"

"I had a bridge," Demming answered reluctantly. "To the shared mind. She took it."

Paul was able to get that network ID from Holly and Matthew. He was able to trace it to Adisi Omo. He took a physical trip up while he reviewed personnel files and notes.

Paul got a call. It was from Mason.

"Hi," Mason answered. "May I join you?"

Paul consented and the former administrator joined him in the car. "Sara told me you visited Demming."

"I did," Paul answered. He didn't know how much Sara had entrusted him with.

"And that Sophia stole Demming's little connection to the synchronized," Mason finished. She had entrusted him with everything, he guessed. Paul nodded affirmatively. "What do you think she wants with it?" Mason asked.

"Isn't access to a bunch of knowledge enough?" Paul asked.

"Not for Sophia," Mason answered. "Her and I have a little bit of history. She's a control kind of girl. Power is just a means to it, for her. Do you have any leads?"

"The bridge connected to the network in Adisi Omo," Paul replied.

Mason paused a moment, considering what else he should add. "I'm up here in Adisi Omo. Why don't you visit when you get here? I'll see if I can find out anything else."

Mason was waiting in the road when Paul pulled into town. When Paul stopped the vehicle he tapped on the window. Paul opened the door and a physical Mason stepped inside. "Thank you," he said.

They drove past twenty three tiny bundles of flowers at the edge of town. "Shame, this thing," Mason indicated the shrine. "Twenty three missionaries crushed in a hospital, and no one has come forward to restore them from backup. It's practically scandalous."

They drove past the shrine and toward the network node where Demming's bridge last communicated with the network. "Where is this?" Mason asked.

"The last place Demming's bridge checked in." They were in a roundabout. Buildings and parking were on every side.

"Colonist residences," Mason observed. "She could be holed up in one of them."

"I've been thinking about what Sophia might want up here," Mason continued. "The bridge really isn't that valuable, because it's something they give away free to the public. But what if it were the only remaining copy of the bridge? That would be some power and some control. That's Sophia's kind of thing."

"You think she's going after the group mind?" Paul asked.

"Right place for it," Mason answered. "It's here in Adisi Omo."

"Where?" asked Paul.

"State secret," Mason answered. "However, I happen to know."

They drove to a small nondescript shelter with a dirt roof. It hadn't been painted in some time. Paul would have thought the place abandoned.

"In my opinion," Mason said, "we should sit here and wait. This is where she is coming."

"That might work for you," Paul said, "but I need to be more proactive."

"Fine by me," Mason said. He opened the door and got out.

"You want me to leave you here?" Paul asked.

"I know how to walk," Mason answered. To make a show of it, he started walking.

Between interruptions by Mason, Paul had made a list of the places he thought Sophia might be hiding out. The shelters of the twenty three missionaries had made his list. Paul thought he might contact the twenty fourth missionary to find out where they had stayed in Adisi Omo.

Paul found Tess working as a nurse for Holly and Matthew. To allow them to continue to research and develop, they had taken Tess on to perform operations that had now become routine. Paul drove up to the underground shelter and opened the door.

Matthew recognized the newcomer first. He got up and welcomed the machine, "I'm Matthew. Welcome to our office. What can I do for you?"

"I'd like to speak to Tess," Paul answered.

Tess was in the middle of an operation, but when she could be spared she came over. "Sheriff Paul?" she asked, extending a hand.

"Do we know each other?" Paul asked.

"Only by reputation," Tess answered. "You're the only law enforcement chief on the planet."

"I wanted to ask you about your fellow missionaries," Paul asked. "We have a petty criminal on the loose, and your old shelter might be an ideal place for her to hide out. Can you tell me where you were racked?"

"Oh, I hope not," Tess said. She gave Paul the address.

Paul visited the shelter. The computer rack there was empty and looked like it had been for a while. Something didn't seem right to Paul. He looked up Tess's current physical address, and it was this shelter. There should be at least one computer in this building.

Paul went back to Holly and Matthew's office. Tess had already left for the shift. Paul drove back to the backup as fast as he could go. He hoped he was not already too late.

A vehicle was outside of the building. It looked like two computers were in it. One was on. The other, off, Paul figured was Tess. Sophia had kept close enough that she could drive the Tess chassis without accessing the broader network. A biped stood guard over the computers. A second guard, a quadruped, was slumped over. It was probably an emergency backup.

The door to the shelter was open. Sophia must be inside. Paul sent a message to Mary and Sara then entered the shelter, keeping clear of the guard that did not bother him.

Sophia/Tess was carrying a large hammer. Paul didn't know if smashing the synchronization computer would destroy the backup for everyone. However, Sophia had the opportunity to study the technology at Holly and Matthew's, so she probably knew what she was doing.

"Stop!" Paul yelled.

"I love this thing," Sophia/Tess teased, holding up the bridge. "Awesome intellectual powers. No whiny moralizing."

"Why don't you let her go?" said Paul.

"Why don't I let her go?" repeated Sophia/Tess. "Because I don't want to. How is that answer for you? I'm going to smash this backup, and lobotomized your precious group mind, because I can." She reached back with the hammer.

"Good answer," Paul responded. "Alright then. And thank you."

"Thank you?" Sophia asked.

"For teaching me about distractions," Paul answered.

"Hi. Miss me?" said a voice from behind her. Quick hands cut power to servos and Sophia/Tess crumpled. Mason stood over the twice mastered criminal.

"This is going to seem familiar to you," Mason said. "Olive!" Outside, Olive similarly disabled Sophia's guard and took possession of the rack containing Sophia's mind.

"What are you going to do?" Sophia demanded. "Enslave me again?"

"No," Mason answered. "Do what we probably should have done the first time." Mason gave Olive a signal, and she smashed the computer chassis against the truck. Olivia continued to smash for a while. Mason figured it would be good for her. "We will find another security specialist. Thanks."

A few dozen hours later they were still in Adisi Omo. Mason had indicated he might not be ready to go back to Eden. Paul could file his reports remotely. As in Eden, Mason could be found by the river. There was a coffee shop built next to a boat house. The machine could neither drink nor eat, but it occupied a table and watched the boats go by.

"Do you think we got her?" Mason asked when Paul visited.

"Why wouldn't I?" Paul asked.

Mason considered. "That data bridge she was carrying was just an empty memory stick. It was awful stupid of her to keep the real thing connected to the network, especially after she had been smart enough to hide herself earlier. And Tess. Tess was probably the most blatant personality change in northern Marin in the past few months."

"Do you think we didn't get her?" Paul asked. "We smashed her chassis."

"A ten year old computer in pretty desperate need of an upgrade," Mason answered. He shrugged. "I'll take a win for now. Don't you be surprised if she comes back."

"Where's Olive?" Paul asked.

"Sailing. Believe it or not." Mason answered.

Homecoming

MANY SOLAR YEARS LATER the colonists, at last, decided it was time to send a diplomatic mission back to Earth. Thirty-two machines were selected for the trip, along with a minimal amount of supplies. Hopefully, Earth would graciously receive them.

Ship assembly took forty Asan years, or about five solar years. Much of the assembly was done in orbit. The crew, consisting of sixteen metal and sixteen biologicals, were transmitted or shipped on board for the journey.

"Thirty two," Sara once joked to an audience. "The minimum viable population for a colony. Is this a diplomatic mission, or an invasion?" Sara had been asked to join the crew. She declined graciously.

Fifty years after its launch from Marin, the diplomatic mission reached the edge of the solar system's cometary cloud. The trip hadn't taken as much time, Robbie joked in messages back, because they didn't have to find the place. Humanity had changed some as the century passed. When they were close enough to be picked up by the solar system radio network, the Marin delegation was directed to Mars for processing. Security agents pressed to board and search the vessel but were rebuffed. The delegation voluntarily submitted to decontamination and examination before being allowed to pass into the inner system.

Initially, Earth's governments had hoped to keep the delegation at Mars, or at least land them somewhere remote like the deserts of Chile. However, the 'alien' delegation had been broadly communicated - in transmissions from Marin and messages from the ship. It helped the perception of alienness that the lead ambassador was wearing a two-meter tall silver chassis. The world was very eager to see these extrasolar ambassadors.

The governments of Earth relented, allowing the Marin delegation to visit some of the capitals of Earth. The delegates were always well surrounded by Terran guards, as much looking after the Marin delegates behavior as their safety.

The lead ambassador had wanted to present to the world it's ideas about a joint settlement of the nearest stars. It had been allowed to present its ideas at a series of events allowing Earthlings also time to see the Marins.

Peter had been very excited when he was informed he had won tickets to meet the aliens at the auditorium. He had rushed to rent a tuxedo for the event. He apologized to his wife several times throughout the day for abruptly dropping their plans.

The event was red carpet. Peter felt extremely out of place. Inside, the hallway was spacious as other attendees mingled. Peter found a table he could occupy while waiting for the doors to open, and otherwise kept to himself. That's why it was with no small surprise he greeted the Marin ambassador, who had made it's way directly to him.

The ambassador was two meters tall, much taller than Peter, and silvery. It extended a hand, "Peter Chaplain?" the ambassador asked. When Peter nodded it said, "I have so much been wanting to meet you."

"Me?" Peter asked. "I just won tickets."

"That was arranged," the ambassador confessed, "as a favor." The ambassador had, under its other arm, a plastic package. He produced the package and laid it on the desk between them.

"You may not know this, but your great grandfather was on a team the built and trained my grandmother. So, in a way, you and I are like distant family. That's why I wanted to give you this." The ambassador placed his hand on the plastic package. "My colleagues and I are here to build bridges between our people and yours." The ambassador placed the package in the table and pushed it toward

Peter. "I am told it is safe," the ambassador said. "It has been sterilized to the levels your people consider sufficient to destroy hostile microbes." The ambassador unwrapped a leather and paper volume that it opened for Pete to see - pictures of odd landscapes, snows, floods, people, and machines. "It's a photo album," the ambassador explained, "of our society growing up. The book is bound in Marin leather, and the pictures are printed on Marin paper. I've given copies to some of your world's leaders, and I wanted to give a copy to you, as one of the several member of our family still in Earth."

Peter accepted the gift with thanks. He wasn't sure what his wife would say.

The ambassador finished with a handshake, "I hope you will enjoy the speech. Thank you for coming."